THE
LEGEND OF RED
ROSE CIRCLE

Other Books by Larry Serfozo

Nora Telegdy

Insult and Revenge

The Bronx Affair

Cara Negra

The Gangster and the Hangman

The Tales of an Irreverent Eros

The Revenge of the Ineptitude

The Painting

THE
LEGEND OF RED
ROSE CIRCLE

A Novel
By
Larry Serfozo
Author of *The Bronx Affair*

iUniverse, Inc.
New York   Bloomington

The Legend of Red Rose Circle

Copyright © 2009 by Larry Serfozo

iUniverse books may be ordered through booksellers or by contacting:

iUniverse
1663 Liberty Drive
Bloomington, IN 47403
www.iuniverse.com
1-800-Authors (1-800-288-4677)

ISBN: 978-1-4401-4026-6 (pbk)
ISBN: 978-1-4401-4027-3 (ebk)

Printed in the United States of America

iUniverse rev. date: 4/20/2009

For all the

True and innocent

Young lovers

Who are compelled to

Endure unbearable

Anguish and sorrow

Chapter One

Anyone, who cared or slowed down enough to notice, would have had only one remark, and even that with a hint of criticism, about Percy Grimsby, a young adult resident and native of Darien, a blessed and happy little town in Connecticut.

That Percy Grimsby, he has very modest ambitions in life. He is a good person and we have to give his parents credit for that. But he is pathetic and he's not getting anywhere unless he changes his attitude.

Percy would have answered this imaginary person, as one never existed and nobody took the time to seriously consider his qualities, with confidence equaling the inner strength of a Buddhist monk.

"What do you know about life? You are too busy to make money, money that you spend on vain possessions anyway. Don't you worry about me, I'll make it one day and it'll be without having to sell my soul to the devil the way you traded in yours."

Years ago, in the mid 1990s, back at the Darien High School, Percy received good grades only in two subjects, English and physical education or specifically in playing tennis. In the rest of the academics, let's not talk about that, he barely received a passing mark. He never got close to taking physics or chemistry, not to mention calculus or trigonometry. So any serious college education seemed out of the question.

After high school, Percy had been taking classes, mainly English literature and creative writing at the Norwalk Community College, but after six years of on and off attendance; he got nowhere near collecting enough credits for an associate degree.

But Percy was born under lucky stars, his father, a hard working engineer owned a big, center hall colonial style home on Red Rose Circle in Darien and although Percy's older sister and brother still lived in the house, Percy had the remaining fourth, the smallest bedroom just for himself. He paid his parents a nominal, minimum rent and everything stayed quiet and at peace.

Everybody in the house except Percy, of course, had a regular 9 to 5 job. His father had two jobs. He had a demanding daytime job as a chief engineer for a small but profit hungry local consulting engineering company, and after dinner he worked out of his basement, sometimes passed midnight, producing complicated calculations and design drawings for the competition as an independent subcontractor.

On the other hand, Percy didn't thrive on being a professional slacker; he hasn't taken pride in making a nuisance of himself. He seemed to be an easy person to get along with. He had no interest in listening to loud music, despised heavy metal, rap, and reggae and never went to a concert. He preferred quiet activities. He had his computer on for hours and hours, mostly when nobody else was in the house or all other decent hard working souls, with daytime jobs, were deep asleep. Percy wrote down anything he could think of. He produced massive amounts of quasi-literary work on his word processor, but outside of a few dozen rejection slips, he could not demonstrate any results. But he loved to write; writing represented his main means of communication and expression of his peculiar or perhaps, we might say, slightly twisted ideas.

If we want to say anything bad about Percy, it would be he didn't really care to please his peers, he rarely went to a bar to hang out, didn't go to Weed Beach to smoke pot, Percy acted way beyond his own age. His parents had no complaints about him, he took odd jobs, cut the grass, raked the leaves, shoveled the snow, made runs to the garbage dump, repaired doors, replaced screens, but mostly, he gave tennis lessons.

He's been playing tennis since ten years old and he strived to excel in it. He could have become a full-time tennis pro, but of course, Percy had no ambitions besides eventually producing a literary masterpiece, so he never bothered to contact any of the nearby country clubs. He gave lessons on town tennis courts. His private enterprise, but of course, permitted doing so, by the town's Department of Parks and Recreation.

Handsome and tall, Percy looked slim and impertinently young. Not a forced growth, steroid fed muscle freak, he was not too strong but quick on his feet and fast with the swinging of his arms. He worked his way up to be a favorite amongst the town's middle-aged housewives and aging spinsters to take tennis lessons from, but lately, he set the limit on his tennis instruction time to not more than ten hours a week for he had to have enough time to write and think about important issues affecting mankind in general.

In late May, with the grass growing abundant and vigorous, it needed to be cut twice a week. Percy had plenty of work and on this fine late morning hour he was mowing the grass of next-door neighbor, Pamela Leicester, a tall, well-built woman, somewhere between forty and fifty years of age. She had enough strength to cut ten times as much grass as she had, but she preferred watching Percy work and sweat. Especially, when he removed his shirt and exposed his splendidly developed fine upper body muscles; she liked to observe him with delight.

Pamela had one son, Joshua. Attending junior high on Middlesex Road, Joshua wasn't due back home for many more hours. Joshua's father, a rich criminal trial lawyer, took off ten years ago to marry his much younger colleague. They lived in New York City and he made partner in a lucrative law practice. Although being a good provider, Joshua's father didn't have much energy left for his only child. His demanding upper class, real New York, lifestyle and social obligations kept him so busy that he didn't mind not seeing his son or his ex-wife for many months at a time.

Pamela didn't want to jeopardize the splendid alimony and the house payments she kept receiving, by doing foolish things like marrying again, so she remained a divorcee and concentrated on local gossip and raising Joshua.

Blessed with inner happiness, Pamela lived for small indulgences. She prepared a large pitcher of lemonade, filled it up with ice and sat out on her back porch. Being close to noontime, the sun climbed high and nearing to the zenith of its apparent trajectory, poured down burning rays and filled up every creature and critter of God with warmth and sensual desires of an exuberantly sublime springtime joy.

Pamela already planted her chrysanthemums, petunias, violets, salvias and buttercups. The small baby plants in their large flowerpot boxes looked strong, healthy and proudly represented the youthful phase of our earth's eternal renewal cycle and yearly rebirth.

Pamela put on a pair of gray cotton exercise shorts. She wore no bra, just a matching, tight and sporty looking cotton top that pushed her most desirable breasts into a big, bulging cleavage. In spite of the balmy temperatures she needed keeping warm, she covered her shoulders with a turquoise blue polyester gown, and let the sides of the garment fall. She didn't seem to mind revealing her strong thighs. In short, she did not try hiding the beauty of her plentiful and blessedly feminine endowments.

Observing Percy from a distance she waved at him when he passed by, "Come on, Percy, take a break and join me for a lemonade."

Percy went on for one more round of grass cutting, put the mower near the end of the driveway and returned to Pamela.

"You are very kind, Mrs. Leicester," he said. "I must admit, I cannot resist your kind offer."

"You'd better not. Sit down, and for God's sake would you call me Pam."

Percy sat down, leaned back and stretched his long and suntanned legs. Still out of breath and holding his sweat soaked shirt in his right hand, he asked, "Pam, what makes you think I'm not a loser?"

As Pam didn't immediately answer, Percy put his pungently scented shirt next to her and proceeded to untie his boots. Pulling them off together with his socks, he continued addressing the lady of the house, "Sorry, I feel much better without them. I hope, you don't mind."

He carefully observed Pam's reaction and didn't fail to note that she leaned forward, and let her oversized breasts be exposed slightly deeper than before.

"The more you take off the better," Pam said finally and put her bare feet on top of Percy's. She pressed down on him and asked with ironic tease. "How can you be a loser, ladies' man?"

"Come on. Nobody likes me except you."

"Liar, I know how popular you are with all those tennis wives."

"That's different; they just play with me I don't get involved with married women."

A big black BMW pulled into the next-door driveway. Pam and Percy glanced over and saw Captain Spencer Shrewsbury. Wearing his elegantly suave dark blue airline pilot uniform he was getting out of his car. He smiled with neighborly friendliness and saluted them, but after getting his overnight bags out of the trunk proceeded, without hesitation, into his house.

Percy thought that Captain Shrewsbury's feet seemed a

little wobbly and as he walked, he needed to try hard to keep his balance.

"He is back," Pam said. "He's been away for a week at least. He flies all over the world. Now he has at least a week off. Not bad. He must be making a lot of money."

"Would you like him to be your wedded husband?"

"No, I've had a husband already. Now he pays me good alimony and I don't have to take care of him. My needs of men, at my age," and she winked at him, "can be fulfilled by a young groundskeeper, just like you."

"You lucky woman," Percy stirred the ice cubes in his lemonade cup and glanced pensively at his employer, "you've got one living right next door."

Ignoring the rude and impertinent reference directed at her sensuous feelings toward her young neighbor, Pamela continued her crafty nudging a subtle degree more forcefully, "Percy, I need you to look at the curtain rod in my bedroom. It keeps falling off."

Percy didn't answer, and she continued, "Could you fix it?"

Percy still took his time. Pamela knew his answer was obvious. She knew he couldn't break away from the simple philosophy practiced by all males. Never say no to a lady when she asks you a favor.

"Sure," Percy said, "I'll fix it, but let's enjoy this cool lemonade a minute more."

They both took long, elaborate sips from their straws and inhaled the overwhelming fragrance emanating from the large honeysuckle bush in full, glorious blossom next to the porch. The overgrown rhododendrons almost reached the bottom of the second floor windows and were heavy with large pink, red and white flowers. Finely intricate branches of azaleas spread wide and rich, flowery carpet decked all corners of the house with smiling, honey-laden pleasantry.

There was no need to rush the moment, the world being as perfect as it could possibly be, needed no adjustment nor deserved criticism. Seeing the embodiment of mature sexuality in her, Percy eyed Pamela with lecherous desire. Obviously interested, he thought, she looked willing and available to play. Maybe due to or in spite of having no steady girlfriend of his own age, Percy had a reputation with women. He had the time, the looks and somehow older women considered him less dangerous and freely flirted with the town's private tennis tutor.

Percy was an idealist and as a writer he needed a muse. In his creative mind Percy couldn't possibly transfer experienced and cynically pragmatic Pamela or anybody like her into one of his own heroines. But giving due respect to all his devotion to perfectionism, Percy was still human, a procrastinator who didn't have the urge to rush life along. He didn't have the compelling need to find the angel of his dreams today or for that matter next week or next month. It seemed all right to explore a game of tease with his next-door neighbor. In his mid twenties, Percy had not experienced yet the power of passing time, he thought that he would be young forever, his muse would not get any older and there was no biological clock ticking away the grains of opportunity allocated for each of us.

As a fledgling writer, Percy treated the entire world surrounding him, as the reflection of his own mind, where characters behaved as dictated by the plot with little tolerance allowed for individual will and unpredictable destiny. He thought, he could have an affair with Pamela and she would stand willingly aside when changing circumstances required her to do so.

Confident and relaxed, he told her, "On second thought, I need to dash on. Starting at two o'clock I have to give tennis lessons at Weed Beach Park and before that I need to get a few things from Ring's End Hardware. I'll stop by your house, late after dinner and I'll fix the curtain rod then. But I need money. Would you mind giving me an advance on my lawn maintenance fee?"

"Ok. Hold your horses for a second. Let me go inside. I'll bring it out to you."

She stood up and walked slowly toward the sliding door leading to the kitchen. Her gown draped smoothly and followed the contours of her wide hips and protruding, firm derriere. Each cheek moved individually and yet in unison, promising lascivious and provocative secrets hidden in between. Percy couldn't resist the temptation; he stood up and went after her. Inside, slightly bending over the center isle countertop and reaching for her petty cash box, she was counting out forty dollars. Percy stepped closer and pushed his left hand against her behind. He sunk his fingers into her large and soft flesh and with his other hand grabbing both of her breasts, provocatively whispered into her ear, "Do you want me to put up that curtain rod right now?"

Pamela turned around, smiled at him with assertive confidence and haughtiness, "I thought that you had a tennis appointment, I don't want you do a hasty job. Come on over after ten o'clock, bring over a bottle of good booze and I may let you put up that rod."

Feeling no rejection, Percy smiled back like an understanding coconspirator. He didn't have to make love to

Pamela right now. He didn't have the time and being sure of his qualities, he knew a better opportunity would arise.

His fleeting urge and lust subsided and he retreated with dignity, "I'll be back at ten. I don't mind working the nightshift with you, but I don't want to disturb Joshua, he has school tomorrow.

"Don't worry about him. He will be deep asleep by ten. Just make sure that you are fit and ready to do your duty. I don't want those tennis ladies draining down your energies."

"No way, I'll see you then," he replied and smirking with victorious confidence went back to the porch, put on his socks and shoes, and with the sweaty shirt wrapped around the holding bar, he pushed the lawnmower back to his father's tool shed.

Chapter Two

Captain Spencer Shrewsbury flew around the globe for Delta Airlines almost every week, or if we wanted to be more accurate, at least every other week. He began flying out to the West and then to the Far East, Seoul or Tokyo, after that he stayed over and continued to Australia, stayed over again and flew a day or two later to Johannesburg or London and from there back to New York. If he was lucky, he could get assigned on a plane from Sydney heading back to Los Angeles and from there to New York. That made his overall trip just about a week long instead of the usual ten days. After these long trips, he had a weeklong break and could relax back at home in the elegant and comfortable Darien house he inherited from his mother.

Spencer Shrewsbury already reached his mid forties but he still possessed the looks of a first class lady-killer. Tall, he looked slim and handsome in his captain's uniform and displayed admirably firm, authoritative and assertive manners. He enjoyed flying, and as a young man he flew B-52 bombers for the air force. Last time being in the service, during the first Gulf War, he dropped untold thousands of tons of explosive ordinance on enemy positions and fortifications made of sand and bricks of mud.

He enjoyed being looked upon as a hero and liked being served by stewardesses and porters at Delta or before that by enlisted men and orderlies at the strongest force on earth. Never having to worry about household chores, like cooking and cleaning and other similar mundane and boring duties, being in charge was his lifestyle.

When his mother passed away last year, Captain Shrewsbury didn't have the inclination to upgrade or change anything. He meant to keep the house and his life just the way it always has been. He had no desire to move or sell and buy something new or different. Having spent his entire life in plush suburban surroundings the captain abhorred apartment living. He had the money to hire a cleaning company, any kind of assistance and services to run the big colonial and to maintain his half of an acre manicured lawn and fine shrubbery.

He paid for all those services, but it wasn't enough. He wanted to have somebody at home when he returned from his trips; he wanted to have female company and a female touch for decorating and beautifying his surroundings. He wanted to be looked upon at home by somebody with the same reverence and admiration, and he wanted to hear constant praises of his qualities the same way he was receiving respect on the large plane under his control and command. He wanted to have a wife, or rather a replacement for his dear departed mother, whose adoration he missed so much.

Spencer met Linda at the Flight Crew Lounge at JFK International. She served coffee and pastry for waiting pilots and stewardesses. Spencer noticed Linda the first time she came to work at the cafeteria, and ever since, when he thought she wasn't looking, kept watching her.

A dark redhead, young Linda was a bloomy Irish rose. She maintained a cheerful disposition, owned a cute and intriguing face and in spite of all her natural beauty, she was timid and reticently shy.

She seemed different from the opinionated, noisy, big-mouthed women of Spencer's age. And those women, indeed, they were only involved, exclusively interested, in their own problems. They already had a life behind them, couple of divorced husbands, if not those, at least numerous ex-boyfriends. Spencer thought that this young girl could be completely his, would admire him without ever challenging his authority, wouldn't be asking unwanted questions and would serve him obediently as a loving wife. She would be fun, cheer up the house, would wait for Spencer with flowers on the table and open, willing arms in bed.

The attraction, he felt, didn't want to fade. He imagined taking take her home and taking good care of her. He didn't know where the feeling emerged from, but he knew, this girl was whom he wanted to own.

Spencer decided to approach the object of his admiration.

First, he initiated small talk type, limited conversations,

trying to find, groping for an edge, any personal information regarding her.

"I like your accent," he asked, "where are you from?"

"From the Midwest."

"Midwest, where?"

"Kansas City, Missouri."

"That's nice; I've been there many times. What made you come here? Wait, let me guess, you've got married and your husband is from Queens."

"No," she smiled hesitantly, "wrong guess."

"What, is he from Brooklyn?"

"No, I'm not married."

"Do you still have family there?"

"Sort of."

"Come on, what kind of answer is that? Either you have family there or you don't."

Linda didn't answer. She walked away and left the much older man, obviously trying to make a cynical pass at her, alone.

She came back a half an hour later and asked politely, "Can I get you anything else?"

"I'm sorry." The captain fixed his eyes on her, "I was too pushy. I didn't mean to pry. I'm sorry if I offended you. Let's start all over again, please. What's your name?"

Linda was lonely, she turned nineteen only a month ago and as soon as she received her papers, she left the State Orphanage in Kansas City. She hated her life there, constant fighting, frequent psychiatric evaluations, bad food and bunk beds with a dozen other girls in the same room.

She finished high school, had part time jobs, saved a little money and she bought a bus ticket to New York City and the day after her arrival she took the first job that the State

Employment Agency found her. Her father left when Linda was five years old and her mother was serving a life sentence for poisoning her live in boyfriend a few years later. Linda instinctively didn't trust any strangers but this tall, handsome pilot, showing interest, impressed her.

She eased up, pointed to her nametag and said, "Linda."

"Of course, silly of me, I'm Spencer." And he pointed to his nametag on his overnight bag, "Captain Spencer Shrewsbury."

"Anything I can get for you, Captain Shrewsbury?"

"Yes, please get me a scotch on the rocks. And get one for yourself."

"I can't drink. I'm not twenty-one yet. I can't even serve you an alcoholic drink."

"I'm sorry; can I get you something else then?"

"If you insist, get me a coffee and a slice of pastry, but not here. I'm on duty; they would fire me if I sat down and enjoyed a piece of cake with one of the guests. I'll have my lunch break in about an hour. Meet me in the bakery shop across the main gallery."

An hour later she was waiting for him in the pastry shop. Spencer bought two napoleons, ordered two coffees and brought it to their table indicating that it was not beyond his dignity to wait on a young girl like Linda. Linda enjoyed the tasty treat and listened to Spencer, a sweet smile brightening her face.

He began, "I used to live with my mother in a big house in Connecticut. She passed away last year and now, I live there all by myself."

"I thought that there was a Mrs. Captain Spencer and a bunch of little Spencers. What happened? Did she kick you out?"

"I've never been married."

"How come, why?"

"My mother took care of me and the house. I was too busy flying airplanes. I didn't have the time to go out with women."

"What about all those flight attendants, I have seen you with all the time."

"Those? Most of them are already married. The rest I know too well to consider them good wife material."

Linda was very naïve; she believed that an old bachelor like Spencer could fall into true love with somebody, easily, just by sight and a few words of niceties. She had nothing, perhaps her looks and youth, maybe her virginity, but she had no experience running a house, no marketable job training or special skills, no money, no rich father or inheritance coming from grandparents. She didn't have her own place; she slept at the YWCA and paid for her room once a week from her meager paycheck. But in her wishfully thinking and inexperienced mind she wanted to believe that Spencer was serious and had only honest intentions.

She asked, "Who do you think is a good wife, quoting your words, material?"

Spencer rested his eyes on Linda; *she was young, attractive and innocent,* he thought, *she must be easily controllable and apparently has no nearby relatives to worry about.* She was the exact embodiment what he wanted.

He decided to take a direct approach. He stared at her and answered, "You. I think you are good wife material."

Linda blushed and became purple red, "Me? Captain Shrewsbury, is this a joke?"

"No, I'm serious. I would like to have a date with you. Give me a chance, please."

She trusted people in uniform. She had a good feeling about Captain Shrewsbury. She had been at too many different, temporary places and been exposed to far too many different situations. But she was barely out of childhood and none of her adult experiences told her not to trust this handsome, uniformed father image type man.

She said, "Ok, just a chance to talk. Not a real date."

"Fair enough," he replied, "I'll be on leave for a week starting tomorrow. Where can I meet you?"

"Pick me up at the Jackson Heights YWCA, the day after tomorrow around noon, and if you wish, we can have lunch together."

Two days later, at the YWCA, Spencer was waiting for Linda. He arrived in his nearly brand new, big and luxurious shiny black BMW 745L minutes earlier than the agreed time. He was in civilian clothes, with an open shirt collar and sport jacket. Dark sunglasses on, absolutely, devastatingly handsome, directly out of a fashion magazine, he was a dream coming true. Linda bought a black satin dress for the occasion. The inexpensive, yet elegant choice of youthful outfit properly displayed her delicate and desirable body, rather large breasts and wide, provocative hips. Her abundant, dark bronze hair, freely falling down past her shoulders, surrounded her intelligent, oval shaped face. Shadows of sad melancholy, her hair provided the perfect frame for her pensive and sweetly unoffending lapis lazuli eyes.

Spencer drove her to the elegant colonial style Inn of Pound Ridge Restaurant in Westchester County. They took a seat near the fireplace by a picture window that had a pleasing view of the full bodied, flowery bloom of the English Garden outside. Linda has never seen a place like this from inside, she was impressed and loved being treated as if she were a rich suburban girl. The heavyset stonewalls and the brick arched windows enhanced her beauty and she smiled at Spencer and a happy and trusting disposition brightened her face.

Spencer ordered grilled fillet mignon with broccoli and Cabernet sauce for both. For wine, he selected a bottle of French Le Haut-Medoc du Prieure. Eyes gleaming enamor with anticipation, she watched the waiter uncork the bottle and pour a dash for Spencer.

Spencer took a swig, sloshed the taste about in his mouth and approved, "Good."

The waiter nodded and filled Linda's glass half full. His smile was reserved, polite and noncommittal, "Enjoy, Madame."

He failed to check Linda's age.

The steak was tender and delicious and the red wine served proper justice to deepen its juicy quality. The sublime fumes rose and made Linda's head spin. Cheeks turning red-hot, a lively crimson color painted her face. *I'm enjoying my first tipsiness,* she thought. *So, this is what the good life is all about.*

Observing Linda, Spencer admired her beauty; the natural and graceful elegance of her movements and her childish yet refined innocence. He was sure of his decision but wanted to wait for the right moment. The fire crackled; the massive, fragrant smelling maple logs ignited anew and little devils lurking behind the flames danced with demonic intrigue.

Mephistopheles rose from his fiery dungeons, stepped out of the fireplace and moving invisibly he stopped behind Spencer. Nodding with fiendish joy he snapped his fingers. *Go ahead. Do it. Now, my humble servant, I command you.*

Spencer reached into his pocket and pulled out a small jewelry box. He gently took Linda's hand in his, looked into her eyes and solemnly proposed.

"Linda Taylor, please marry me."

Linda didn't want to believe her good fortune. Barely out of the orphanage, she had nothing but hard struggle in a big, strange city ahead of her, and now, this middle aged, obviously well established man wanted to marry her. At the sideburns his hair had a touch of gray, yet he looked distinguished, attractive, youngish and handsome. And he was mature and obviously financially successful. His confidently sweeping manners diminished her feminine awareness to stay selective. Linda couldn't consider or foresee the serious consequences of a hasty decision. She was in no mood to rudely discourage him with her outright no and, demeanor bashfully encouraging, whispered back, "Captain Spencer Shrewsbury. I barely know you. You don't know me. How can you propose to me?"

He held onto her hand and squeezed it reassuringly. She didn't make an effort to retract and let Spencer pull her hand closer to his heart.

The captain went on, "Linda, sweet little innocent and young, Linda. I've been around enough to appreciate your virtues and to value my luck that a beautiful young woman, like you, is willing to listen to my plea."

She smiled timidly. *No harm in listening,* she thought and let him go on, "I'm here. You can talk."

"Come and live with me in my beloved town, Darien. You'll love our way of life. We have big houses and beautiful gardens. You'll love the neighbors. They're the best people in the world. My house is empty. When I come home I want to hear your voice, I want you to cheer up that empty and lonely place."

Meek, a tamed doe, venturing onto incitingly green, spring pastures, she blushed and dropped her eyelids. "It's a big decision."

"Of course it is. But trust me. I have money. I have a good job. And not in the least, I admire your beauty beyond words can describe. Or you think I'm repulsive and pushy, oh please, don't."

She let Spencer hold her hands and didn't retract them when his grip became stronger.

"No," she muttered under her breath, "I don't find you repulsive."

"What is it then? Am I too old?"

"No. I have no problems with that."

She was weakening and running out of even feeble excuses. She pretended to hesitate while what she truly wanted was not to let this opportunity slip away. She grew up in orphanages and foster homes and nobody ever told her, I love you. And even now she wasn't missing that all encompassing verb. It was perhaps a Freudian slip but there were no exchanges of I love you and cherish you forever expressions of deep feelings. But how could they have said or felt something like that, they hardly knew each other. But this, otherwise obviously important point, was completely neglected. She couldn't rely on the advice of her parents or her siblings. Alone, she was barely hanging on to the last threads of her frayed, evaporating resistance.

Linda tried to procrastinate, but it was to no avail. "Isn't there anything you want to ask me?" she asked submissively and it seemed her resolve was already subdued and conquered.

"I know who you are. I know you grew up in orphanages." He stared forcefully into her eyes and tried to impress her with his sympathy. "Your misfortune is my luck. Can an old bachelor like me get any luckier than to find a young lady like you without a frighteningly protective father and a demanding and inquisitive mother?"

"I do have a mother."

"You do? Where is she?"

"In jail, she is serving life sentence for killing her boyfriend."

The admission frightened her. She didn't intend to give away this embarrassing information. Was she scaring the captain away?

Captain Shrewsbury's character didn't come from a mold that could be easily thrown off balance. He answered as if he possessed vast fortitudes of inexhaustible superiority.

"I know you didn't inherit her genes. That's not in you. You wouldn't hurt a fly."

She felt opportunity being lost. Was she detecting a change in his tone? Was her big chance fading away? She had to make a decision while the offer was still on the table.

She mustered up her courage and boldly declared, "Yes, I'll marry you, Captain Spencer Shrewsbury."

Spencer grinned proudly. Slowly and gently, he slipped the diamond ring on her finger.

"Linda, my dearest," he called her dearest for the first time, "you're not going to regret your decision. I'll be a very good husband."

"And I'll be a good wife," she whispered softly, "be good to me and I'll take care of you and make you happy."

With these words they set on a course from where there was

no return. There was no more chance to alter their predestined path. There was no time machine to bring them back to their previous lives. They committed, for better or worse to the fate they chose. All her fortunes and misfortunes were predicated on the decision, she had made so quickly and under the influence of alcohol and under the enchanting charm of an elegant place. She was to become Mrs. Linda Shrewsbury, the wife of an airline pilot, a respectable position at any age but especially commendable, perhaps too demanding for her age of nineteen.

The wedding, less than a month later, took place in Darien, at the little old stone Presbyterian Church on Post Road. A couple of dozen old ladies and gentlemen represented the groom's family. They were friends of Spencer's mother and father, back from the good old days, when they were active and important members of the congregation.

Spencer didn't have many local friends any more. His work took him to far away places. The big properties isolated him of getting close to his neighbors and the town changed so much since his long forgotten high school years. It grew from the little coastal summer place of big estates to a major and super rich bedroom community of well to do people commuting to work in New York City. If he were to stand on the crowded railroad station platform, he wouldn't have known a soul. He could hardly remember or recall a familiar face.

Her jovial natured and chubby boss, Chef Garcia, presented Linda to the groom and her coworkers sat in the pews, green with envy and with facial expressions of obvious disbelief. Linda wore a long, pure white wedding dress. It looked perfect and she spent her last dollars on buying it.

Her dark bronze hair, crowning her pale face and cascading down onto her shoulders, provided an attractive contrast to the sparkling brightness of the dress and added solemn importance to the event. Spencer wore his black tuxedo and asked his copilot to be his best man.

The young Presbyterian pastor made a long and very inspiring speech about the joys and duties of married life, the importance of love and understanding and the lifetime obligation of care and tenderness. He mentioned the man's responsibility to protect and cherish his wife and the woman's duty to provide a good home and have a hot, tasty meal every night to welcome home the tired breadwinner.

Linda pondered how she would cook a meal every day, first she didn't know how to cook, second her husband was coming home maybe only once in every ten days. But she had no time to develop doubts and the ceremony proceeded on.

The pastor took their vows, the best man gave them the rings and they both congratulated the newlyweds and at close range witnessed the first kiss, they awkwardly exchanged.

The reception took place at the Piedmont Club, rented and decorated for the occasion. The food was excellent and plentiful; a disc jockey provided good music and Linda and Spencer swayed to the lively tunes. Linda swirled around with some of the older men and Spencer danced with some of the younger ladies, especially from the airport, who were provocative and shameless in expressing their shock and disappointment.

They kept whispering into Spencer's ears, "If I knew you wanted to marry I would have married you myself."

Spencer laughed, enjoyed the compliments and returned

them in kind, "It is too late, dear, but it doesn't mean that we cannot be good friends."

They both laughed like members of the same wife-swapping club, and he pulled their lithe body into his intimate embrace. Linda saw the frivolous acts of flirting; the obvious insinuations of lechery and the first hurt and pain entered her married life, even before she had a chance of consummating it.

Around ten o'clock their paid time was up, Manager, Joe Shirkey cleared the tables and started making preparations for the late night crowd. Spencer took Linda home and for the first time she entered his Darien house.

Inebriated, perhaps even drunk, the three miles long drive was no challenge to Spencer, the pilot of jumbo jets. At home, as soon as they entered the house, he rushed to the bar and poured himself a half of highball size glass of his finest scotch.

Gulped it down, and casting at Linda a curious and peculiar glance, he grunted, "We did it, I don't believe it but we did it. We are married. I never thought I would ever get married."

"I haven't forced you. Have I?"

"No. You just were in the right place in the right time."

"Is that all you have to say?"

"Come on. I'm and old bachelor. I don't know how to court a pretty woman."

"I thought you knew everything."

"Of course," he guffawed and drank more, "provided I have enough alcohol in me."

"Then drink and be brave."

"You are absolutely right, my dear, alcohol is the elixir of life."

He gurgled out from the bottle another full glass of Chivas Regal and poured it into his throat without swallowing.

Staring at Linda with unmitigated lust he mumbled, "There, now we enter the fun part phase."

Confused, yet naturally curious and thanks to her youthful and abundant hormones Linda wasn't afraid to have sex with Spencer. She wanted to see him happy and make him devoted to her; she wanted to show this old bachelor, now her husband, the best time he ever had. But her exposures and experiences were limited and she tried to make up for her shortcomings by pretending she knew exactly what was expected from a young bride on her wedding night.

Linda put her arms around Spencer and tried to kiss him. Spencer, now drunk almost beyond delirium, alcohol soaked stench and unbearable breath, his repulsive equanimity stymied her desires. But she forced herself to embrace her husband

To Linda's surprise he pushed her away. "Take off your wedding gown. It is so tight and uncomfortable. You are like a medieval knight in armor. I can't even touch you in that travesty."

She removed her gown and for the first time in her life she stood wearing provocative lacey underwear in front of a man, ready and threatening to make love to her.

Spencer tried to sober up and come to his senses; he took his young wife into his arms and carried her upstairs to the master bedroom. Her bare hands and naked legs dangled, enervated and obediently inert, and he had to catch his breath.

He cursed, "What a dumb customary practice, a stupid habit, why can't you walk on your own?"

She took it as a joke and laughed, "I'm not that heavy, big man. Do what you are supposed to do."

Upstairs he placed her on his bed, stepped back and began to undress. Ready for the inevitable, Linda raised her upper body up, supported herself on her elbows and stared at Spencer, and she had romantic interest and lustful curiosity in her eyes.

He looked back, shamelessly disrobed and, naked as a man-eating aboriginal, he stood in front of her. She bashfully glanced at him and the sight made her ashamed.

"Could you turn off the lights?" She begged.

He turned the lights off and in the darkness things seemed easier. The pale moonlight, shining into the bedroom turned her into a fair skinned Celtic heroine, sitting on a rock and waiting for her lover and ready to submit to his desires.

He came closer, knelt down on the bed and pulled down her panties. She shuddered with primordial female fright but the man was her husband and she didn't want to flee. He unhooked her bra and threw it on the floor. His hairy chest touched her shoulders and she awkwardly put her arms around his neck.

Forty-five years old Spencer pushed his six foot two inches and two hundred pound heavy boned, no fat and bulging muscled body down on her and tried to force her legs apart. Nineteen years old, five foot eight, hundred and ten pounds at the most, Linda only had delicate and long bones, soft and tender tissues for muscles and perhaps a little fat on the right places. She disappeared under him and any resistance was useless.

Spencer passed his age of easy excitement years ago. He had seen and done everything what there was to be seen and done. He tried it with everybody in every which way he could think of. Lately, in the last few years, he noticed that he was losing his spontaneous and ready at command erections and he needed special techniques and situations to stay aroused and hard, techniques Linda could not possibly have known or heard of.

Spencer kept the pressure on. He expertly pinned Linda on her back and pressed his belly against hers. Holding her knees, he spread her long legs apart and placed his half erect but very large and thick penis in front of her entrance. He pushed in, and it didn't go.

Young Linda, wet with sexual arousal and slippery like a bubble bath, yet Spencer couldn't penetrate. Her strong and resilient hymen blocked his way. Spencer kept trying and when Linda realized the problem, she turned carmine red with embarrassment and whispered to her husband, "I'm sorry, Spencer, I'm a virgin; I've never had a man before. I'm sorry, dear."

"Yes, of course, how silly of me," Spencer mumbled and pulled out of her.

She asked. "You are not angry at me. Are you?"

He hated her. *Why did he have to get married?* He thought. *The last thing I need is a condescending little slut in my bed.* He felt like hitting her. Slap her pretentious, cute face, but not yet, not on their wedding night. He couldn't let her discover his weaknesses, his dark side. He had to go on and make his failure look unimportant. Blame it on her.

He said with calm that almost forebode a lasting grudge, "We don't have to do it tonight. I can wait until you get used to doing it. I don't want to force you."

He turned on his back and they lay next to each other, silent and ill at ease. Terrified of provoking the big man's anger Linda didn't dare to say a word. Her heart pounded inside her skinny ribcage and she jumped with eagerness to please when, after a long wait, Spencer spoke, "You could do something for me though. I would like it very much."

"Anything, what is it?"

Spencer had failed as a man but he still painfully desired to have sex with her. He was infatuated by her nakedness and he had to have her one way or the other. He had to disgrace her; he had to denigrate her to teach her from the very beginning that he was in command, in command on his plane and in command in his bedroom.

He said, "Come on the top of me, turn around and let me taste you."

Linda wanted to make up for her perceived failure to consummate their marriage, turned around and did as told. He glued his mouth on her soft, well-developed labium, between her legs and stuck his tongue inside. That gave Linda pleasure, she moaned and feeling relief she relaxed and felt she almost could enjoy the act.

She thought. *After all, he must like me for doing this.*

He pushed her head down toward his limp manhood and Linda followed his push. Soon he was getting strong and thick, that made her almost choking but with relentless force he kept pushing her head down and further down. At the end he wailed like an old woman singing a dirge, let out an inarticulate and prolonged cry and released his load. Close to asphyxiation, she couldn't breathe and forcefully had to break her mouth away from him.

Spencer finished his pleasure and drunken and exhausted, in a minute he snored like a hibernating bear.

His falling asleep concluded the action part of their wedding night.

Having regained her freedom, Linda rushed to the

bathroom. She closed the door and spitting out and spewing saliva, she threw up into the toilet bowl. Still nauseated, she washed her face and furiously searched for an unused toothbrush. Finding one she brushed her teeth with vigorous anger and rinsed her mouth at length. Repeated it, again and one more time using antiseptic mouthwash. Having finished with her mouth, she climbed up on the lavatory, crouched down and, frantically like a macerating brush, thoroughly cleaned out her bottom.

After a half an hour of desperate cleansing she took her nightgown from her suitcase, put it on and lay down next to Spencer.

Tense, shaking with nervousness and at the end of her strength, she couldn't fall asleep. Badly confused, she had to keep confronting her bothersome and doggedly lurking final thought for her wedding night, *Good God, I'm still a virgin and if that's what sex is all about, God help me, I'm not going to like it at all.*

Spencer didn't seem interested in sex for the next few days. He set up Linda in the house, bought all kind of toiletries, creams and soaps to make her comfortable. He was a good spender. Whatever Linda liked and asked he bought. He showed her where the supermarket was, let her fill up a big shopping cart and helped her to put all the purchased items to their proper places in the house. He appeared to be a good, caring husband, although one could have made the observation that he was a control maniac and wanted to have everything the way he wanted them to be, and the same way he always has been used to having them, exactly the way his mother had them for decades.

In a about a week, Spencer left for his next ten days

tour of duty. This time he took a limousine to the airport and left the big BMW for Linda with the warning that she shouldn't drive it around too much with her limited driving experience.

Their marriage hasn't been properly consummated and it remained unfulfilled for some time to come. Linda bought cookbooks, cleaned and decorated the house and made sure to have a good meal prepared when Spencer eventually came home. But he wasn't hungry and ate little from what she cooked. She kept trying, he didn't complain and things started to smooth and seemed settling into a mundane, mutual understanding.

Chapter Three

Percy went home, took a quick shower and put on a pair of freshly washed and pressed white tennis shorts. On top he pulled on a sleeveless shirt and checked his image in the mirror.

His expression seemed pleased with himself, as if he never needed to face problems bigger than teaching tennis on lovely spring afternoons.

Down on the driveway he opened the trunk of his car and made sure he had the ball basket and his duffel bag of extra tennis balls. Taking a relaxed minute, he checked the string tensions and inspected the grips on his tennis racket. When everything looked in order and to his picky satisfaction, he drove to Valala Delicatessen.

"Hi Joe," he told his former high school antagonist, now a polite deli clerk, "make me a Boar's Head baked turkey breast sandwich on a hard roll."

"Anything on it?"

"Lettuce and mustard. And I'm going to grab three bottles of Perrier."

A firm believer in healthy eating, Percy was the living proof of his practices, for he never got sick. Never even sneezed, that was just another filthy thing he didn't do.

After Valala he headed down on Noroton Avenue, turned right by the red brick new Presbyterian Church and made a quick left onto Nearwater Lane, toward Weed Beach. He waved at the young black man, an earring in his right lobe, watching TV in the guard booth. Parked his car and came back to give the guard eight bucks for court number one, from two o'clock until four.

Checking his watch, he saw it was barely quarter past one. *Plenty of time to enjoy lunch,* he thought and took out his hard plastic, light blue cooler box. He went out to the sandy beach area and near the water and under a tree sat down at a picnic table.

Simple or complicated, life must be enjoyed; he mumbled and began to eat.

Taking savory bites from the juicy meat and the crisp lettuce he fixed his eyes, with no particular purpose or interest, across the calm waters of Long Island Sound. The tranquility of the moment filled him with a feeling of priceless luxury. The serenity of the location, and having the busy and bustling hard working world so safely remote and being so securely tucked far away, gave him inner peace. Maybe Percy did comprehend that something wasn't right. In moments like this, he might have pondered that he needed to gather life experiences, or he should be going out to see the world, should meet interesting people and characters, otherwise, and he knew that much, he would never be able to produce the first page of a novel that was publishable.

But what the heck, he figured, life is not a horse or a dog race, it always could be worse. He could be paying child support, for as much he knew, he could have a drinking problem or God forbid, a drug addiction. His thoughts wandered about but basically, he was content with his life and satisfied with himself, the way he was. He has never been bored and never suffered from loneliness, depressed or been in dire need of human company. He reasoned, boredom created all the problems of the world and he; Percy, with his freelance work, tennis lessons and literary experiments invented the antidote. He was not a boring person to be lonely with, after all.

After devouring his sandwich and feeling gratified, he piled pleasure on top of pleasure and bought a cone of chocolate ice cream. Sat down again and pondered about life a little more before packing up his lunchbox and walking back to the tennis courts.

His three students arrived a few minutes before two. Three middle-aged women, Darienates; felicitous, careless and well to do, giggling and talking without taking even split second, squeezed in between breathing, breaks.

They greeted him, "Hello Percy, we are ready for you."

"Hi Susan, Amy, Eileen," Percy spoke with self assured confidence, "remember, first we have to warm up. Please form a line and do the exercises with me."

To garner Percy's attention the three women tried to outdo one another. Standing, stretching and bending down with legs slightly apart they teased him with a witty show of comedy.

"Is there any position, Percy that you haven't tried?

"Show us something that we haven't done already."

Percy kept a serious face, "Ladies, bend down and up, one and a two, let's get moving."

"Percy, how do you meet your women?" One of them asked. The two other chuckled and stifled their bursting out laughs for they knew the punch line.

"He checks in at Howard Johnson and hangs the sign, Ladies' Room, on his door."

"You'd better believe it. He also thinks he runs a galley ship."

"What's wrong with that?"

"What? He is the slave driver."

"It gets worse than that?"

"What way?"

"He is the captain and he wants to water ski."

The three women in their sexy tennis shorts kept chattering but following Percy's lead, swung their arms, lifted their legs and pushed their hips back and forth.

When, with the warm up exercise Percy had tortured enough his students, he brought the ball basket to the middle of the opposite half of the tennis court. He came to the net with a few balls in his hands and pockets and announced to his students, "Today we're going to practice the forehand stroke."

Someone couldn't resist letting out an undignified wisecrack, "Percy, which hand do you prefer when you stroke a few?"

He acknowledged the saucy and disrespectful note with an all-knowing smile, stepped closer to the women and explained, "Hold the racket, use the forehand grip that I showed you girls last week, pull the swing arm all the way back, hold the racket vertical to the ground, hit the ball and follow through by letting the racket swing high in front of your faces."

He checked and corrected each woman's starting position until they all got it right. Walked to one after the other and made sure that he stood in close body contact near their behinds. He personally took their hands, slightly rubbed his body against their buttocks and almost hugged them following the upward swing of the racket. This delightful exercise killed about thirty minutes. Their cheeks flaming with rosy shades of health, the students seemed getting their money's worth.

"Now I'll go over the other side and will start hitting two balls to each of you. Use the forehand stroke, the way we just learned doing it and hit it back to me."

They kept hitting the balls until the ball basket emptied out. Then Percy yelled out, "Ball collection time."

He stayed at the net and watched the ladies collecting the balls. Bending down they seemed to expose to him, on purpose perhaps, their cute, feminine, white cotton panty covered derrieres.

Watching the delightful sight he was at the peak of his happiness when from the corner of his eyes he saw Pamela sitting down on the spectator bench just outside of the tennis court's wire fence.

He tried to ignore her, but her presence didn't go unnoticed by his tennis disciples, "Friend of yours?" They asked.

Percy couldn't whisper. Whatever he was about to say or explain had to be yelled across hundred feet of hard, reverberating tennis court surface, "My good neighbor. Maybe she likes to watch the best of the local talents."

Eileen, the biggest mouth of the group yelled to Percy, "She must be checking on you. You'd better behave."

Susan seconded, "She is checking you out for her daughter."

Percy hit a real hard spinning ball. It curved and bounced up directly at her foot. She had to duck but had time to whisper to Amy, "I sure hope to God, she is better looking than her."

Jokes or teasing, no avail, the good mood seemed to catch a cold. The three paying students made an extra effort to look half way decent beginner tennis players and clearly were annoyed by and disliked Pamela's presence. Percy also thought that it was uncalled for and impertinent from Pamela to show up uninvited. But it was a town park and she could sit wherever she decided to put down the cheeks of her fleshy bottom.

In the second forty-five minutes, Percy introduced the ladies to the art of making a good service smash. He explained the theory, swung his racket, bent his left leg, lowered his right shoulder, tossed to ball straight up brought his racket up and smashed the ball down. He went to each lady, held their arms, pushed their left knees from behind and thrust their hips forward.

Needless to say but the teaching of this technique also required a lot of personal touch and associated close physical contact.

Percy's students were happy with the special treatment. They were delighted to watch Pamela frustration and irritation to grow with Percy's increasing show of his displeasure about her unwanted presence at the tennis instructions. At the end of the session, Percy collected twenty dollars from each student and made them promise, they will meet next week, same place, same time again.

Seeing the breakup of the tennis lessons, Pamela came onto the court and introduced herself to the other women, "Hello, my name is Pam. I live next door to Percy. I didn't want to believe that he was such a good tennis instructor. Maybe I should start taking lessons from him."

"He is the best." The three gave an almost simultaneous supportive reply. "And he is shamelessly young isn't he?"

Percy interrupted the palaver before Pam could go on and reveal more, "Sorry, Pam. I'm all booked for the season."

Pam never really meant to spend money on tennis lessons but she wanted to indicate to the others that Percy was hers.

"Anyway, Percy," Pamela said. "If you want me to pay you, you have to do real work. You know how it goes, don't you?"

Indicating her desire to ignore the pushy outsider, Eileen, the oldest of the tennis students turned away from Pam and said, "Percy dear, remember, tonight we have our weekly prayer session at the Cavalry Baptist Church on Post Road. You are more than welcome to join."

Percy glanced at Pam and answered, "Eileen, I'm so sorry. I have prior arrangements; I can't come to the church tonight."

Eileen saw the near imperceptible exchange of signals between Percy and Pam and retorted with an obvious and intentional hurt in her voice.

"What can be more important than God?"

Hearing no answer, she continued. "Every lost lamb is important to the Lord and I'm afraid that you are one of them. Think about it."

"Sorry, I can't break a promise, maybe next time."

The victory was Pam's, although she couldn't declare it; she couldn't brag to the others that Percy was coming to her house, late tonight to put up a curtain rod. She wished that she could yell, out loud, that Percy belonged to her, but in this small town, she still had to make sure that she complied with the perceived morals and followed accepted standards of behavior. She had to be content with having planted a tiny seed of suspicion that she had something to do with Percy after all. Having an enigmatic, victory implying smile on her face, she walked back to her car.

The three women chat amongst them, pretending disinterest, until she drove away then turned to Percy, "See you next week, young man. Watch out for her. She is in love with you and she is the jealous type."

"That's her problem."

"She is going to make it your problem. Trust us."

"Don't worry. I know what I'm doing."

"Oh really, then tell us, how do you get rid of her when you change your mind? She isn't going to move. You may have to."

Percy collected the tennis balls into the duffel bag. Together with the wire basket he put them into his car and drove home. At home he sat down at his word processor and wrote the next chapter of his current novel. He worked nonstop until he heard his mother yell, "Dinner is ready, everybody, come down to eat."

Percy came down and sat down on his chair at the family dining room table. His father, already sitting at the table and seemingly deeply absorbed, was reading the editorials of the New York Times. Hearing Percy sitting down, he glanced up and saw a chance to express the opinion he has been formulating since lunch.

"They're pushing it too much. This gay marriage issue is out of control. Marriage should be legal only between a man and a woman. Those unmoral liberals are wrecking the very foundations of this country."

Percy loved to debate; he always presented a dissenting opinion regardless what the issue was or what his personal opinion happened to be. His basic instinct wanted to bring out the true feelings and personal thoughts from everybody, so later he could form his characters and include anything said or implied into his writings.

He challenged his father, "Dad, what do you expect them to do? Back in the 1980s they were over-promiscuous. Everybody did it with everybody. Then came the AIDS epidemic and they were told to have a steady partner. Have a lifetime significant other and stop spreading the disease. Now they want to be faithful to each other, they want to have a commitment and we're telling them again, that is wrong too. What do you care if they are married or not? Before the 1964 Civil Rights Act, interracial marriages were banned in most states because they also were considered immoral."

Mr. Lawrence Grimsby stared with righteous disapproval at his youngest son. He didn't like his dissenting opinions. As an engineer he was used to dealing with facts, numbers and unchallengeable realities. Liberal minded, as he thrived to be, he accepted his son the way he turned out to be. He always looked for the best qualities in any man. He knew Percy was a good person, perhaps too much of an independent thinker, perhaps somebody who could never afford to own a house like his father, but Mr. Grimsby knew that humanity took all kinds and he willed himself to tolerate behavior on the odd side. But this time, Percy's hardheaded and well-informed opinion about gays surprised and annoyed him.

He tried to lecture his son. "I think the Moral Majority should return our nation to its Christian constitutional origins."

Percy had given a lot of thoughts to this subject during his writing sessions and had his reply ready, "Why should the fundamentalist have the right to rule our diverse country and dictate how everyone shall live?"

His father let his indignation expand, "Son, you are going to get into a lot of trouble with this kind of reasoning. You will pay the price for your liberties."

"I don't have liberties but I cannot silently stand by as the xenophobic majority sanctions discrimination against and allows injustice done to certain minorities. I'm worried that the Moral Majority is trying to stop anything they deem objectionable. They will impede my free thinking as a writer seeking truth and justice for all."

The father had no recourse but launch a personal attack at his son.

"Are you trying to defend the rights of queers?" He raised his voice.

His oldest son, David, already a self-confident certified public accountant, in spite of his young twenty-eight years of age, interrupted them.

"Maybe he is one of them. He doesn't have a girlfriend. I've never yet seen him with a woman."

Percy snapped back, "I haven't found the right person yet. And I don't like to pay for whores like you do, if that's your criteria of high morals?"

Percy's mother Rosemary called out, "Boys, stop it. Dinner is on the table; start passing your plates."

She served plenty to her family. Bowls of potatoes, rice, vegetables and a platter of neatly arranged pork chop slices filled up the middle of the table. The food smelled delicious and the tasty meal and the quick stuffing of the empty stomachs stymied all further disagreements and accusations.

After dinner, Percy volunteered to do dishes and clean up the table. He collected the plates, pushed the food scraps into the garbage disposal and placed the china, the glasses and utensils into the dishwasher. By the time he completed the cleanup, his parents were already comfortable and settled in the family room and were watching a movie on Cinemax. Percy sat down with them for a few minutes and after seeing them getting too much involved in the simplistic movie plot, he climbed back to his feet and quietly walked up to his room. He checked his watch. It was only half past eight.

For Percy it was the perfect opportunity and chance to recharge his batteries. He took a nap but made sure he woke up a few minutes before ten.

Like a stealthy eavesdropper he listened to the noises of the house. Parents were still watching TV, and the siblings were yakking on the phone in their rooms.

Like a tomcat on the prowl, Percy tiptoed down the stairs, passed by the door of the family room and, not expecting any answer, told his parents.

"I'll be out for a little while."

Chapter Four

Now, after he acquired what he wanted, a lovely wife; a faithful beauty in his house waiting at home while he was far away on long trips, Spencer wasn't bound to change his celibate ways. Her sunny and youthful disposition, watching and absorbing her cheery presence, seemed to be enough for the man in him and they did not consummate their marriage.

Spencer didn't feel like begging for sex. Married or not, he had to stay in total control and that was the only way he could have imagined leading his life. In his heart he chose to remain a bachelor, but when talking to more serious and family oriented colleagues, he proudly boasted having a young and attractive wife.

He said, "She is not only young, beautiful and sexy but

she is a delightful person to be with. I got very lucky for my older years".

When directly asked about their marital life in bed, he dismissed the inquiry, "I don't look at things that way." Or. "What do you think? Just look at that fresh flower full of zest."

Gone on long trips and enduring his lonely airline pilot life, Spencer reverted back to being a single man, the one he always has been. In Seoul, he visited the same Geisha house as before and all over the world he kept frequenting popular health clubs and hot water spas. He made friends with strangers just like when he was a celibate. That's the way he liked it and to please young Linda, he wasn't about to change his addictive, obsessive habits.

On his first trip, after his wedding, he had two days layover in Budapest. He checked himself into the modern, recently built Hotel Liget, had a comfortable night sleep in his clean and air-conditioned room. By next morning, Budapest time, he got rid of his jetlag, had a substantial English breakfast and passing by the famous Heroes' Square walked over to the attractive Szechenyi Baths Spa.

Spencer had been there before. The Szechenyi, his favorite place in Budapest was one of the largest health spas in Europe and offered watery relaxation on a grand scale. Outdoors, in the middle of a great city park, a ring of three story high buildings surrounded a vast courtyard that equaled paradise. Three large pools with different temperatures, restaurants, liquor bars, ice cream and noshing stands and rooftops secluded for naked sunbathing, all facilities were isolated from any intruding city noise. The resort was indeed a tranquil place of carnal indulgence.

Inside the massive circle of buildings was an intricate maze of thermal baths, steam rooms and saunas. Spencer could exercise and laze about all day long; alternate between admiring the beautifully laid out architecture of ivy clad walls outside or indulge in naked hedonism inside.

Complete with arches, domed roofs and spiked towers of former minarets, the baths of Budapest were the finest reminder of the city's otherwise lost Ottoman architecture. Lolling in the warm water, while the rays of the morning sun were cutting through the rising steam, he easily could have imagined himself being a Turkish Pasha, in his harem, reviewing newly purchased wives.

Outdoors he could watch young girls in tiny bikinis but indoors where nakedness was allowed the sexes were separated. Spencer preferred indoors.

It was Tuesday; a day reserved for men only in the complex indoor labyrinth of the steam bath area. He bought his ticket, walked through the gate and handed over the stub to the young, linen jumpsuit clad, chubby attendant. In return he received a white, well it was white once but now yellow and aged, tiny apron. The attendant showed him to the changing room where he completely undressed and tied the little piece of cloth around his waist.

Next, Spencer walked along a long, brightly lit and clean corridor with new tiles and freshly painted walls. Entered the main bathing area and went directly to the showers. Removed the apron and thoroughly soaped his body. Glancing at the pool, he noticed two, late middle-aged men, looking at him with interest and peculiar curiosity.

After the shower, Spencer went to the hottest pool. It was at least 104 degrees, sparkling clean and constantly replenished from an abundant hot spring belching up thermal water from thousands of feet below. He stretched his legs, spread his arms and fixed his eyesight in front of him, as carelessly and as relaxed as he possibly could, he pretended disinterest.

Soon he noticed one of the men, who previously observed him, came, sat down just around the corner and tried to make eye contact. Didn't like him, avoided his eyes and waited. Disappointed, the guy left but less than a minute later a second one replaced the first and positioned himself closer to Spencer.

Spencer didn't move and didn't look. The stranger slid his hands carefully and touched the tip of Spencer's fingers. Spencer still didn't move; he left his hands there, making his move look inadvertent and unintentional. From the corner of his eyes, Spencer glanced at him. He looked younger and physically better fit than the first. The stranger extended his legs, straight out in front of Spencer, and just under the water surface, temptingly, wiggled his toes.

They played the international male pickup ritual game by the rules described in the unwritten book of homosexual conduct. Spencer liked him and decided to respond. He reached with his leg and touched the other man's foot. A bold move on his part; it couldn't be construed as an accident, a mistake, or an inadvertent touch. It was obvious and deliberate. Now they exchanged glances, the stranger signaled Spencer that he understood his intentions but needed time to make their temporary friendship inconspicuous and unnoticeable by other bathers.

He left and waited a few minutes until Spencer had enough of the hot water and went to the moderate temperature main pool. It also had sitting benches all around. Spencer sat down and within a minute, his new friend, just like and old acquaintance, sat down next to him. They were sitting next to each other, as two good old trusty buddies engaged in casual discussion.

The stranger began the conversation in Hungarian.

"*Jo meleg a viz.*" He said.

Spencer smiled politely and shook his head. "I don't speak Hungarian."

Hearing the reply, his new friend, still a total stranger though, changed to a heavily accented, but understandable, broken English, "That's good, gives me a chance to practice my language skills."

He pulled his apron aside and showed his already half erect penis to Spencer.

Using one eye Spencer glanced at it and cautiously asked, "Is playing allowed here?"

"No," the man grinned conspiratorially, "but nobody is watching?

And he reached and touched the tip of Spencer's penis.

He said, "My name is Leslie. I don't have any diseases. I like you very much and I like to meet you somewhere in private."

He spoke and acted straightforward, needed no courtship, bonding, character references, nothing. He had gotten to his point right away.

Spencer didn't want to have a date with him and didn't respond. The same time he didn't want him to go away and let him keep playing with the head of his pecker.

The stranger, Leslie, obviously encouraged, kept talking and pushed on with his verbal advances from a different direction, "I like this place, there are not that many people here, and there are no young prostitutes, desperate people from Romania or other places. One can easily get a disease from those. It is safe over here, between us, older guys. I'm married, I have a wife and family, but this thing is coming on me. I can't resist it and I don't want to resist it. What about you?"

The feeling of excitement, seething forward and unstoppable, made Spencer hyperventilate. With his arousal building up, a pleasing sensation indeed, he liked this forbidden game of high testosterone. He ceased to be a respectable airline pilot; he wasn't the honored Darien residence, the newlywed; he was a desperate and reckless faggot picking up another one.

He said, "I am married too. But I like to fool around just like you. I don't mind to play."

Leslie pushed on while the game was hot and things seemed being on the move. "Let's go to the steam room." He suggested.

They left and entered the foggy, dripping hot room, but another guy, old and wrinkled ancient relic, was already sitting there. Seeing him they didn't want to leave right away and pretended that they came in for the steam and the heat and, first putting their aprons under their butts, sat down on a wooden bench.

They talked again. Spencer asked, "Are you still making love to your wife?"

"No, she doesn't like sex anymore. She thinks that I'm completely impotent."

"Are you?"

"No, way," Leslie replied and they both laughed.

Leslie continued, "Come over to my place, I let you make love to her. I've always been telling her to have sex with other guys. I like to watch."

"Is she making out with other guys?"

"No, she is old, she doesn't like sex any more, but when she was younger she had a lot of boyfriends."

"Did you approve it?'"

"She never told me. I would have approved it but women are habitual liars. They fool around and they deny it. They feel better that way."

Spencer thought for a second about his young wife, Linda. He thought about how young she was, she appeared to strongly desire sex and he couldn't satisfy her. A cold whip of cruel jealousy gripped his heart, but Leslie, oblivious to Spencer's introspection, suggested, "It is getting too hot over here. Let's go into the cold water pool."

Having had too much from the wet heat, together like two playful boys, they rushed out and jumped into the refreshing seventy-five degrees water of the pool in the next room.

They vigorously splashed around in the cold water that quickly cooled them off. Later they tried the sauna room. Large, unused and with the temperature turned down it had tiered wooden bleachers and plenty of room. But most importantly, nobody was inside.

They closed the door. Spencer reached down and started to stroke Leslie's penis. It grew long and hard. Leslie reciprocated, bent down and put his mouth on Spencer's penis.

With his erection stone stiff and his voice wavering with excitement, Spencer whispered to Leslie, "I want you to fuck my wife. She is young and sexy."

Inflamed with arousal and delight, Leslie voice trembled as he covetously viewed Spencer's ass, "I prefer fucking you."

"Right here, and now," Spencer asked but gave no consent or indicated protest.

In lieu of answering Leslie turned Spencer around, pulled his buttocks apart and entered him from behind. His dick slippery with hot water and sweat, foreskin retracted almost to the base, he easily slid into him. Shameless and unconcerned with dangerous infections, Spencer enjoyed the prostrate massage he was receiving from behind. The throbbing inside tingles and the overpowering strong thrill of the unnatural stimulation reached almost unbearable levels. Leslie rode on Spencer rising pleasure, reached out and with expert technique jerked him off. Moaning and out of breath the two men ejaculated the same time. Spencer came onto the floor, but Leslie shot his load way inside into the anus of the newlywed, airline pilot.

As soon as the male coitus came to an end, Leslie rushed out of the sauna and left Spencer standing there. Surprised by the abrupt conclusion of their friendship, Spencer lingered on for a short while, and in a minute, as a lamb of innocence, ambled out from the room. He couldn't see Leslie anywhere. He had disappeared and Spencer couldn't find a trace of him any more even if he wanted to have him for a follow up.

Spent and having lost his lust, Spencer felt stupid; he took a shower, thoroughly scrubbed himself and went to the towel room. He picked up one from the rack of large, warm and dry fresh towels and lay down on one of the cots that stood there to provide rest after bath. He fell asleep and woke up an hour later.

He still couldn't see Leslie but he didn't care any more. He had to go on, and tomorrow, next week, in a different town he was going to find a different new friend anyway.

Spencer dressed up. Rested, his carnal passion satisfied, he left the spa. He walked across the great park of Varosliget, back to his hotel. Had a good lunch and headed back to the airport. His Budapest adventure was over. He may have regretted it now, but in a few days he had the same urges and desires for he never had any willpower to control or delay his dangerous, compulsory and instant sexual gratifications.

One thing he never did think about and denied to acknowledge, that Leslie or any of his fleeting partners were lying about their free of diseases condition. He reasoned that married men was supposed to be infection free and was all right to fool around with them.

Chapter Five

Taking a narrow path through the dark bushes Percy went over to Pamela's house. Approaching from the backside, he lightly tapped on the kitchen window. Waiting for his arrival, she pulled the curtains an inch apart and peeked out. Seeing Percy she unlocked the sliding door and, just barely enough to let him in, pushed the handle. The heavy door glided with ease and he silently entered her house.

Inside Percy flashed the sleek bottle of burgundy to her he brought with him and with a girlish curtsy she acknowledged the tribute, "Put the bottle on the cocktail table in the family room," she said, "and come back. Let's relax and unwind for a little while."

Percy took the corkscrew from the kitchen drawer; he

knew where everything was and popped the cork. Filled up two large wine goblets and they sat down, Pamela on the sofa and Percy in a large armchair directly across from her.

Thirsty tongues sticking out, like a pair of lion and lioness at a midnight water hole, they wet their lips with the chilled, sweetish-tart tasting liquid. The strong wine flooded their conscience; heads became dizzy and light, and the alcohol urged them to talk.

"Percy, dear," she asked, "do your parents know you are here?"

"No," he sipped cautiously from his wine, "why should they know or care where I go?"

"You are not ashamed of me. Are you?"

"It's not that," he savored the joy of inebriation, that pleasantly began blurring the better part of his brain, and mumbled. "They just don't have to know everything."

"You should be proud that I take interest in you." Pamela talked with a trace of petulant hurt. "Have I told you how big of a wedding I had with my husband? My parents were rich, they spent a lot of money on my wedding, and my fiancée was handsome like a movie star. We had many good years together. Joshua was a cute little boy. Believe me, those were good days."

In his uncaring mood, head buzzing with proverbial bees, Percy interrupted her sentimental tirade with uninterested irony. "Too bad I missed it." He took another long sip from his glass and suggested in a bored, impatient tone. "Maybe we should take a look at that curtain rod now."

"Slow down, cowboy," she wasn't ready and hesitated, "just because I'm older than you, it doesn't mean that I will jump when you have the urge."

"I don't have the urge," he backed off sulkily. "I just

wanted to look at that curtain, you've been complaining about so much."

She kicked off her slippers and raised her right foot, high, way up into the air. Reaching out, she wiggled her toes and touched Percy's strong bulge between his legs.

"Pamela badly needs a massage," she said incitingly, "massage it for her. Please."

In the dim light Percy sized her up. Saw her reflection in the wine glass and gently took her foot into his hands. He didn't have to say a word. He knew she was serious but he denied acknowledging that she was in love with him.

Massaging her foot, he stared at her big, heavy thighs. He clearly could see her laced black panties and underneath the silky material her enormously big and fat pubic mound. He could judge by the protruding amount of thick black hair that it was unshaved and splendidly covered with sexy and animalistic fur.

"Is Joshua sleeping?" He asked; voice throaty and full with stifled eagerness. He was losing reason and care to abide by the rules of conventional morality. His lusty libido, properly put into gear by her raw display of mature genitalia, but considering little Joshua in the house he didn't feel comfortable to make love on the sofa without the security of locked doors.

Pamela, seeing his easy arousal and readiness, saw the opportunity to break down the last vestiges of his hesitation.

She said, "Yes. He is. Let's go up to my bedroom, quietly though."

He didn't object; the effect of the alcohol made his brain float with unhinged, foggy easiness. They went upstairs, Pamela first, Percy after. Her big behind wiggled inches away from his face. He massaged the mounds of her undulating flesh and she stifled a giggle and let out little squeaky cries of phony protest.

In the bedroom Percy asked, "Where is that curtain you've been talking about?"

She hasn't turned on the lights yet; she pulled Percy close to the window, pulled the curtains slightly apart and said, "That's the one."

Percy stepped closer to investigate and he saw, across the dark patch of bushes, in the neighboring house the light was on. Not prying, rather by instinct, he looked and saw Captain Spencer Shrewsbury.

Standing tall, grasping the end of his leather belt in his raised fist he was hitting a lump on the floor. Through the open windows, Percy could hear a low, almost imperceptible female weeping of humiliation and pain.

He looked again, more focused this time, and saw a young woman, probably Captain Shrewsbury's wife on the floor. Curled up on her knees, with her clinched hands, she tried to protect her head and hinder the blows she was receiving.

Than Percy heard the captain's voice, "You've been unfaithful to me again. Haven't you. Tell me, who is it? Or I'll beat it out of you. One more time, who is it?"

The miserable poor creature on the floor just moaned and begged the big, obviously drunken man.

"No, no, ouch, owww, please no," she cried.

He hit her again. "Tell me that you had enough and you don't want to see him again."

She wailed with pain in a low almost inarticulate plea, "I have nobody, I swear. I've been always true and faithful to you; please stop."

He lifted his foot and with his heavy duty black Dock Martin shoes still on pressed down on the fragile woman's arm.

"I'll rip you apart if you do. Why don't you behave like any other wife?"

Pamela came closer and resting her chin on Percy's shoulder whispered to him, "When he is drunk he always beats up the poor wretch. He gets drunk as soon as he comes home from duty. He can't drink while he is flying and he is an acute alcoholic. He takes it out on her. And the worst part of it, she never even goes out, less having an affair with anyone. She is so shy and timid. Sometimes, I don't think she can even talk."

Anger made Percy's blood boiling. Utterly sorry for the victimized little woman he felt each hit on his own skin and her cries penetrated down to the deepest bottom of his soul. He couldn't see her face, and for that matter he couldn't even recall what she looked like but he knew she had to be protected, it wasn't right to hit, abuse and torture a woman by anyone. A big lump lodged in his throat, Percy's adrenalin level shot up to painful heights. His heartbeat speeded up with raging anger at the abuser and with sympathy for the victim.

He grumbled to Pamela, "No one should hit a woman, ever. He is going to kill her, we should do something."

"Do what? That's their business," she tried to trivialize, stymie his unjust overreacting. "Mind your own problems. You don't want to mess with Captain Shrewsbury. He is rich and well respected in this town. You are nobody. What do you want? She is not your wife or your sister. Forget it."

The beating stopped. The lump in the crouched position, Linda, remained on the floor. The captain went to the bathroom and making rattling noises, he was apparently throwing up.

Judged by the bangs and the thuds he made, he could hardly stand on his feet.

After minutes of eternity the little woman stood up. With cautious care she slowly lifted her sleeve and looked at the contused, deep purple wound. Massaging her arms and shoulders she limped over and climbed into the king size bed. She held her head up and when Spencer came back from the bathroom she forced a forgiving smile on her face.

Spencer tried to make up; his drunken glare became friendlier and he spoke in a conciliatory tone. She lifted the corner of the comforter and timidly prompted Spencer to lie down next to her.

Now, he was begging her, "I didn't mean to hurt you. If only, you could come with me on those long trips. I get so lonely sometimes. I miss you and I get jealous. Please forgive me."

He kicked off his shoes, pulled down his pants and tried to get into the big bed. With his head already spinning out of control, he took another big swig from the whiskey bottle he had on the night table. He couldn't live with himself without getting drunk. He had to drink until he collapsed, down and unconscious on the bed. Soon, Percy could see the captain's jaw dropping, and, across the yard, he could hear his strong snore.

Percy kept looking. He saw the young woman reaching and turning the lights off. The room became dark and quiet except for Spencer wheezing that reminded him of the grunting of a well-fed, sleeping swine.

Pamela tried to pull Percy away from the window, "The show is over," she warned. "He won't remember a thing tomorrow. Anyway, the day after tomorrow he is going to go away for two weeks and that little, feeble rickety pile of misery will have a break. Do not pity her; she knew what she was doing when she got married to that rich, much older guy. Now she has to bear the consequences. That's all. Forget about her. Pay attention to me. I'm strong and healthy and I don't have a husband. You don't have to fight for me."

"Pamela, please! Don't you have any compassion for her, feelings of sympathy?"

"No, none for her, but I think, my friend, you have your silly concerns and commiseration in spades but apparently none of your deep emotions are meant for me."

"No, it's not that. I just feel sorry for her."

"You have taken it too much to your heart. Haven't you?"

Percy looked at Pamela; there was sad melancholy on his face. "She is a saint," he pleaded. "She didn't fight back. She took her punishment with dignity; she didn't lower herself to the level of that animal. She is like a true Christian martyr. I really wish I could help her somehow."

His unreasonable concern upset Pamela. She set her heart on this evening with Percy. She planned the wine, made sure Joshua was in bed early. She put on her special perfume and she wanted to have Percy in her bed. Now that little sorrowful waste of humanity next door was spoiling her fun.

To save the evening she made one more attempt, "Come on. Let's go to the party room. Let's dance. Don't you want to dance with me?"

Percy didn't feel like touching Pamela, not any more. Lustful and filthy female in heat, he began despising her. Percy's thoughts were somewhere else; he was floating high in a celestial sphere of noble and heavenly feelings.

He murmured his answer absentmindedly, "Not now, maybe on the weekend. We can go to the movies or something."

Pamela had enough. She wasn't willing to take any more humiliation. She had to show she still had the upper hand, "In that case my friend. Get out of my house. Worship her. Put her on a pedestal. She won't give you anything. I don't think she has anything to give. And you will have to deal with that captain. He is going to teach you a lesson and you'll deserve it."

She had a vicious and infuriated grin on her face. She was angry and indignant. She was insulted in her feminine pride. This young gigolo betrayed her; he dared to notice another woman, impertinently somebody close to his age.

She opened the door for him, "Out, or I'll kick you out. There is nothing for you here tonight, you ungrateful bastard. I had enough of you. Out you go."

Percy was already on his way. Until her last words he was walking silently and stealthily, but now he didn't care any more. He rushed to the front door, flung it open and burst into the cold springtime night. A blessed feeling, he found a worthy muse for his secretly cherished poetry.

At home he sat down at his computer and began to write. The words effortlessly flooded out of him. Suddenly his main heroine came to life and an angelic muse kissed him on the forehead. He worked nonstop until dawn arrived. An awfully heavy burden of physical lust and promiscuous lewdness lifted off from his inner psyche and liberated his genius. Now, able to write about love and true passion without being chained down to earth by carnal and filthy desires, he began to create. From his preadolescent age he recalled his true love, an imaginary young woman, depressed and silenced by her tyrannical father and not allowed to meet with her one and only sweetheart, of course Percy, who else. He put her into eighteenth-century England, dressed her up in a tight bodice and a skirt with large hoops and covered with an elegant gown with long vertical pleats falling from her shoulders to the ground. He created a dreadful Northeastern stormy night where she had to wait for her lover to return from the raging and dangerous sea. He imagined that her father wanted her to get married to an old friend of his, for money and fortune and settling her father's debts. He wrote about the dramatic return of her young and invincible boyfriend and her rescue and their escape together to colonial America.

The burst of creative power, that kept him going all night long, finally ran its course. His eyes closed and sitting by his computer, he fell asleep on the keyboard.

Late next morning he woke up as a different man. He had purpose in life now. He had found himself. He was in love.

Chapter Six

Few days after the beating incident, browsing for his power bars in the Stop and Shop Supermarket, Percy thought he saw Mrs. Shrewsbury. Pushing her shopping cart between the isles she was slowly picking up, scanning and putting back items to and from the shelves. Percy hadn't yet met her face to face and wasn't sure if it was her.

He wanted to check. Rushed down in the next isle and came back up in the isle where he could see her from the other direction. Still a distance apart, he slowed down and looked.

Her facial expression seemed depressed and sadly unhappy. Her skin shined pale and her large, innocently blue eyes reflected dreary remoteness and concealed fear. As she moved, step-by-step and inch-by-inch closer and closer to Percy, the curly ringlets of her freshly washed, dark bronze hair floated around her shoulders like prairie grass undulate in the wind.

When she almost passed behind him, Percy turned around and called out.

"Mrs. Shrewsbury, fancy seeing you here."

She stopped and raised her subjugated, dreamy sight at him. He saw the fright and the unpleasant surprise in her eyes that someone noticed and exposed her. Percy almost froze, his smile turned awkward and shy, but he wished very much she would not resentfully keep on walking away.

Linda didn't remember Percy. She had no idea who the stranger greeting her was. At first, she thought, somebody, from her past, from the numerous orphanages or foster homes, recognized her. But then why would he be calling her Mrs. Shrewsbury? She looked at Percy with cautious interest. Saw a young man, maybe a few years older than her, kind of simple and unthreatening. Strange man frequently greeted her, mostly insolently and sometimes intruding cleverly, she spent a lot of time alone and without being escorted by her husband. At her young age most women were still unmarried and most of the times were in the company of their parents or their friends. She had to reflect rejection; she was an insecure loner and had to suspect wrongful intent. She didn't reply.

Percy however saw in her hesitation a chance to continue, "I'm your neighbor. I live almost next door, in the second house on your right. My name is Percy."

Linda remembered now. Unfocused eyes telling surprise and dreamy confusion, she was caught off guard and didn't know what to say. A foggy image from a freeze-framed silent movie, she hesitated to respond.

Riding on her indecisiveness Percy pressed on with his monologue, "I'm sorry if I startled you. I mean no harm. I thought, since we are neighbors, I should say hello and introduce myself."

Finally, Linda gathered her composure. She didn't want to look overly impressed that somebody greeted her from her street. She wanted to say something to make this encounter a simple and trivial, neighborly coincidence.

She smiled bashfully and her lips began to move, "Percy is the name, isn't it? That's right. I remember seeing you. You're cutting Pamela's grass. How do you do?" she said and offered her right hand to the young man.

Percy took her hand. He held it a second longer than modest politeness should have approved. He felt her warmth, the blood rushing under her skin and perceived the irresistible electrical current, through their touching fingers, passing from her soul to his heart. Percy's legs turned to soft mush with weakness and he fought with effort to control the tremors shaking them. Linda noticed Percy's lingering hold of her hand. She noticed the trembling of the boy's body and sensed the developing affinity. She never experienced this emotion before and she didn't know how to handle the effects confronting her. Frightened, she pulled away her hand and cut the encounter short.

"Say hello to Pamela for me. She is such a nice person," she said demurely and slowly, but at a steady pace started walking away.

Percy stood there, he tried to open his mouth, say something, make Linda stay longer but he lost all his self-confidence and his usual bold intrepidity.

He couldn't say anything more than a feeble and meek, "It's been nice meeting you."

She kept on walking but over her shoulders turned her head back and looked at Percy, "Linda. Call me Linda, please."

Percy didn't move until she turned the corner and disappeared. She was real. He has seen her face, touched her hand, she wasn't only his imagination. She had a voice. A warm, superbly elevating and heavenly cleansing feeling of happiness inundated Percy's insides. Linda, that's her name, and she wanted him to call her, Linda. For now he blocked out of his mind that she was married and had a big, mean and strong husband. Percy only saw a delicately beautiful young woman in distress and in need to be rescued from evil predicament. He made a loop with the cart and saw her at the checkout line. But he didn't dare to queue up behind her. Didn't want to bother her now; didn't want to take a chance and spoil the moment by rushing matters. He knew what destiny intended and, soon enough, it would bring them together again.

Linda, under the façade of her melancholy sadness, felt happy inside. She couldn't resist the urge to encourage the young man, but her action also frightened her. On second thought, she knew she shouldn't start a flirtation. What if this, uncaring young man is going to bother her and Spencer finds out. Remembered the beatings and her shoulders shuddered with horror. That's all she needed, an admirer. She tried to think that maybe she was just imagining and this next-door young person only tried to be a friendly neighbor. Not having a better reasoning, she could rationalize the encounter this way, at least for the time being.

Toward late mid afternoon, towering cumulus clouds

gathered above Darien. The strong sun beating down on the vast surface of the Atlantic Ocean lifted warm vapors up into thirty thousand feet heights. Immense amounts of energy, released through massive condensation, formed towering, dark, rain-laden clouds and blocked the sky, horizon to horizon. The sun disappeared and the day became night. In a minute, drenching rain poured and visibility dropped to distances not extending beyond one's nose. Jagged lighting strikes illuminated the darkened sky and deafening long rolls of thunder shook the earth. The wicked tempest appeared to center itself directly above Red Rose Circle. All living souls and animals sought shelter and trembled in mortal fear.

An enormous lighting bolt struck the gigantic maple tree on the front lawn of the Shrewsbury residence. The heavy trunk split almost in half and an enormous limb came crushing down on the ground and blocked the driveway. Under the fallen branches, rainwater rushed in thick sheets and in mad urgency the gurgling storm drains swallowed the flood. Doomsday threatened, but for one more time a perceived last judgment passed, and in an hour the storm departed as fast as it came. Leaving colder but cleaner air behind, it allowed the sun to reemerge.

Linda came out, through her back sliding door, and observed the damage at the front. The fallen branch missed her house but hopelessly blocked both her front and garage doors. With its gnarling bulk and thousands of smaller twigs and leaves it rested snuggly on the driveway, after all it was the most natural place for a tree to fall. She couldn't move a single piece and didn't know what to do. Just looked at the monster size pile of timber and debris and lamented. *Poor tree, I'm sorry that you had to perish like this. But you are blocking my way and somehow I have to cut you up.*

Linda went back to the house and searched for a bow saw. When finding one, she put on a pair of tight blue jeans and a white tee shirt, reemerged again through the backdoor and started to work on a mid size branch. Cutting it forcefully, the little woman was half way through when from behind her she heard Percy's voice.

"Linda, let me help you with that. That's a lot of work, far too much for you."

Linda straightened up. Out of breath she had no strength left in her arms. Wiped the sweat off her forehead and looked at Percy, "It's you."

"Please step aside," the young man said, "and let me do the work."

Percy had a fourteen inch long chainsaw; pulled the cord and revved it up. Stood expertly on the tree, and cut one branch after the other. The sharp chain chewed into the stiff wood and in a graceful arc, the ripped shavings showered away. He cut through the bulk and made a huge pile on the lawn and sawed the larger limbs into short pieces and neatly stacked them up along the garage wall.

Linda helped him carry branches and the smaller wood pieces to the piles. They worked diligently and didn't talk.

After an hour, the job was all done. Linda swept up the remaining debris and filled two large plastic thrash cans to the brim.

Percy talked. "Tomorrow I'll pick up those for you. I will take them to the garbage dump. It's closed now. But tomorrow morning they'll open the gate at seven."

Linda saw how hard Percy worked. She saw he was soaking wet and sweaty. Sawdust covered the exposed skin on his neck and arms. Clinging on, sticky bits of leaves were embedded in his disheveled hair. She liked his messy appearance. She liked him for being there for her. It seemed polite to offer something in return.

"Percy, let's take a rest. Let's sit down on the back porch and I'll get us something to drink. You've worked hard and you must be thirsty. I have cranberry and raspberry juice mix. Can I get you some?"

Dehydrated by the strenuous physical effort, Percy was in dire need of some liquid refreshments, but most of all he didn't want to miss this chance to sit down with Linda and talk.

"Perfect. Please and thanks," huffing and trying to catch his breath, he agreed.

Linda went inside. He walked to the back and put his chainsaw down. She soon returned with a large jug of the red and sweetly tart tasting cold delight and poured a glassful for each.

Percy drank, put down his empty glass and looked at Linda refilling it.

"How is your arm?" He asked.

Long silence followed. Then she asked, "What arm?"

Percy just gulped down his second cup of the sweet and sour tasting drink but his throat was dry and he stuttered under powerful emotions overwhelming him. Reflecting his deep concerns about his rude intrusion and forcing his words out he struggled with his articulation, "The one that was kicked."

A cold fear grabbed Linda's heart. She was a child caught doing something bad; something that nobody should have not known about. How on earth this young man knew? It wasn't any of his business. She let him help her clean up the fallen tree but he had no right to intrude so callously into her private problems. Her arteries constricted and cut off the blood flow to her heart. Iron spikes of angry pressure wrenching her innards, she detested his condescending discovery.

Linda's lips moved silently and she could utter her protest only after several, silently futile attempts.

"I don't know what you're talking about." She said.

Percy knew he went too fast and too far. But he'd crossed the Rubicon and returning ceased to be an option.

"I saw him beating you."

"You saw nothing."

"Linda, please, let me help."

"You should leave. I'm sorry. I have things to do. Thank you for the cleanup. But you must leave now. Please."

"Linda."

"Leave me alone."

She stood up, went inside and locked the door behind her. Percy stared after her and through the sliding door, he saw Linda looking back at him. The wet glass altered her fading reflection and in her white tee shirt and with her long and loose auburn hair she was like a pale and pitiful apparition begging for help from a dungeon below an icy grave.

Chapter Seven

Percy showed up early next morning. He parked his father's old Ford pickup on Linda's driveway and began loading the branches. Linda saw him from inside; she turned off the coffee pot, quickly put on her blue jeans and a thick cotton sweater and rushed outside, "Thank you, Percy." She said, "Very nice of you doing this messy cleanup, but at least, let me help."

Remembering the sharp rebuff he received yesterday, he tersely replied, "If you insist, Mrs. Shrewsbury."

The pretense of no commitment was to no avail. The sight of her stirred up his longings, the few non-belligerent words she spoke, eradicated his blues. Together they finished stacking logs and larger branch pieces by the side of the house and loaded the truck with the leftovers.

Getting into the cab of his truck Percy turned to Linda and smiled. "Help me unload at the dump and I'll buy you a coffee." Confidence revived, he proved once again, he was a lady's man who did not miss opportunities to further his advances.

Linda was in a better mood this morning. She regretted her last afternoon's abruptness; she couldn't sleep well; kept tossing and turning and wished she hadn't hurt Percy.

"It's a deal," she said. "I owe you that much."

They drove to the dump and passed Pamela standing at the school-bus stop with Joshua. She waved at them, saying something her lips moved, but Percy didn't slow down, he waved back but left her standing on the corner, puzzled and seriously disappointed.

At the town garbage transfer station they dumped the twigs and emptied the thrash cans. After finishing the task, Percy drove Linda to the Uppercrust Bagel Shop on Post Road. There he bought two large coffees, orange juice and four warm and deliciously fragrant bagels. He took them all to Linda, who already, like a regular couple doing a familiar routine, got the napkins, loaded up with sugar and cream, and secured a table by the window. They sat down, prepared their coffees, sipped a taste and bit into the softly sweet bagels.

Keeping the delicate distance of emotional separation, Percy spoke first, "How is Captain Shrewsbury?"

"He is fine. He is in Tokyo. He'll be back in about a week."

"How long you two have been married?"

"A year."

Percy stopped questioning Linda. He was afraid of prying and asking for private information and was truly concerned she would clam up again and he would lose her for good. Staying quit he pretended to be fully occupied with spreading jam on his sliced bagel.

Linda broke the silence, "What made you help me?"

"I'm a writer."

"What has that got to do with helping me?"

Her smile broke through her solemn and serious countenance like the sun coming out from under a dense, three-day long cloud cover. Her disposition changed to a cheery and youthful temperament more befitting her age.

Percy saw it. He couldn't comprehend why and how but he already talked to her like he never talked to anyone before. He let his unspoken secrets and desires bubble to the surface of their friendly, mutual tryout.

Trusting she would not ridicule him, he answered, "I'm searching for the truth."

"What truth?"

"The truth in everything, the truth in love and the truth in relationships."

"And what would you do with it if you found it?"

"I would hold onto it and would never let it go again."

Linda wondered wistfully if his truth had abundant dark bronze hair and greenish-blue eyes but didn't dare to challenge him by further inquiring about the details.

The more they talked the more they drifted into risky territory. They knew so little about each other and yet, driving hopelessly on a slippery serpentine without a safety rail, they were attracted undeniably. They were both young and naïve. Lacking equal peers they had no opportunity to learn to be rough and reinforce their own attitude with callousness or indifference. They shied away from young people their own age and they both lost touch with reality. Percy lived in his own world and Linda never knew what a loving family was. Now they saw the ocean of emotions in front of them but they did not have a boat to sail on it, they had to retract and stay away from the inviting and challenging waves.

Time passed and Linda gathered enough courage to confront his advances and rein in her own fledgling emotions. The time for small talk was over.

"What do you want from me?" She asked and her face turned serious.

"I wish I could explain it to you, but I don't want to frighten you."

"I'm married. I have a husband."

"I know, but you are still the one I've been searching for."

"I'm not an easy lay, just because my husband is away and I'm alone. I'm not a slut. Don't dare to think of me like that."

"No, of course not. I don't want you physically. I only want to adore you. You're my main heroine. My muse, my goddess, for me you are every woman condensed into one person. I feel I have known you for centuries. You are everywhere, in every book I wrote and every book I'll ever write. I know I shouldn't expect you to share my literary enthusiasm, but let me worship you. I know you don't feel the same toward me. And you don't have to. I love you and that's enough for me. You don't have to love me back just let me have you as my dream, my reverie, please."

"I cannot get involved with you. Please leave me alone."

With a sudden move he secured both of her hands and stared into her eyes, "I can't leave you. I love you. Please forgive me. I know you don't love me and that makes me love you even more. I know you don' have feelings for me."

Linda looked down. She blushed and pulled her hand away and talking softly but with unwavering determination she whispered to him.

"You are wrong about that. You are very wrong."

Later in the day, Percy was cutting his father's grass. Pamela saw him working and came over to his side of the property line. She stood in Percy's path and grabbed the lawn mover away from him. The machine stopped, a turtledove sweetly cooed in the distance and a rose bug buzzed by Percy's face, but tendons of angry silence, stretching to a point of breaking, oscillated between woman and man.

She stood far too close to him; he saw her plump face, fatty skin and the greasy powder of her makeup reminded him of a corps lying in a casket at a pompous funeral.

She demanded, "Hey. I want to talk to you."

"About what? I'm busy."

"I saw you."

"So."

"You were not alone. You were with her."

"With whom?"

"I saw what you were up to. And I'm telling you, you're not going to get away with it."

"Get away with what?"

"Linda Shrewsbury."

"So, I helped her to clean up a fallen branch. What is the big hullaballoo about it?"

"I'm warning you, I'm not a used shoe that you can throw away."

"Who wants to throw you away?"

"My husband did it once. He left me for a younger woman and he's still paying for it. I took him to the cleaners and he has to work hard for the rest of his life. I'm not stupid; I know what I'm doing."

Percy had to laugh. The jealous rage of this older and cynical woman amused him. As far as he was concerned he wasn't obligated to her in any way.

He tried to handle her irate furry with a joke, "But I have no assets. Are you going to put a lien on my lawnmower?"

"I'll make you pay otherwise. You'd better leave that wretched heap of unhappiness alone. Her problem is none of your business. I told you that before. You are going to be one sorry ass if you didn't."

"I have to help her. She is my muse."

"She is your what?" in her self-righteous wrath Pamela gasped for air. She hyperventilated and her chest cavity looked ready to explode with stifled hysteria. But she took a deep breath, muffled her anger and forced herself to speak. "I cannot figure out why you have the hots for her. I don't find her attractive at all."

"You wouldn't understand. You have no feelings besides your senses. You feel hunger, you feel cold or warmth, you feel physical pain and you feel lust but you don't even come near to comprehending what love is."

"And you do, with her."

"Yes, I love her. I never touched her but I love her."

"You son of a bitch, you low life scum, you fornicating loser. You can touch her but you're never going to touch me again."

That made Percy ad nauseam. He felt throwing up. Now, the thought to touch or make love to Pamela repulsed him. A noble and pure feeling of ethereal love filled him and there was no more room left for any lewd and lascivious sex with this vulgar woman. He reached the upper regions of celestial bliss. He needed to cleanse himself of earthly dirt. He wanted to get Pamela out of his life. He had to stop beating around the bush. Rude as it might be, he had to be firm with her.

"I'm sorry, Mrs. Leicester." He said firmly but without raising his voice. "It's over between us. There never was anything between us. Come on. I'm twenty years younger than you. I have my pride."

"Your pride, what am I to be ashamed of? You've been lucky with me. You could have had your fabled golden goose. You're throwing a real treasure away; for what, somebody else's wife? You're walking on thin ice, you fool, don't come back to me and beg for my forgiveness for old times' sake. I'll never take you back. I have my pride too."

She was angry; she was near tears, but not weak and emotional tears, she had tears of profound anger and raging tensions, dangerous tears of a hurt but headstrong woman.

Pamela walked away and turning her head back, she spat her words at Percy, "Don't blame me if I have a word with Captain Shrewsbury. He's going to have fun with you. You haven't heard the last of me."

Chapter Eight

Percy wanted to share his world with Linda. He wanted to tell her she was the dream woman of his creative desires. Tell her that on a flimsy barge he was sailing in aimless search through a dark sea of black ink, pouring senselessly over the white paper in front of him. He was lost until he saw her sitting on a rock and holding in her hand a frayed, white flag. Waving with grace she was beckoning him to come. With consecrated devotion and humble trembling he shivered at her Godly image. He died for her and she resurrected him and now he was going to follow the calling of her white banner forever. He had a mission now. He had to pursue his destiny leading to her messianic altar.

Next morning he cut across the backyards, went over to Linda's house and knocked on the kitchen window. Linda looked out and saw Percy. The mere sight of him implied unpredictable and frightening possibilities and her own feelings terrified her. She rushed into a marriage with Captain Shrewsbury and had no love she could remember of. She had no family who loved her and whom she could love back as a child. Her feelings toward Percy were new to her. She had been lured into this relationship without seeking or wanting it. She knew her life had been terrible so far and she never had a single moment of feeling good and secure, neither before nor after her marriage, but now she encountered something wonderful that she never knew existed. In her still blossoming youth she couldn't resist the temptation of getting a taste from the sweet honey of true love.

She pulled up her window. Her eyelashes fluttering, going from diffident to acting amused, she gave Percy a quizzical look. "Percy, to what can I owe the pleasure of seeing you again, so soon."

"Linda, I thought," he hesitated meekly, "I mean, you should, we should, why don't we take a walk. A long walk together, a hike; you need some exercise; you're so pale. Don't wither inside in this beautiful weather. Come on out. Don't afraid of me."

"Walk?" She asked cautiously, "Where?"

"It's more like a hike," seeing the opportunity to convince her, Percy rushed his words as if he was afraid to lose a once in a lifetime opportunity. "I know a wonderful place in Pound Ridge. Dress in shorts and put on a pair of good sneakers. You're not going to regret it. We should be back by late lunchtime."

Linda made her decision in the spur of the moment. She

didn't think. Maybe subconsciously she wanted to make up for yesterday. Maybe she had been waiting for something like this to happen. Maybe she thought it was perfectly innocent to go out and hike together with this young man. She didn't know why, but definitely this was what she wanted to do right now. To Percy's pleasant surprise she agreed, "Ok. Give me two minutes. Wait for me by the garage door. We're going to take Spencer's BMW."

Slip of the tongue or blatant warning, she used Spencer's name.

Linda drove and Percy gave directions. They went north on Mansfield Avenue, took the Merritt Parkway and turned north again on Long Ridge Road. After crossing the New York State border, the winding road became narrower and ran between forest-covered hills undulating on both sides. About a mile later, Percy told Linda to turn off the main road. They crossed an old wood bridge over a charming small river and passed by a two hundred years old red mill building that had a working paddlewheel. A moment later they arrived to the entrance of the Mianus River Gorge Preserve.

There were already a number of other cars in the parking lot. At the rustic information shack, a group of hikers looked at the directions and the brochures. The sunny scene seemed perfectly safe and benign. Linda stopped the BMW and they got out. She stretched her body and inhaled the oxygen laden, sharply fresh air. Century old hemlock trees surrounded them, the sunrays beat down on their heads with merciless strength, but inside the forest, the air remained cool with deep, dappled shades and strong fragrance of decaying leaves and pungent scents of tree fungus.

Percy looked at Linda; his adoring smile resembled a triumphant gloat and said, "My favorite place."

"It's nice. I see why you like it. It is so peaceful and tranquil. I already like your magic forest."

Between the trees and bushes a narrow dirt trail led to the left and continued along the riverbank. Percy let Linda go first. Her shorts were cut high and allowed glimpses of the top of her legs, almost where the curvature of her derriere began. Fine and long muscles twitched and, as to avoid the muddy soil of the trail she stepped from tree root to rock and back, the sways of her body seemed to compose a cadence that reminded him of the harmony of a classic symphony. Her hips were wide but her buttocks were firm, round and not even half the size of Pam's. Her shoulders looked strong and her arms showed lithe, playful physique of perfect proportions. There was not an ounce of fat on her he could see. Jumpy like a little girl she giggled and flushed and seemed to enjoy the feeling of abundant health and the pleasure of being out on a hike. When she saw a flower here and there, she crouched down and smelled the delicate aroma with delight.

With incessant easiness and without being prodded, Linda talked to Percy. She didn't need to be nudged or asked. Happy in his company, the words just floated out of her like tiny songbirds flying aimlessly on happy days of a balmy spring.

"I grew up in the orphanage," she chattered, "When I've become an orphan, I mean on paper, I was already too old to be adopted. They put me into foster care homes, several of them. I never lasted long anywhere. Once I lived with a rich family, they used me as a maid. I was thirteen years old."

She skipped her feet playfully and jumped across a

bubbling brook rushing into the river down below at the bottom of the deep and wide ravine.

"When the Lady took a bath I had to hold the towel for her. When I took a bath, they washed the bathtub after me with bleach."

She laughed and kept walking with jumpy, dancing steps. "Imagine that. Dirty. They thought, me coming from the orphanage, I must be filthy. The husband was a big, fat and bald guy. Never said anything just watched me with his fishlike, bulging eyes. One day he reached out and touched my behind under my skirt. The next day I was back at the orphanage. I told the lady on him and she yelled at me. Not at her husband."

Percy just absorbed her cheerful yet so serious voice. She was a child now, who couldn't just let her unresolved childhood issues go away. She needed to talk about them. And she confided them to Percy. They became soul mates. They were bonding and feeling more at ease in each other's company.

She continued. "Next they put me up with a family of religious nuts. The wife had a cluster of children of her own, small ones. I was supposed to help her take care of the kids; there were four little ones, all wicked brats. The husband was a carpenter, big, muscular handsome guy. He liked me too. He made me sit next to him on the porch steps and talked to me a lot. He never touched me but he told me many things.

"What kind of things."

"Like he never loved his wife, they were only good friends but she became pregnant and he had to marry her out of moral obligation. I told him that was better than putting the child up for adoption. Do you know what he told me?"

"No, but I can guess."

"Guess."

"Marry him."

"No silly. I was only fourteen. He said it would have been better if he hadn't fooled around with her. He had sinned and he was being punished for his transgressions."

"How did you leave them?"

"I just left, packed up my things and sneaked out in the middle of the night."

"Why?"

"They wanted to christen me in a tub of dirty water. Submerge me, and make me their slave for the rest of my life. No thanks."

Percy kept listening to Linda. They were already about a mile inside the forest and he thought they should turn around. He loved her stories, they happened in the past, they were safe to tell or listen to and they seemed to have no bearing whatsoever to her present state of mind or situation.

In the majestic silence, under the towering primordial ancient trees, in the safety of this enchanted old forest, Percy had the courage to ask. "What about Spencer? Do you love him?"

Percy held his breath. He couldn't imagine that Linda loved Spencer but he wanted to know why she was staying with him.

A long silence followed. Linda quieted down and pondered about Percy. She had her doubts of letting Percy into her secrets. Yet she needed him. She felt that he was simple and straightforward, she was sure that he had no ulterior motives and as naïve as he was, he meant what he said yesterday.

They walked almost a half a mile more without saying a word. Then she asked, "Why do you want to know?"

"Nobody should beat a woman. Nobody should beat his wife. He especially shouldn't beat you."

"He just does it when he is drunk."

A blinding wave of irrational impulse seemed to override her rationale. Almost trusting him she began dismantling the wall between caution and confidence.

She continued, "It is all right. I always recover. He is a good person, a good provider. I never had a life like this, ever. Spencer is a decent individual otherwise. I just have to stay out of his way when he is drunk."

"I'll talk to him."

"You will not do such a thing."

"I love you and I'll protect you."

"Don't get involved. I'll handle it. I had worse abusers than him."

"How can you make love to someone who beats you?"

"I'm not making love to him."

"No?"

"No. I'm still a virgin."

Percy's mind froze and his legs stopped moving. For him, this private, casual sounding, revelation elevated Linda into staggering stratospheric heights. She became an angel, an innocent victim; in Percy's poetic mind she turned into a saintly symbol of pure chastity. A knight fighting for his Lady he had to rescue his muse now and regardless of consequences or cost.

"Linda, I love you. Leave Spencer and I'll marry you."

"You'll do no such nonsense. You can't marry me."

"Yes, I can. We can move down to Florida. I'll take a full time job as a groundskeeper you can take a job at the airport. Rents are cheap down south. We can live happily thereafter."

"No. You are a fool. You don't know what you are talking about."

Percy had to have Linda as a mate for life. But he realized who he was and respected she didn't want to give up the known for the unknown. He loved her nevertheless. It was better this way, unfulfilled love being the best for a poet. Love somebody else's wife is the best inspiration. Just watch that husband, he silently mused over the possible implications of this paradox, but out loud he agreed.

"Ok. I respect your wisdom, but one day I'll show you I'm worthy of you. And on that day I'll beg you again to marry me."

Linda smiled approvingly, "That's better. But in the meantime keep your distance and don't let Spencer know that you are in love with me. If you really loved me you'd do that. Wouldn't you?"

"I accept your terms. But don't hate me for loving you.

"I don't hate you. I just can't marry you. One marriage after a week of courtship is enough for me. I promised myself, I'd be more careful next time."

"I see." Percy winced in pain. "And I admire your fortitude, your perseverance, Linda. I love you. Your words are the gospel for me."

They arrived back at the trailhead. There they pumped up ice cold artesian water from the cast iron well; used the palms of their hands as cups and were back to being two happy little puppies frolicking about on a beautiful, warm, late spring day.

Linda drove home. On the main road, a half a mile away from Red Rose Circle she let Percy out of the Spencer's BMW.

Chapter Nine

Later in the afternoon of the same day, Linda drove the BMW to Weed Beach Park. She got out of the car and placed a blanket on the sand. From the trunk she took out a red plastic cooler, put it on the blanket and sat down next to it. In a distance away, flicking a glance over her shoulder and across the parking lot, she saw Percy giving lessons on the tennis courts.

She kicked off her sandals, raised both feet in the air and lifting her bottom wriggled out of her shorts.

As if it were too much of an effort, she took a pause and just stared at the afternoon sunlight reflecting off the wide waters of Long Island Sound.

Later unbuttoned her red blouse and removed the glossy

garment. Like a toreador waving his cape at the bull, she took her time to fold the flimsy nothingness before finally putting it down next to her shorts.

There she was, in nothing but her tiny, sky-blue color bikini. Cut way below her belly button and very narrow in the back it barely covered a third of the silky skin on her so round and so delectably firm buttocks. She lay down on her back; her stomach flattened and a narrow slit, stretching under the elastic top of her panties, dreamily revealed the upper edges of her dense, black pubic hair below. Stretching wide on the front, her bikini covered enough and let out only a few unruly curls on each side.

Her breasts, befitting her age were round and small, did not sag onto the sides but thrust firmly upward and the two little pieces of triangular cloth barely covered their tips.

She closed her eyes and waited. Nothing happened. The strong sunrays made her sweat and beads of sparkling water formed around her belly button. She turned on her stomach, reached back and unbuttoned her bra. She let the bra fall and didn't mind exposing the sides of her polished alabaster bosoms.

She glanced up and saw the tennis players leave. Turned her head down, closed her eyes and waited. With her heart pounding against the firmness of the sand, she didn't move a muscle and yet she could hardly breathe. Butterflies danced in her belly and she didn't dare to look up or raise her head an inch.

A soft shuffle of smooth footsteps approached. Someone near her sat down and placed a bag on the ground. She pretended to be asleep. Then she heard Percy.

"Hello, Linda. How nice, seeing you here."

Glancing up at an askew angle, she squinted and saw

him sitting on a wooden bench and smiling at her. She lifted her head and shoulders, smiled back and with her left hand covering her chest she spoke in a surprised, but sweeter than dripping honey tone of voice.

"Percy. What are you doing here?"

Percy saw her move. Fleetingly, perhaps he imagined it for a split second, she revealed her breasts on purpose, but he discarded the thought as filthy and disrespectful. His angel had nothing on but the tiny bottom of a bikini but she had the right to sunbathe and enjoy the caressing sea breeze on her naked skin if her heavenly body desired so or the velvety semblance of her shiny skin needed the rays of sun to keep its rosy luster.

"My creative intuition told me that you were going to be here."

She giggled, "Your creative what," then she made a mockingly serious face. "Turn around, would you. How old are you anyway?"

Percy turned away. She buttoned back her bra, sat up and pulling her legs underneath her buttocks asked him again.

"I asked, how old?"

"Twenty-four, why?"

"Then you can have a glass of wine with me."

"I could, but where is your wine and how old are you?"

She opened the cooler, looked around, for it was against city and state ordinances to have any alcoholic beverage on a public beach, and said.

"Here is the wine. And I'm nineteen. But it is not my wine. I was just carelessly allowed to gain access to it. Isn't that a shame?"

Linda remembered something she read a long time ago and in a place very, very far away. She filled up two glasses, gave the larger to Percy and with lofty pathos recited a few lines for him.

"Drink up, Percy. The world doesn't last forever. But while it does, do something good or bad but doesn't stand idle. Put your soul up to a great task, a great love of yours and if you see it ripped apart by evil forces, drink again and forget and start all over again until you succeed. Don't ever give up."

They drank and Percy felt small and pitifully insignificant in the company of such a profoundly great, heaven inspired philosopher.

She poured another glassful for each and sounding a notch more intoxicated, came down to his level. "In case you don't have a dissenting opinion, Mr. Tennis Instructor, we shall conclude our outdoor drinking with the consumption of the second glass of this magnificent liquid and should press the stopper back into the neck of the bottle."

They drank again, slowly this time. She put the bottle and the glasses away. Just in time, a second later a police cruiser pulled into the parking lot.

Then she said, "With your willing, we shall finish this bottle indoors, my place, ten o'clock. Make sure nobody sees you coming in. I'll leave the front door unlocked for you. Don't forget, ten o'clock."

"Indoors, your place," Percy wondered dreamily, as if he were a street pauper discovering an abandoned treasure chest.

"Sure, yes. You don't want me to break the law by getting drunk in a public park."

An hour later, they sobered up and drove home in separate cars. Linda took a nap and when she woke up she went to the bathroom and filled up Spencer's oversized bathtub with hot water. She threw off her clothes and submerged to her neck. Looking and admiring her own nudity she soaked for a while and then reached for the soap and a body cleansing brush. Scrubbed her skin everywhere, including her back, the insides of her thighs and between her touchy cheeks. She shampooed her long hair, rinsed it off and got out of the tub. Dried her body with a fresh towel and stood naked in front of the huge mirror. Blow-drying her hair she looked at her full size reflection in the glass and saw a beautiful, fully matured woman. She wasn't a child, not even a young girl any more; she was a young and married woman.

"You are still a virgin," she stuck out her tongue and disapprovingly sneered at her own image.

Virgin or not she liked what she saw. Put on expensive perfumes and applied smooth creams on her skin. Colored her lips bright crimson and brushed her eyelashes with dark mascara. She put on lacy red lingerie and a long black dress with sides slit up all the way to the prominently protruding top of her strong femur bone. Put on matching black high heels and happily noted she looked like a true femme fatale. She never, ever dressed up like this for anyone, but she did it tonight, and she did it for Percy, the young poet from next door.

Near ten o'clock she sat down in the living room and waited for him to arrive.

Percy followed his routine. He finished dinner, took his late evening recuperating nap and headed out, saying only a brief goodbye to his TV watching, tired parents. He walked past Pamela's house and, behind the darkened curtains, failed to notice her peering eyes.

Pamela watched and instantly recognized Percy's special

gait in the dark. Secretly expecting Percy to come and visit her, she thought, he wanted to beg and ask for her forgiveness. When she saw Percy passing her house and approaching the Shrewsbury residence, she cursed him and there was hatred between her clenched teeth.

"You son of a bitch gigolo, that's where you are going, to that little tramp. Do it. You're both going to be very sorry you ever existed. I'll make sure of that."

Percy silently opened the door and let himself in. He saw Linda sitting on the sofa and the sight mesmerized him. In the dimly lit living room, she was a love deity, a divine queen draped in the dappled shadows of the mist, a benevolent sorceress merging out of her humble, unrecognized hiding and about to claim her rightful domain in kingdom of witches and celestial seraphs.

Percy couldn't say a word. He never thought to face his muse live and never hoped to meet her in the flesh. But there she was and his trembling legs turned into feeble mush. He dropped on his knees and tried to kiss the edge of her skirt.

Linda reached down and softly beseeched him, "Come on, Percy, it's only me, Linda."

He put his head into her lap and said, "My love, you are so beautiful, I'm not even worthy enough to be your slave."

She didn't answer; in silence, she gently caressed the head of her impassionate, love stricken young naïve writer.

He continued and poured out the innermost secrets of his unfulfilled love. "Linda, I'm a flaming painful gash, I'm burning. The light tortures me; the soft dew of the early dawn tortures me. I want you. I've come to you. I wish more pain. I want you. I want your flame to glow white, my kisses hurt me, my desires hurt me, you're my pain and my purgatory,

I want you, I want you badly. My desires had torn me apart. My kisses bloodied me. I'm a red-hot wound. I'm hungry for new sufferings. Give me misery, misery to my starving self. I'm a scar slit open, kiss me and burn me. Burn me please."

She lifted his head, toward her face and saw the unfathomable depth of true love in his eyes. She saw the lonely man, the genius trapped in an earthly body fallible to mortal sins. She knew he was telling her the truth, his true and most sacred feelings and placed a light kiss on his lips.

It was their first kiss. It was her first kiss of love, as she never knew what love was before. She married Captain Shrewsbury and there was no love between them, especially not after the way he treated her, after the abuses and the beatings. She was trapped in a loveless marriage and she had no place to go except to the battered women's shelter.

Tonight Captain Spencer Shrewsbury was flying his airplane on the other side of the globe and this night was Linda's night. It was her revenge for her upside down life, abandonment by her father, her mother promiscuous behavior and the asininely impulsive poisoning of a worthless boyfriend topping off her attitude and for the tears she shed seeing her mother rotting away in jail for murder. It was young Linda's revenge for all her years in the orphanage, for the many foster homes and for all the neglect she'd suffered. This moment was her vindication, exoneration for the sins of progenitors and she wanted to share her absolution with Percy.

She said, "Let's finish the wine."

She took the wine out of the cooler and put two glasses on the cocktail table. As she moved around and bent down, Percy watched her long silky dress fall and to reveal the contours of her superbly formed youthful body. The side slits opened high and he glimpsed the whiteness of her thighs.

She sat down and crossed her long legs; raised her glass and said. "You want me to torture you," she paused and rested her eyes on him. "I'll give you torture and pain. I'll show you paradise once and you'll never even get close to it again."

Percy took her long and delicate fingers into his strong suntanned hands and begged her again, "Linda, look into my eyes. The flaming bonfire in them may burn out one day, but these sad eyes will never look at anyone else. Linda, you may chase me away but you can never get away from these faithful, pleading eyes. Maybe one day another fire of love will inflame your blood, but it would be in vain and for nothing. Maybe new horrors will come, but these sorrowful and lonely eyes would never let you go. They will look at you forever."

If she had any doubts of what she was doing Percy's poetry swept her off her feet. They both drank from their glasses, stood up stepped next one another and Linda said, "Hug me."

Percy put his arms around her and held her tight in his embrace. She thrust her hips forward and pushed her pubis against his. A hot scorching flame ignited and flared up inside him. Through all their clothing he pressed his hard erection into her.

Her deliciously full lips were already moist from the wine. First he cautiously and slowly leaned closer to her face, enough to smell her perfumed fragrance and absorb her wine scented breath. He hovered inches from her lips to see if she was in agreement and when she still presented her lips ready, he pressed his mouth on hers. She let out a tiny, tenderly lustful whimper and willingly parted her lips. He thrust his tongue into the depths of her expecting mouth and reached down the side of her dress and slid his fingers underneath her loose panties.

Dangerously close to having his explosion, the feeling the woman of his dreams so intimately close to him was like a tidal wave of undiluted intoxicating ecstasy that put his senses into overdrive.

Linda pulled her lips away and, still thrusting her belly against his, whispered into his ears, "Upstairs."

They separated and Linda led the way up the steps. He followed her into the master bedroom and she showed him the beautifully made king size bed with whipped cream white sheets, fluffy pillows and a flowery patterned cheery comforter.

"Don't worry," she assured him, "everything is freshly washed. I did it yesterday."

The venetian blinds were closed; curtains stayed drawn and only a small bulb, left burning in the hallway, provided dimmed illumination. Necessary precaution, as Pamela was capable of using infrared goggles to watch them, if she needed to.

He pulled down the zip at her back and she stepped out of her sexy delight of a dress and he saw her for the first time in nothing but her lacy underwear. She unbuckled his belt and his pants slid to the floor. He took off the rest of his clothes and she saw his flawlessly slim, free of fatty tissue body, his perfect and lean muscles and the huge and thick erection he had. She wasn't afraid. Time, for her to become a woman had arrived. She dropped her panties and he unhooked her bra. Both naked, nothing could have made them stop.

They smiled no more, she lay down on her back in the middle of the huge bed and he expertly mounted her. They used no protection; they trusted each other and unexpected consequences had not entered their minds.

Percy guided her legs apart and she followed his wishes. Her never shaved, young pubic hair completely covered her privacy and pubic mound. On the sides the velvety skin was soft and shined with luminous luster in the glow of the moon that appearing from the clouds peeked through the skylight and seeing their passionate enthusiasm seemed to smile approvingly.

Percy let his weight rest on his elbows and pushed her legs widely apart with his hips. He reached further in and was at the soft entrance of her vulva. Completely wet and inviting, a river of her love juices flowed out from deep inside her womb. Percy knew what he was doing; he gently pulled apart her outer lips and placed the head of his penis half way in.

Linda wiggled with pleasure and anticipation. She kept lifting and pulling back her hips and together, carefully squeezed her thighs. This was her moment of fulfillment. She wanted him more than anything else she ever wanted to have in her life.

Percy pushed in and he couldn't. Something kept blocking his way. Her hymen was indeed strong and resilient. He tried again and again to no avail. He was long and throbbing hard, a perfect fit and yet it wasn't going in. Getting too close to his climax he had to try it harder. Seconds later he felt his avalanche coming and he couldn't hold it back any more. He moaned with pleasure and she whimpered with joy. Linda had her orgasm in the same time and he thrust forward with full force. Sliding deep inside, breaking through her virginity, for better or worse, he completed the task that was not legally his.

She felt no pain; her erotic pleasure stymied all other feelings and her emotions boosted by her carnal afterburners erased any fears she might have had.

For minutes they lay there kissing, whispering and making no promises.

She pondered about the consequences. What if Spencer ever finds out? Inevitable regrets and afterthoughts, was she ready for new commitment, and start an adulterous affair behind her husband's back? What if Spencer doesn't understand her sacrifice? What if Percy truly loves her? What if the fool wants her to get a divorce?

This breathtaking experience, a once in a lifetime irreplaceable feeling that only a crime of passion could give, filled her with joy and yet confused her. Was she right? Was she careless? Will play Percy the designated role of a secret admirer?

Unable to see the future she turned to Percy and shyly whispered to him, "I'm a woman now."

"My woman," he replied and kissed her lips.

Then Linda gently pushed him off. She reached down between her legs and showed him her blood-tainted hand. They both looked at the first tiny but rapidly growing red spot. She had a white towel under her; she wiped herself clean and gave the bloodstained rag to Percy.

"Souvenir," she said simply and the magic of the moment shattered to shards of reality.

Percy picked up his clothes and dressed up. Linda put on new dark colored cotton panties and a plush bathrobe. Without turning the lights on they walked arm in arm, down to the living room. Before letting him out of the house she turned toward Percy and said.

"Thank you, Percy."

He turned back and slightly resisted being pushed out the door, "It was the most wonderful thing I've ever done." He replied, "I want to make love to you again."

She softly warned him. "Remember what I said, once and never again. You wanted me to torture you. This is your torture. You can't have me again. You may love me as your muse, as a woman of your dreams but you cannot physically have me again. I'm married to Spencer Shrewsbury."

Her resolve devastated him. It threatened his dreams of eternally fulfilled and happy love. He knew he truly would not be able to love anybody else any more. He knew he would write about her again and again a million times but that wouldn't be near anything he experienced tonight. He knew he wasn't worthy to kiss the ground she walked on. He had a long way to go before he could measure up to her heavenly qualities.

Walking home in dreamy despondency he completely missed Pamela who approached him like an irksome guard of morality.

"What did the two of you do?" She confronted him, "Did you have her?"

He was tempted to hit Pamela. The arrogant low life fat cow, he thought and yelled at her in a muffled but dangerously angry voice.

"Stay away from me. I don't want to have anything to do with you."

She saw his unchallengeable indignation. His angry stance spooked her. Cautiously retreating back to her house she mumbled with vengeful hate. "I swear, Percy Grimsby. You will pay for what you have done to me."

Chapter Ten

"When are you going to pay up? The boss has a helluva tough time to understand why your debt is growing a lot faster than your payments can cover. He can't comprehend why you can't afford to pay him more, much more. Look at this office, luxurious furniture, classy location, big lunches, nothing but the best."

The visitor leaned forward and pressed his knuckles on the top of Dwight's desk. His swarthy face hovering inches away from Dwight's he lowered his menacing voice. "Dwight. It's about time to pull your act together. We don't want to hurt you unless we have to. The boss likes you. You've got him off the hook, more than once. But you've been disrespectful.

You took advantage of his generosity. You've borrowed too much money from him, way beyond your limit."

A deftly intelligent man, a successful lawyer, Dwight Leicester's perception of situations and understanding of matters was lightning quick and flawlessly efficacious. He had a big law office on the 14th Floor in the elegant Fred F. French building in New York City. He was one of the four senior partners and his corner office had windows facing both Fifth Avenue and 45th Street. He knew what his guest, Sal Sclafani, was talking about. And he knew Sclafani meant what he said. With caution, not to aggravate his accuser, he made a two handed palms up and tried to explain.

"I make a lot of money, but I have expenses. I can't have a shabby looking law office and expect well paying clients and lucrative cases. This is for show only. All the furniture is leased and the rent is very high."

Sal stood up, at 280 pounds and six feet he was a big guy; he revealed the magnum 45 in its holster under his arms and raised his voice, "I know, and I also know that you have a bad gambling habit. You lose and you pile debt upon debt. And you expect us to pay for your pleasures, for your hobbies. We're nice people but not that nice. When it comes to money we're especially not soft hearted. You've bummed off one half a million from the boss. You had your fun and you lost. Now you owe us, and you ran up a million dollar tab with us." His chipped front tooth and dark gums showing, Sal grinned cynically and added, "With interest and handling fees included of course."

Like a juggler on a carnival Sclafani jerked out his gun, tossed it in the air and forefinger on the trigger caught the weapon with ease. Aiming the barrel between Dwight's eyes his surly voice thundered as he grabbed the lawyer's neck, "I don't want to hear any small talk. When are you going to start making serious payments? You have huge escrow accounts, take the money out from one of those and pay us."

"That money is not mine," Dwight pleaded. "I'm accountable for every dollar. I have partners and we have an accounting firm handling our transactions. It would be stealing and I'd be caught with my pants down."

"Any other suggestions," The big goon looked deadly serious.

"Give me a chance, I'll win a big case, and I'll pay off everything."

"We can't wait. I've heard you making these pathetic excuses before. It must be a lot quicker. You have a house in Connecticut. Sell it and pay us and with a clean slate we can start all over again."

"I can't sell it. My ex lives in that house with my son. As part of my divorce settlement I have to let them live there rent-free. I have to pay a huge alimony to her, and she doesn't want to get married again. That's the main reason for my money problems."

"We can easily solve that for you," Sal lowered the gun and let Dwight's neck go, "We'll do two birds with one stone. We remove her from the picture, the house is yours, no more alimony; you sell the house and pay us. Exactly a million bucks, our fee included"

"I don't want my son to get hurt."

"Of course not," Sal said cajolingly. "We are not that kind of people. He is going to move in with you."

"I have to think over something like this."

"There is nothing to think over. It is either you or she. I trust you don't love her that much any more and it is not a difficult choice."

"It's not that. There is no such a thing as a perfect crime. You guys will fuck it up and I'll go to jail."

Sal reached out and lifted Dwight Leicester out of his seat by his throat, "We are going to do what?"

"Not that I don't trust you."

"Then it is settled. We're going to make it look like an accident. We'll not leave behind a trace of evidence."

"Not good enough. Make it look like somebody else did it."

"Anybody special in mind?"

"Yeah, a boyfriend, you can blame it on the boyfriend."

"Does she have one?"

"I don't know, but she is fucking the kid next door. I know that much."

"Good. We're going to take a close look at that possibility. Now it's Wednesday. Call up your son and invite him over for the weekend. He'd better not be there when we drop in to call on her mother."

Dwight loved Pamela at one time, years ago. She was voluptuous and had fat on every right place. In his younger years, Dwight was into big things. Pamela huge and youthful derriere filled out all his imaginations and consummated all his fantasies, days, evenings and nights. She was an all-nightlong double feature, he played her back-to-back, and she proved herself to be genuine never-ending sensual delight. But many happy years later, Dwight finished law school; worked hard, bought the big house and met Joyce. Tall and thin, Joyce had pale white skin and she acted sophisticated and talked intelligent. He loved her Scottish accent and blondish red hair. He thought she had talent and surely, she came from a good family. Her father, a rich lawyer took Dwight into his own law practice. Dwight never could understand any more, how he could have spent all those years with plain, heavy set and vulgar Pamela. The choice looked simple. He proposed to Joyce and left Pamela. He figured with his law experience he easily could outsmart her in the divorce settlement. But like a pit bull defending its turf, Pamela fought back. Joshua insisted staying with his mother. She produced evidence of Dwight's infidelity and won a big alimony and the use of the house. She proved that her lifestyle was indeed an expensive one and down to his last dime she cleaned out Dwight. Dwight became a pariah within the firm. His father in law treated him with disdain and even Joyce made him feel, every opportunity she had, that he brought nothing to his second marriage. And of course, high-class New York socialite, Joyce had a lavish lifestyle, loved big parties and Dwight had to keep up with her high standards. He borrowed money and heavy sums of it. He loved Joyce and hated more and more the source of his troubles, Pamela.

Joyce didn't care and didn't want to know about her husband's debts. She didn't know he owned money to the mob. She just assumed that Dwight had all the money she needed and when she needed it. But reality caught up with Dwight. He didn't want Joyce to find out about his money problems and his father in law to find out anything about his gambling habits and mob related friends. Sal's idea of doing a double whammy, presented so compellingly by his charming manners, seemed indeed very attractive.

Reaching for the phone Dwight thought, *come to think of it, Sal Sclafani's idea might solve most of my problems.*

Dwight dialed Pamela's number. He didn't even have her on his speed dial. Using his nicest lawyer voice he played on her gullibility as if she were a sweet and caring orchestra flute.

"Hi Pam, it is Dwight. Joyce and I," he wheedled first and took a theatrical, convincing pause, "we had a wonderful idea. Why don't you send Joshua down to New York for the weekend? I can pick him up on Friday evening at Grand Central and I'll send him back on Sunday evening."

"What's your big interest in him all of the sudden?" Leery of an unseen trap, Pamela asked. "You haven't spent a minute with him for six months. And now you want him for the whole weekend."

"The Ringling Brothers are in town. We, Joyce and I want to take him to Madison Square Garden. We want to show him around, a little father and son bonding. We've a long way to go mend family misunderstandings; we should make an effort to develop a closer relationship."

"I don't believe it. You, I thought you didn't care about him at all."

"Why don't we ask him, at least, let's see if he wants to come."

Pamela cupped the mouthpiece on the receiver and called out to Joshua. "Joshua, your father wants you for the weekend. Do you want to go?"

Joshua rushed in from outside and picked up the nearest extension. Excited about seeing his father and the opportunity of a great weekend in New York he was out of breath and yelled into the receiver. "Dad, of course I want to go. Cool. I'm coming down with the five thirty train on Friday night. Pick me up at the information booth."

Pamela took the phone from Joshua and told Dwight. "It's settled than. I have something planned for the weekend anyway."

Dwight couldn't resist answering, and his disrespectful pitch was full with eerie forebode, "You do, really."

Sal pushed down the button on the telephone receiver pad and told sternly to Dwight Leicester Esq. Attorney at Law, "Good decision. You just saved your life. We take over from here. Make sure you spend every minute of the weekend with your son and your second wife, Joyce. That's going to be your alibi."

"What about you?"

"We don't need an alibi. We have the perfect man for the job. He is untraceable. Nobody knows him. As far as the government concerned he doesn't exist."

"He had better not."

Sal pulled a Cuban from his breast pocket, flicked on his golden lighter, took a deep inhale and blew the smoke into Dwight's face. "After we're done, put the house on the market. Sooner is the better, no more than a month. We already have a buyer."

"Will be even then?"

"Yes, until you have the fucking urge to gamble again."

Chapter Eleven

Without a hitch, Captain Spencer Shrewsbury put his Boeing 747 airplane down on the east-west runway of John F. Kennedy International Airport. He gave the huge bird over to the assistant maintenance crew supervisor, Rick Mellon, explained a few problems he experienced during the flight from Seoul and finally walked over to the terminal building. He went directly to the crew lounge bar and gulped down a double Johnny Walker Black, authentic Scotch drink on the rocks, and that made him feel much better.

Long hours of intense concentration, and lack of alcohol, frayed his nerves, overcharged him with a feel of tense hostility, and caused sharp pains in his neck, right below his nape. The skin twitched on both of his temples and persistently throbbing headaches tortured him. Rankled to the limit and his state of mind bordering insanity, he was ready to explode with rage.

He swore at the limo driver, from Queens to Connecticut, for taking the Van Wyck Expressway instead of the Cross Island Parkway, for taking the Whitestone Bridge instead of the Throgs Neck and for taking Interstate 95 instead of the Hutchinson Parkway. He cursed the traffic, the construction delays, and the stinking noise and hated all the stupid people for being on the road when he was trying to get home.

He was dog-tired; had jet leg and in general was in a pretty bad, angry at everything mood by the time he arrived home. A sour dryness irritated his throat and his clogged ears hurt. *For sure*, he thought, *he must have caught a bad case of Asiatic flue.* He damned all the disease carrying passengers and coworkers and couldn't wait to start his alcoholic remedy.

Linda greeted him with her sweet and youthful smile and took away his overnight bag. She put on, for him, an olive-khaki silk safari shirtdress and underneath she had a set of sexy, stretch-satin, floral patterned seamless push up bra and matching, hi-cut style panties. She smelled like a bouquet of fresh spring carnations and her cascading reddish bronze hair sensuously caressed the silky pinkness of her skin on her delicate shoulders.

Her enthusiasm got quickly stymied when she got a taste of Spencer's gruff disposition. She didn't feel like kissing and hugging him more than the initial welcome and he wasn't asking for seconds. He went straight to the liquor cabinet, got out a bottle of dry Cinzano Bianco Vermouth, a bottle of sweet Cinzano Rosso Vermouth and a bottle of eighteen years old Chivas Regal. Then took out two rock glasses, yelled to Linda to fill up the ice bucket and mixed two Perfect Rob Roy drinks, one for him and one for Linda.

On the big comfortable light greenish-blue sofa and love set they sat down in the party room, crossed their legs and put the bottles and the drinks on the cocktail table in front of their dangling feet.

After chin-chinning with the glasses, Spencer gulped his drink down and Linda followed him modestly with small, suckling type dashes of swigs and sips. Spencer made another one for himself and Linda turned off his offer for a refill. The first went straight into her head. Its alcohol content already put her into a good talkative mood and intrigued her into wanting to tell Spencer the big news, with happy pride of course that after all, she, finally, got rid of her virginity problem.

Then she didn't dare. Instead she asked with coquettish tipsiness in her voice, "How was your flight, Spencer? Have you been missing me?"

"Terrible. Is there any particular reason I should have missed you. It is my life to fly. It is my work and you knew I had to be away for long days when you married me."

She ignored his callousness and after suppressing a tiny burp she asked, "Do you want something to eat? I have excellent roasted pork loin and potatoes meal prepared, still hot in the oven."

"No. I ate already."

"When?"

"Hours ago on the plane, but there is something not right in my stomach. I don't feel good at all."

"Then you shouldn't drink."

"Do not tell me what to do," he glared at her with possessive and bossy anger. "Stop bugging me?"

A grotesque demon awakened by the alcohol and sitting on her shoulder nudged Linda to share with Spencer the biggest news of her fledgling adult life. She knew how jealous and abusive Spencer could be and had been in the past but she pressed on maybe hoping to get her husband to play a game of imagination and tease.

"Do you want to go upstairs? I have a surprise for you."

The drinks, the multitudes of shots Spencer had since the airport, already made him two sheets into the wind. He didn't know what he wanted. He just wanted to pick a fight and retorted, "I don't like your fucking surprises. Is it a new damn bedspread?"

Inebriated, bad enough, yet she didn't miss this beginning signs of the brutal abuse coming her way. Now she had to withdraw and be on the defensive. With a touch of hurt in her voice and retreating into sulky reticence she said, "No. Not a new bedspread. It is something what I don't have any more. And something that you're not going to miss, my dear husband."

Spencer lost all his rational perceptions. He could not have understood a direct explanation, let alone a subtle reference. His arteries started to unclog and his lack of alcohol fix headaches were going away, he stood up and announced with the pride of a drunken sailor staggering into his port of call, "Whatever it is, I'll look at it later. First I want to go down to Smokey Joe's."

A lot less alcohol than her husband consumed turned Linda into a drunk. But she became mild mannered, laughingly funny and benign.

She giggled a little and slapped Spencer slightly on his shoulder blade, "It's not something you look at, silly. But anyway, it..." and she took a long theatrical drunken pause,

"…I'll keep it ready for you. Go. Enjoy yourself at Smokey's. After all you are home. You are back in Darien, your beloved birthplace and town."

Spencer stood up. All of his six feet four inches, still in his Captain's uniform, he wobbled to stay on his feet, tried to stop the spinning of his head, then he fell down on the sofa and woke up only hours later, just after ten o'clock at night. Having a terrible hangover, he needed a drink and feeling hungry, he wanted to eat. But Linda was already sleeping upstairs. After she cleaned up all the glasses, put away the drinks, locked the liquor cabinet and put the leftover food back into the refrigerator, she called it quits.

Spencer shook her shoulders. But to no avail, she only moaned and turned to her other side. No chance, he thought, and decided to leave her alone. He changed into his fashionable stonewashed blue jeans and put on his expensive Darien Sportshop purchased polo shirt, took out the BMW and headed down to Smokey Joe's Bar and Restaurant on Post Road.

Smokey Joe's didn't have many customers for a Friday night and surprisingly only a few regulars were hanging out past ten o'clock. Spencer first headed to the downstairs buffet, asked for a pulled pork sandwich and selected potatoes and broccoli for the side. The older Joe served him and slipped a couple of chunks of cheap lard onto his plate. While smiling, he overcharged him at the cash register and in his heavy, southern Italian accent complemented him.

"Looking good, Captain Shrewsbury. I give you brake. Ten percent. I so happy see you back."

Spencer saw that Joe overcharged him; he regarded it as a

tip and let it go. He took the plate upstairs and sat down by the bar.

Vika, the young Russian born, most attractive barmaid we must admit, left the two guys sitting by the end and making insolent passes at her and went to tend on Spencer as soon as saw him sitting down.

"Captain Shrewsbury, what's your drink tonight?" She asked.

"Amstel light."

She gave him the beer, opened it up and pouring it into a big frosted stein mug added, "Why the long face. You are back. Be happy."

He took a long swig from the foamy liquid. She waited, hasn't moved but leaning forward on the bar gave him a scrutinizing look.

He didn't flinch, squinted back, quickly finished his beer and demanded even before put his mug back on the counter.

"Hit me with another one."

Vika was a good person, she knew the whys and the wherefores of every drunkard or inebriate that sat down in her bar. "Is it that bad?" she asked, "How is your wife? Is she ok? I never see her here. Why don't you bring her here sometimes?"

"Never mind her; she is too young to drink. We shouldn't be talking about her. Let's talk about you. What about your boyfriend?"

"Which one?"

"The Brazilian."

"That one, he is ok and so are the other six of them."

"Come on, Vika, you don't have that many boyfriends."

"No, I was only kidding, you are the one and only."

Spencer saw someone sitting down on the barstool next to him. And he heard her voice.

"We should be talking about your wife."

He turned around and stared at the impertinent and uninvited commentator. He saw Pamela Leicester, his next-door neighbor.

Pamela kept watching the Shrewsbury residence all evening. She saw Spencer coming to the master bedroom and turning on the lights for a few minutes. She saw Linda sleeping in the bed and Spencer dressing up and going out. She figured; he must be heading to Smokey's place. She dressed up and followed him. She settled her big bottom down on the barstool next to him and eavesdropped on the conversation the captain carried on with Vika.

After getting her neighbor's attention, she relentlessly pressed on. "If I were you I would watch her very closely."

Spencer never liked Pamela, he didn't like her when Dwight was still around and especially didn't like her after she got divorced. He was clearly annoyed by the intrusion.

"Say that again."

"You've heard me. While you are gone she is warming her own dish of goodies in the oven."

The blood drained from Spencer's head down to his toes. Angry fear gripped his heart and his worst nightmare hit him head on and banged against his frontal lobes. He became mad but the same time he was relieved. At least he had reason to be ascertain, he had the proof that Linda was unfaithful. No more excuses being a nice guy. He just received a license to abuse his wife. But he hated the messenger.

He turned to Pamela, "What do you know about her?"

"Nothing. I only know what I see. She has suitors, late

night visitors, and she goes out during the day with local playboys."

"Who?" Spencer roared like an African lion speared by Shaka Zulu in the jungle. "Who is it?"

"The young gigolo next door, Percy Grimsby, he is in love with her and she has the hots for him."

Spencer jumped up. He hit Pamela across the face and yelled, "Liar, you fucking-double-dealing tramp."

He charged out of the bar, jumped into his BMW and screeching the wheels and exceeding speed limits by bi-fold drove home. Pamela followed him and didn't see the dark car with New York plates that were stealthily making the turns after her.

Chapter Twelve

Spencer burst into his house, didn't say hello and headed straight to the liquor cabinet. Ripped open the locked door, grabbed his Chivas Regal and drank with big urgent swallows, lips clenching the bottle's mouth as if he was thirsted in the desert for three days. Wiping his mouth clean he hollered for his wife.

"Linda."

"I'm here."

He saw her. Standing under the archway between the living room and the entrance hall in her nightgown she was holding her doll, the one she brought with her from Kansas City.

"What are you doing with that crap?" He asked hoarsely.

"I'm putting Lily into the family room."

"It doesn't belong there." He bellowed and ripped her cherished raggedy friend from her hand. He threw Lily across the room and saw somebody who didn't belong there, not in his house, not ever, Percy Grimsby.

He turned to Linda, lowered his voice to a menacing calm and asked.

"Are we having a guest in the house?"

She didn't answer.

He repeated his demand, louder this time. "I asked you damn it. Are you entertaining while I'm not here?"

Linda turned to Percy, "Please, go home. You shouldn't be here. It's my own problem. Don't get involved."

Spencer raised his arm and stepped closer to his wife. Near tears, dread and fear of a horrible confrontation made Linda's face white as a burial linen covering a coffin. Her voice panicky and her small body shaking with trembling fright, she desperately wished to defuse the situation.

She tried again, "Percy, you have no business of being here. Spencer and I, we need to be alone. It's far too late for us."

Spencer saw his wife's predicament and he liked it. He thought. *I'm going to have fun with the two of you.* To keep his balance he leaned against the wall, calm and composed, and said with benign disinterest, "The young gentleman doesn't bother me. He can stay."

A long and uneasy silence followed. Exerting the confusing power of the alcohol the Chivas damaged Spencer's reasoning. Feeling dizzy he couldn't decide what he should do next. He only knew that he had to stay in control. He was missing something. Ice, yes, there was no ice in the bucket.

He raised his arm again and tried to hit Linda, "Get the ice, now, damn it, woman."

Then Spencer couldn't move his arm. A strong and brave grip got hold of his hand and he felt a force restraining him. Percy grabbed Spencer's arm and held it back. His demanding voice reflected contempt and although voice subdued, his hatred was obvious.

"Nobody should hit a woman." He warned.

Spencer was fifty pounds heavier than Percy; he had stronger bones and broader shoulders. He easily shook off Percy's grip and ridiculed him.

"Have you got a problem with that, punk? I'll hit my wife when I need too. What do you know about marriage anyway?"

Spencer raised his arm and hit Linda in the face. She saw it coming, pulled back and the blow barely touched her mouth. But caught on the upper lip, the skin broke and tiny drops of blood oozed from the wound.

Percy's eyes blazed with insane resolve. He moved between Spencer and Linda, pushed him back and yelled, "You will not hit her again."

With his tightly clenched fist Spencer landed a hard blow on Percy's head. He absorbed the impact and as hard as he could he punched Spencer's nose.

Spencer jabbed back and Percy tried wrestling him to the floor. Staggering, he tripped and Spencer kicked his ribs. Percy jumped up and lowering his skull ran into Spencer's chest. He grabbed Percy's head with his right hand, gave him a nelson and pounded his face and neck with his left. Percy freed himself and charged at Spencer one more time. Taking a great swing he tried to take him out with a double-handed haymaker. He missed, lost his balance and Spencer grabbed the whiskey bottle. Using unrestrained strength, no mercy or caution, he hit Percy's temple. Percy collapsed, tried to get up, but Spencer kicked his chest. Percy couldn't breathe. He was bleeding, bruised yet he tried fighting on.

Linda cried and pleaded the two men to stop. She saw Percy getting weaker and pushed into the corner. Spencer kept hitting him. Uncaring the damage he was doing Spencer turned raging mad and looked ready to kill.

Then Percy was out. Down and out he couldn't get up any more. Spencer sat down, his point made and he felt awfully tired, and bellowed to Linda.

"Ice, damn it, don't make me ask you again."

Linda rushed to get the ice. Spencer mixed another Rob Roy drink and ordered her, "Sit down, whore."

Trembling and week, Linda sat down and listened to the violently jealous man.

"What have you been doing with him?"

"Nothing."

"Come on. You've been fucking him."

"Who told you that?"

"Pamela, next door."

"Whom do you believe? Me or her."

"Than what is he doing here?"

"Because, Pamela told him you've been beating me. He came over to talk to you. He meant well. I begged him to leave but he wouldn't listen. "

"That slut Pamela again."

"Can't you see what a snake she is?"

"We'll see about that. I'll ask her tomorrow and if it's true what she says you are out. You pack your tiny suitcase and move back to the YWCA."

Percy was regaining consciousness. In his confused and

dazed beaten up state he barely could comprehend any more what transpired. He tried to remember. Pamela. Of course, she must have ratted on them, the revengeful bitch. Then he heard Spencer.

"We have to get him out of here. Grab his feet."

Linda didn't move and Spencer pulled up Percy. When standing straight, using his bare knuckles he hit Percy's head once again. Percy fell down like a sack of potatoes and hit his head against the edge of the cocktail table. Spencer grabbed Percy's shoulders, dragged his lifeless body out of his house and a few feet away from the house threw him on the front lawn.

Wiped his sweaty hands against his pants and sighed, "Better. That's where he belongs and not with somebody else's house messing with somebody else's wife."

Percy just lay there, silent and motionless. He was no concern to Spencer any more.

Spencer went back to the house. Finished his remaining Chivas Regal; sat down and didn't feel good. First he shivered and then his body began to shake. His acute alcoholism and his overworked global schedule took their destructive effect. His blood pressure dropped and making his teeth chattering, the alcohol sucked away his body heat. The fight and the blows he received depleted his strength. Exhausted, and head spinning dizzily, he had to lie down and desperately needed warmth.

On the top of this, for the last twenty-four hours, he has been coming down with a serious flue, a vicious virus or something. Now he wanted Linda's help. He moaned arrogantly and demanded her attentive care.

She came, didn't say a word of complaint or reprimand.

Undressed him, guided him into his bed and made him a hot tea with lemon. She took his temperature and it was 103 degrees. She didn't smile hasn't made any comments, only did her duty. When she saw Spencer quieting down she picked up her pillow and took it into the guest bedroom. Spencer saw it, touched her skirt and pleaded. Now he behaved like a gentleman.

"Sleep with me, please. I love you. I'm sorry. I had to protect you. I defended you because I loved you. I had to defend your honors."

Linda caressed his flaming red face and feverish forehead with saintly compassion and noble forgiveness, "I know. But I don't want to catch your virus. We should sleep separately until you get better."

Spencer fell asleep and for the rest of the night, things remained peaceful in the house.

Giacomo Pugliese followed Pamela to Smokey Joe's. He hoped to catch her earlier and quickly finish his business, but in the dark suburban streets of Darien he mixed up the directions and arrived a minute too late. She was already heading out and Giacomo cursed his luck. Going out of his way meant more exposure and more risks. He didn't like to deviate unnecessary from his planned course of action. He angrily drove his rented Chevrolet Avalanche after her and parked in the dark lot by the river.

There, ready to jump but patient as a cat in front of a gopher burrow, he waited. Later he saw a guy running from the bar and drive away like a crazy lunatic in the BMW that was parked next to him.

"Shit," he said derisively and spit a broken toothpick out

his window, "Dude, I guess, if you've got to go, you got to go."

Then saw Pamela rushing out and turned his engine on and followed her. He observed the woman to enter her house, didn't want to leave his car nearby, made a circle and parked in a dark spot on Raymond Avenue.

Like a casual stroller doing exercise he walked back. Just in time to see Spencer throwing Percy out of his house.

The lights in Pamela's house went out and Giacomo mumbled, "*Bona fortuna, amore mio,* time has come to make my move on you."

After all, he gloated contentedly, things might work out much better this way. He went over to Percy's limp body, laying motionless in the dark and kicked him in the head.

"Sorry, pal. I don't want you to make a sudden move while I'm checking out who you are."

Holding Percy's wallet he didn't want to believe his luck. The man resting in the grass was the kid from next door, his second target. Finding him saved time, a lot of waiting and perhaps the difference between a perfect crime and a botched up job.

He glanced sideways toward the Leicester residence. Pamela still seemed moving around, she was turning lights on and off, maybe couldn't sleep, maybe she knew what happened next door and she contemplated coming out and help Percy.

Giacomo waited. *If she comes out,* he thought, *I could whack her and make it look like it was a bloody fight between the two.*

Giacomo waited more, then figured Pamela wasn't about to come out. He had to revert back to his original plan to bump her off inside the house. He kicked again Percy's head and picked up his lifeless body.

An avid weight lifter, 150 pounds felt featherweight for Giacomo. He carried him to the front door as if the boy were a feather in the wind. Leaned him carefully against the door, rang the bell and then hid on the side.

Pamela came to the door, she thought the late night ringer must be Percy, asking her for help or offering an explanation, have an argument and than kiss and make up. At any rate it was better to be with him than being alone. Maybe this was a chance for a sweet reunion, after Percy had learned his lesson from Spencer.

She peeped through the side glass and saw, it indeed was Percy. He looked dazed, beaten and in bad need of help.

Good, she thought; *that served him well, now he wants my compassion and assistance.* She opened the door and with a reflex she caught him as he fell forward. Her hands full with Percy's heavy body she didn't see the second man emerging from behind.

Giacomo Pugliese pushed in, put his hand on Pamela's mouth and grabbed her upper body. Let Percy fall on the floor and with his foot kicked the door closed. Pamela fought hard, tried to bite the hand but he was far too strong and she could cause no trouble for him. He made it inside and there was no way of stopping him.

Chapter Thirteen

Percy woke up with a terrible headache. His body hurt and he hardly could breathe. The bones of his ribcage ached as if they were broken and pried apart. Daggers of sharp pain, each time he attempted to inhale, the gurgling sounds of air gushing into his blood ravaged lungs seemed to tell, he sustained serious injury. Wheezing and rattling through collapsed air passages, he craved for oxygen, and couldn't move without bringing punishing tortures of excruciating pain on him.

In the darkness of the night, he had no idea where he lay crumpled up and defeated into a bloody mess.

Opened one eye and saw the insides of a house. Indoors, definitely not outdoors and not in his room and not in his father's house for sure, he could figure out that much, but how did he get here, wherever he was?

One of his eyes was swollen shut but could wipe the blood away from the other one and saw better. He was lying on a carpet in somebody's living room. It seemed familiar. Eerily quiet; not single source of light in the house. He must have been in the dark for a long time. In the near full moonlight, filtering in through the curtains from outside, with his widely dilated pupils he could differentiate between the colorless shades that surrounded him.

He was in Pamela's house. But what was he doing there? And where was she?

Percy set up and, enduring pains of damaged nerve endings forced himself to stand. She must be upstairs, sleeping, he hoped.

Then he remembered. He was at the Shrewsbury's, he tried to protect Linda and Spencer beat him up. And Linda didn't help him at all, she just stood there and let Spencer thrash him, but on the other hand he, Percy, was the one who should have protected her.

Percy thought with some solace. *But I have done it. He didn't beat her. He beat me instead.*

Went to the kitchen and turned on the lights, and then saw her. She was lying on the tile floor. Her posture seemed terrifyingly unnatural and her open eyes were strangely bulging out of their sockets. He examined closer and there was no life in her fishlike eyes. They were immobile and fixed in a single, inanimate direction and they accusingly pointed at Percy. He moved but her eyes did not follow him.

Her face was looked pale. Ashen pale but unusually grayish and scary, then he saw her hands, her fingers were gnarled and tried to break a white rope away from her neck, her fingernails were broken and furrowing deeply in a wide swath all around, deep purple bruise marks covered her skin. Her tongue dangled out lifelessly and she bit off almost half of it. She must have struggled against death and must have suffered terribly in her final agony.

Percy touched her skin; it felt cold, frighteningly and surprisingly cold. He just touched a dead body, Pamela's dead body.

No need to panic, Percy reasoned. *I must help. Maybe Pamela isn't dead. I have to get help, now.*

He went to the nearest phone in the house and called 911.

"Darien Police Department, Sergeant Cahill," a calm voice replied.

Pronouncing his words in raspy gasps, Percy had to use force pushing each syllable. He needed help and he trusted the police.

"I'm Percy Grimsby,' he said, "I live at 14 Red Rose Circle. I'm in Pamela Leicester's house, 16 Red Rose Circle. I think she needs help. She needs help right now."

"Anybody else is there?"

"No"

"Are there any weapons?"

"No."

"Domestic violence?"

"I don't think so."

The sergeant was deliberately keeping him on the phone and he motioned to his partner, already listening in on the other line, to dispatch all available units to the scene.

"Can she talk? Can she come to the phone?"

"No. She isn't moving."

"Is she breathing?"

"I don't know."

"Son, go to the door and open it, the police should be there by now. Don't hang up."

Percy saw the flashlights at the front and the shadows moving about by the back porch. Put the receiver on the counter and let two officers in through the front.

One of the officers opened the back door; let the others in and they asked Percy, "Where is she?"

"In the kitchen."

The officer stepped into the kitchen. He looked at Pamela and said.

"I see," he pushed Percy away, "stay back. We'll take it over from here."

The officer bent down and checked her pulse. His partner called an ambulance. The first signs of dawn were breaking through the darkness and the town began waking up.

Ten minutes later plainclothes detectives and a crime scene photographer arrived. They took pictures and marked the body on the floor.

"No signs of forced entry," someone said.

Percy stayed standing near Pamela and nobody cared about him. The doctor who came in with the ambulance examined her neck.

"Cause of death, asphyxiation by strangling with a rope. About six hours ago."

The senior detective called Percy.

"Son, come to the dining room. We need to talk."

They went to the dining room; he sat down and made Percy to take a chair in front of him.

"How did you get into the house?"

"I don't remember."

"What do you remember, tell me; tell me all the details."

"I woke up in the living room. Then I saw her body and I called the police."

"Who beat you? Did you have a fight with Mrs. Leicester?"

"No, I had a fight with Mr. Shrewsbury next door."

"Captain Shrewsbury, when?"

"Last night."

"What time."

"Around eleven."

"Are you usually going around in the neighborhood at night and pick fights with people?"

"No."

"Why did you come to Mrs. Leicester house? Did you have a problem with her too?"

"Yes, no."

"What is it, yes or no?"

"It's a long story. I didn't hurt her."

"Yeah, who did it then? Empty your pockets, everything on the table."

Percy emptied his pockets, he took out his wallet, keys, change purse and he found something unfamiliar, he reached deeper inside and pulled it out. Looking dumbfounded he held it in his hands.

"Come on son, show it to us; put it in on the table."

He placed the item down and it was an open plastic bag and in it was a folded up long piece of nylon, maybe quarter inch thick white rope, the same kind imbedded in the skin around Pamela's neck. Its end had a rough cut and the cut matched the cut on the piece used to strangle her. The detective inspected both ends, shook his head and turned to Percy.

"Percy Grimsby; put your hands behind your back. You are under arrest and anything you say may and will be used against you in the court of law. You are entitled to seek advice from an attorney."

Percy stood with his back turned toward the detective; he put the handcuffs on him and went through his wallet. Showing no sympathy and out of routine he asked.

"Have you been arrested before?"

"No, never."

Already seven o'clock the sun began climbing above the horizon and morning commuters emerged from their homes. The police pulled a yellow crime scene tape around the house and more neighbors came out and stood curiously outside their front doors.

Linda woke up to the commotion, checked on Spencer; he appeared deep asleep and breathed heavily with high fever. She didn't need to babysit him.

She dressed up and went outside.

"What's going on?" Linda asked the old man from across the street.

"Someone murdered Pamela and they are keeping the Grimsby boy inside. I guess they must be questioning him."

A cold sensation of fear tingled down on Linda's spine. Maybe Percy had gotten mad and killed Pamela. Then she dismissed it, it's impossible. He couldn't even have hurt a gadfly. *He only wanted to protect me last night,* she thought, *and that was a noble cause. No way could he be the murderer.*

She wanted to see Percy and tried to get inside the house.

The young police officer guarding the door stopped her, "Who are you?"

"Linda Shrewsbury. I live next door. I know these people. Let me in. Percy was with us last night."

On his two-way radio the guard called the sergeant on duty inside the house. He talked to the detective. The detective left Percy, came out, looked at Linda and told the guard, "Let her in."

He led her into the family room, far away from Percy. She couldn't see him. The detective told Linda to sit down and putting his notebook in front of him asked her, "What is it what you want to tell us?"

"He didn't do it."

"He didn't do what?"

"He didn't hurt Pamela."

"What makes you think Pamela is hurt?"

"I saw the police activity and someone outside told me she was dead."

"If so, what makes you think that Percy had anything to do with her death?"

"I said; he didn't do it. Percy was with us last night."

"Until when?"

"Midnight, eleven thirty, maybe. My husband was drunk and they've got into a fight. My husband was much stronger than him; he threw him out of the house and left him unconscious on our front yard. He was in no condition to move, let alone fight big and strong Pamela."

"I see. What were your husband and Percy fighting about?"

"Spencer was jealous; he thought I had an affair with Percy."

"Who is Spencer?"

"My husband, he is an airline pilot."

"Aha, him? I know him. We went to high school together, great guy. I didn't know he'd got married."

"He had. We've been married almost for a year now."

Lucky bastard, detective Sean Doherty thought, but it would have been very unprofessional to have a comment reflecting his personal opinions. Furthermore, he thought, she knew a lot more than she was telling and he needed to get that out of her without revealing information beyond the minimum she needed to know.

He asked, "What made Spencer think you had an affair with Percy?"

"Pamela was spreading crazy rumors."

"Like what?"

"Like Spencer was beating me. Percy came over to protect me and Spencer assumed we had some sort of relationship going on."

Doherty hasn't shown any outward signs of his inner elation but he knew he was onto something. Linda realized she was implicating Percy. Feeling bad she tried to control the spin she caused.

"Percy and Pamela were good friends. I usually keep to myself I'm relatively new in town."

Bingo, she did it again. Doherty figured and said, "Hold that thought for a second."

He left the room and called his colleague, Detective Murphy away from Percy.

He informed him in a low, accusingly hushed voice, "I think we have a motive. Percy had an affair with Pamela and he wanted to sack up with Linda Shrewsbury too. Pamela found out about it, she went berserk and told Captain Shrewsbury, the captain beat Percy and the boy went bananas, he confronted Pamela and in a mad rage strangled her."

Murphy had a slightly different opinion, "That doesn't mesh. The evidence against him indicates premeditated murder. He purchased the cord, cut it and strangled her in cold blood. There are no signs of any serious fight inside the house. She let him in and they didn't fight. It looks like a professional, premeditated and well-planned job.

"That is not for us to figure out." Doherty shook his head, "We already arrested him and from here on let his lawyers do his defense."

Doherty went back to Linda, "Sorry, Mrs Shrewsbury, police procedures. Could we talk to your husband?"

"He is very ill. He suddenly came down with a vicious flue."

"All right, we're going to talk to him when he feels better. You two don't have any problems we should know about."

"What problems?"

"Is he a good boy? Is he treating you nice? He is not abusing you, is he?"

"I have no complains. He is a very good husband.

"Well then, you may go now, Mrs Shrewsbury. We'll contact you if we need you. If you remember anything else, don't hesitate to call me."

He gave his detective card to Linda and politely escorted her out. Outside, after she was safely far away, he asked the crowd of spectators.

"Does anyone know where Percy's parents are?"

"Right here," a late middle-aged distinguished looking couple spoke up. "We would like to talk to our son."

"I don't think it is possible right now," Doherty shook his head, "but I need to talk to both of you."

"By all means."

"I would like to see his room" The detective nodded approvingly and asked with a tentative smile, "Can we go inside your house?"

Chapter Fourteen

Lawrence and Rosemary Grimsby were in denial. They could not find it conceivable that their son committed a serious crime. Once inside their house they unexpectedly confronted detective Sean Doherty.

"You are making a serious mistake."

Doherty's eyes went from benevolently benign to ice cold and his until semi friendly face turned straight and official. "I don't make mistakes. But let's assume for argument sake he didn't do it. Then who did it and what was your son doing in the house with a dead body?"

"That we don't know; we didn't know Mrs. Leicester well. She could have had enemies, affairs; she is a divorcee, we mean she was a divorcee."

"She had an affair all right and her sugarplum sweetheart was your son. Does your son have any temper problems, any history of psychotic behavior?"

"No, absolutely not."

"Was he home last night?" The detective made a checkmark in his notebook and glanced toward the steps, "We need to see his room?"

They escorted Doherty upstairs and Rosemary opened Percy's door. His neatly made bed clearly indicated that last night he hasn't slept a minute in it. Doherty grinned and there was irony in his voice.

"I see. He likes things tidy and neat. He made his bed already."

Lawrence and Rosemary didn't have any answers only a timid and meaningless excuse. "He never stayed out all night before."

Although confident that he already knew enough to justify Percy's arrest and the Grimsby couple's son was presumably the murderer, Doherty still felt fragments of sympathy for the tragedy stricken parents and as he continued he tried to keep the mocking and threatening out of his tone.

"Have you heard any strange noises in the neighborhood last night, have you noticed anybody loitering around, any unusual cars, anything out of the ordinary?"

Lawrence grabbed this last straw of opportunity. He foolishly thought that assuming Percy's guilt, at best, was presumptuous and Doherty unfairly discarded other opportunities and he misguidedly decided to challenge the detective.

"Mrs. Grimsby and I," the jittery father began, "we are very sound sleepers, we haven't heard any noises and we haven't been checking the neighborhood all night long for prowlers.

But let me say that, if the Darien Police Department is not making a through investigation and does not properly scan the crime scene and for that matter, the entire neighborhood, we we'll hire an independent investigator and private detective to prove our son's innocence."

The unwarranted accusatory tone angered Doherty.

"You do that," he replied and, contempt and disdain now palpable in his clipped voice, rebuked them, "But I'm warning you, we caught him with the murder weapon in his possession and he is the only one who had been in the victim's house last night. You'd better get prepared, mentally and financially, because we're taking him in. You should get a lawyer to handle his defense. Your son can talk to his lawyer as much as he wants. Other than that you may come to his arraignment at the Stamford Superior Court when he is going to be formally charged and the date for his preliminary hearing will be set. We will recommend that the State charge him with first degree murder."

Having blown the uncooperative parents out of the water Doherty left the devastated and speechless couple. He walked out of the house but turned back from the open front door, glared at them and using a terse, confrontational voice sharply confronted them, "We need to search the house, do you want us to do it now or shall we come back with a search warrant?"

Lawrence Grimsby despised Doherty self-righteous attitude. He became defiant and told him off.

"I you must, come back with a warrant."

That made Doherty outright unfriendly and belligerent, "Don't move a thing." He warned the parents and his stance projected irate calm, "That will be tempering with evidence and could bring you…" He stopped and raised a forefinger to emphasize. "You both will be charged with obstruction of justice."

Doherty came back in the afternoon with a two plainclothesmen and a search warrant to look for evidence of drugs, weapons, and signs of conspiracy to commit murder. For the two hours the evidence team was in the house he avoided eye contact with Rosemary. They were digging into closets and drawers, emptying everything on beds and tables, pouring out boxes of cereals and bags of flour. They threw everybody's clothes on the floor and spread pieces of papers all over the place.

They confiscated Percy's computers, his manuscripts and carried them into a police van parked outside. They took all the pills from the bathroom cabinets to be tested at the police laboratory. They turned the lives and the home of the entire family upside down and spilled their privacy to be viewed by callously prying and pretentiously disinterested strangers standing outside and peeking in when the door opened for a few second.

When Lawrence, David and Stacey, Percy's sister came home they found Rosemary crying and trying to put everything back in place. Going from upset to enraged they cursed and fumed. The family unanimously blamed Percy for the embarrassing mess.

"He had to fool around with that older bitch. He couldn't get a decent job, work during the day and sleep at night. Now we're going to be in the local papers. The Darien News will have a field day with this case. We're going to be ostracized and people will whisper behind our back."

They felt no sympathy for and refused to understand

Percy's plight. And the issue of money hasn't even been raised. After six hours of hard work, finally the house looked clean and back in order and the infuriated family sat down for dinner. They had pizza delivered and ate it. The pie and the double cheese on it smelt good, the savory bites were delicious but the anger that wrenched their insides still ruined the enjoyment.

David led the predominant tone. "How much is this going to cost us?"

Lawrence had the numbers at his fingertips. "Fifty thousand, we have to get a lawyer. We have to post bail and we may have to put up our home as collateral."

Not a second hesitation to reconsider or debate, David and Stacey answered in unison, "No way. What if he skips town and we lose the house."

For a few minutes they gnawed in silence on the chewy pieces of the pizza and David again took the lead with a sobering suggestion, "Let him get a public defender. They are free. And it wouldn't hurt him if he spent some time in jail. That's where he was heading anyway. We should not go into bankruptcy just because he committed a crime? Remember the perfect cliché; if you can't do the time don't do the crime. Jail will turn him into a man. Finally he will have a chance to grow up."

Rosemary interrupted the ugly tirade that her oldest was belching forth, "What if he's innocent? What if somebody else did it? We should get at least a private investigator and challenge the police report."

"On what money," the rest spoke in unison. "That is a bottomless pit. Everything we worked for in all of our lives could go down in the drain because of him."

Rosemary had no power in her own family. She may have

felt pity for his youngest, but the others saw an opportunity to get rid of him, and to get rid of him without spending too much money on it. They threw him to the proverbial dogs. The decision has been made. They left Percy to his own devices and the prognosis for a cloudless outcome didn't seem promising at all.

Percy Grimsby's arraignment took place on Tuesday. Lawrence Grimsby had an important meeting he couldn't miss. He couldn't get himself to tell his boss and coworkers that he had problems at home, that his son had been charged with murder.

David couldn't care less; being due for a promotion he couldn't possible skip a day from work.

Stacey had a lunch date with her boss and prospective boyfriend and she wouldn't have postponed that for all the treasures in the world.

From the family only Rosemary showed up for the arraignment. The heavily overscheduled court was running late. The judge speed-read the charges, set the bails, almost disregarding the seriousness of the offense and one after the other new detainees were brought in. After many cases and a long wait, accompanied by a guard on each side, Percy arrived.

For the first time since his arrest, Rosemary could take a close look at her son. She saw a stranger. He lost weight; seemed worried and didn't have his usual confident disposition and healthy color. Rosemary came to the front and cast her pleading eyes at the venerable looking middle-aged, black lady judge. After reading Percy's folder for a minute, the judge looked up and stared at Percy. She had no hatred in her eyes just compassion and pity.

"First degree murder and conspiracy to commit murder," she stated solemnly and asked. "Do you understand the charges?"

"Yes," Percy said almost imperceptibly. He knew; he wasn't getting any sympathy, not even from his mother.

"Do you have an attorney representing you?" The judge asked and regarded Percy with traces of kindness, "If you don't, the court will appoint one for you."

"I don't have an attorney," Percy said and he felt his life ceased to exist. He asked for suffering and he was getting it. He was innocent, at least he thought he was innocent but he didn't remember exactly what he did. He resigned to his fate and hoped to see Linda coming to his defense. But she seemed to be nowhere in the court.

A small-framed, grayish looking man, appearance lacking any significant attributes or encouraging qualities, rose and introduced himself, "Robert Schwechter, attorney at law, public defender. I have been assigned to represent Mr. Grimsby."

The court set the initial bail at two hundred thousand dollars, Schwechter asked to have it reduced and while the judge pondered the request, the assistant district attorney, a slender woman of about forty with a somewhat unattractive and masculine looking face, jumped to her feet and objected. "The seriousness of the charges, the likelihood of the accused fleeing prosecution and the danger of his freedom presents to society, warrants and justifies the higher bail."

The judge fixed her eyes at Schwechter and asked, "On what grounds do you request reduced bail?"

"The accused has no prior criminal record, he was born and raised in this area and he is not in the financial situation to flee prosecution. He doesn't have any known history of violence."

The judge looked into her papers. She wrote down a note and ten seconds later, without lifting her eyes and looking at the defender or the accused, smacked down her gavel.

"Bail set at fifty thousand dollars. Preliminary hearing will begin twelve weeks from today."

Two guards grabbed and led Percy away without letting him talk to his mother. He didn't feel inclined talking to her. He didn't want to hear her castigation and reproach for causing all this humiliation and trouble to the family.

Schwechter stepped closer to Rosemary and asked, "Are you going to post his bail?"

"No, we can't afford it."

"I can set you up with a bail bondsman."

"No, thank you, we don't have the cash and we don't want to put up our house as collateral. I'm sorry, family decision."

"All right, lady. It's your son. You know what you're doing. I'll do my best. He looks a good person to me; anyway, as I said, it is your choice. See you at the hearing."

They parted. Schwechter didn't shake her hand and had nothing but contempt for the decision she made.

Chapter Fifteen

The day after Percy's arrest Spencer's flue took a turn for the worse. At nights his pajamas soaked with drenching sweat; he had dry coughing and suffered of constant shortness of breath. Linda took his temperature and noticed the swollen lymph glands in his armpit.

She touched them and they felt hard. "You must have an infection. I don't like those lumps at all."

"When I get better they go away. What was about that big commotion next door last night?"

"You don't remember?"

"Remember what?"

She didn't dare to mention Percy's name. Alone with a monster, sick with a flue as he was, she didn't want to provoke him. She wasn't sure how much he didn't know and what would trigger his rage.

She spoke cautiously, "The woman next door was murdered last night."

He seemed to recall that something last night really made him mad and asked hesitantly, "Pamela?"

"I'm very bad with names." Linda avoided a straight reply.

Spencer tried hard and remembered seeing Pamela in the bar and remembered a fight. He thought. *Maybe, I did it* and making a startled phony face asked. "I didn't do it. Did I?"

Linda shook down the mercury in the thermometer. She didn't make eye contact and spoke ponderously, "Probably not."

Spencer remembered Percy. "But I had a fight with someone. Haven't I?"

"That wasn't her."

"Who was it?"

"I don't know. An intruder, I guess. You threw him out."

"Wasn't that your boyfriend?"

Linda put a cold towel on Spencer's forehead. "Don't start with that nonsense. I don't have a boyfriend."

"Better not. Are they suspecting anyone?"

"Yes, her groundskeeper. They arrested him."

"I see, the young Grimsby boy."

"I guess so. As I said I'm very bad with names."

Now Spencer remembered everything. But he was too sick and too sober to pick a fight with Linda. He just nodded agreeably. "Good. That serves him well."

Linda felt awfully bad. She thought she'd betrayed Percy. Not only she implicated him to the police, but also now she didn't have the courage to stand up for him. She had fights in the orphanage, defended the honor of her mother or fought over which bed to take, but that was different. Back then she thought she protected some childishly perceived higher moral grounds and possessed no feelings of true love for her mother. She could look cool and play tough and that was the end of it. The fighters got punished and next day they became friends again. But now she hated Spencer and loved Percy and yet she had to pretend the opposite.

She thought. *I have better change my attitude.* Otherwise, she reprimanded herself, *I'll be a doormat of everyone and life wouldn't be worth living.* She made a promise. *Enough, from here on I'll set the rules of the games that life forces me to play.*

Two weeks passed and Spencer still looked miserable. He had chronic diarrhea, noticeably lost weight and became depressed. He hardly could eat and looked frighteningly emaciated.

Linda went outside to bring the mail in. After Percy's arrest and Spencer being so sick she didn't want to hear any phony opinions and didn't want to tell anybody about Spencer's acute illness. With the immense inside resentment she was harboring, she was afraid she would snap at any gossiping jerk. She remembered her mother being dragged away and screaming and she didn't want to end up like her.

Walking outside she fixed her eyes at the ground three feet ahead of her and avoided talking to or even glance at anybody coming her way in the neighborhood.

Feeling sorry and nostalgic about Percy, sadness and wishing to find remedy she looked at the spot where he lay beaten and unconscious. Didn't feel like going back to the house and listen to Spencer's coughing. To sort the mail out she sat down on the woodpile that Percy stacked up for her so neatly and not so long ago.

She dropped half of the junk mail and when picking up saw a small piece of yellowing and withered paper wedged between the logs, something that didn't belong there. She bent down to investigate and pulled out the piece.

It looked a sales receipt. She took it inside and put it on the kitchen table. Sat down and carefully studied the weather washed fading print.

It was a Home Depot sales receipt. It originated from the New Rochelle, New York store, stated the sales number, the date of sale and the item purchased, dollars spent and indicated a VISA card purchase with approval code and exact down to minute time of purchase.

She looked at again and read: ¼" Thick Nylon Rope, 50 feet length, May 28, 2003, 11:40.

Percy was walking with her at the Mianus River Gorge Park, on that day at that exact time. He didn't purchase the rope. *Somebody else did,* she thought, *and that somebody brought the rope here; put it into unconscious Percy's pocket and in the process inadvertently dropped the sales receipt.*

She pondered about her responsibility. If she didn't encourage Percy he wouldn't have come over and wouldn't have been thrown on the lawn and Pamela perhaps would be alive today. But who dropped the sales receipt.

She missed Percy's love and devotion, the faithful and idealistic look in his eyes, and she hasn't forgotten their walk, the way he desired her, and the passionate way he made love to her. She felt she had to help him.

She decided to make the first step of her new life. She used computers before and had no problems of getting on the Internet. Turned on Spencer's computer and looked up the Connecticut inmate information site. She typed in Percy's name and the system gave him his number, date of birth and present location, Bridgeport Correctional Center. She clicked on the directions and in an instant she knew where Percy was and she knew how to get there.

She needed minimum of three hours to drive to Bridgeport, find Percy, talk to him and return. First she called the jail's information number to get the visiting hours and then she went into Spencer's room.

"Spencer, dear," she told him softly, "I have to go out for a couple of hours. Do you think you are going to be all right on your own?"

"I manage. What do you have to do?"

"Shopping, I would like to go to the Trumbull Mall."

"I guess you need to get away from me. I don't blame you but, please, hurry back. I'm sorry to be this sick. A wicked flue, I'll be better soon and we'll have fun, together. I promise."

"Sure we will. We will have a lot of fun together and I'll be back soon." She said but inside she thought. *You son of a bitch wife beating scumbag, now you are nice to me that you are sick, you going to get better and start everything all over, the drinking, the abuses, the beatings, you savagely beat that unlucky Percy, who knows what happened to him and now he is in jail, thanks to you.*

She took the BMW and drove to North Street in Bridgeport. The Correctional Facility was a drab looking; yellow colored one story building and had a huge parking lot. She found the visitor center and with a group of other women emerging from a bus entered.

They checked her identifications, she had to open her

handbag and a uniformed female correctional officer padded her down including between the insides of her upper thighs. Then they allowed her to enter the cavernous visiting hall. First the human stench and smell shocked her senses, and then she saw it all, the desperate and pitiful crowds of friends, relatives, wives, mothers, husbands and children trying to communicate with their loved ones. She waited long minutes and she heard her name called and she sat down in a booth, in front of a glass and a phone receiver at her right side. She stared across and saw Percy being escorted in shackles to his seat. He looked different. In two weeks he changed into another man. More mature, despondent and seemingly resigned to his fate.

She picked up the earpiece. She had to try to restore his self-esteem. She intended to change his desperation into an optimistic notion in what he could place his trust and hopes.

Percy's life at the Bridgeport Correctional facility settled to a daily survival routine. They locked him into a cell with an elderly white male who wasn't willing to divulge the nature of his offense. But, apparently for his own safety, he was semi isolated from the rest of the prison population. The prison food didn't taste too bad and the guards brought it to their cell. Percy had no exercise privileges until the warden's office could come up with a safe routine, devised just for him.

The old man didn't talk. He kept to himself and only once, on the first day ventured in superficial communications when seeing the others leaving for exercise privileges he commented with self pity. "If I ever went out there, they'd kill me just for fun."

The old inmate seemed to have nice priestly manners but

didn't seem wanting to share with Percy any information regarding his past.

Percy's mother brought in her son's manual typewriter; bought him a box of typing paper and Percy begin to write. He wrote down his feelings but he never wrote about his recent experiences, he created his own reality, far away from his current gloomy and frighteningly dire existence. The assistant warden carefully read Percy's writings every day, seemingly appreciated its quality and decided that she had nothing to report to the District Attorney's Office.

Percy's memory improved with each passing day. Now he remembered that someone picked him up from the grass and hit him again. He remembered regaining consciousness inside Pamela's house, and then he recalled the force of a hard blow and the sharp pain of the impact. He remembered being forced to swallow a pill and almost choking on a bitter taste before he was clubbed again and then nothing between that and waking up and finding Pamela.

Dangling his feet down from his upper bunk bed he pondered his sorry future and limited options when the stern faced, steroid enlarged, daytime guard called into his cell. "Grimsby, you have a visitor."

He led him through a series of heavy gage wire mesh and steel gates, unlocking and locking them in sequence and finally letting him into the prisoner side of the visitor's hall. Two guards put shackles on his feet and led him to a seat and he saw Linda on the other side of the thick glass.

Weak and feeling disgraced, he trembled under a presumptuously accepted guilt. Constricting coronaries tortured his heart and he hardly could force air into his lungs. She could easily perceive his sadly solemn demeanor as an unhappy surprise.

She was already holding the receiver and Percy slowly picked up his.

Linda," he began haltingly, "Nice to see you," and he seemed to struggle finding his words, "but what brings you here?"

"Percy, you didn't do it." She cut straight to the point. "There was somebody else there. He must have done it."

"Linda," He tried to speak again but his faltering voice was raspy and the teardrops of shame felt like swollen lumps in his larynx. "I know that you are saying that from the bottom of your heart. You are such an angel. But you are the only one who says that. I wish that somebody, anyone really would believe you."

"Oh yes, they will believe me. Look what I've found."

And she showed him the receipt, close enough that he could read the date and the item printed on it.

He looked and his expression turned into astonished bewilderment. "I never purchased a rope like that. Truthfully, I never had one. I had no use for it."

"Look at the date, that is the date and time when we were walking together in Mianus Park. I could testify to that. You couldn't have been possibly in New Rochelle, 30 miles away. Plus look at the credit card number; they can identify the purchaser through a credit card. You didn't do it. Come on. Even if you don't remember anything for that bastard Spencer beat you up so horribly."

"Would you give this information to my lawyer?"

"I would, don't worry. I will and I'll see to it that he is going to use it. I'll find out who that guy is and why did he kill Pamela and why do they want to frame you for it. I have a lot of experience with jails and judges. My mother is in jail. For many years I've been visiting her."

In his precarious state of messed up affairs Percy still worried about Linda, he asked. His voice was full of genuinely heartfelt concern. "How is Spencer treating you in these days? Is he still beating you?

"No, he has been very sick lately. A serious flue virus, he has chest problems, coughing and his lymph glands are badly inflamed."

"His lymph glands?"

"Yes."

"Linda, listen. Over here they gave us an HIV education and prevention course. He seems to have symptoms of HIV infection. I hate to break bad news to you, but you'd better go and get yourself tested. I hope to God, he hasn't yet infected you."

Percy's warning gave Linda a sobering realization. She knew what an HIV infection meant. It sounded like a death sentence, and one given to her at her barely nineteen years of age. She has never been promiscuous and she married Spencer as a virgin. She didn't deserve an incurable disease. Nobody does. So far she had nothing but raw deal after raw deal in her life. Her father abandoned her when she was five, her mother didn't care about her and she got a life sentence for killing a boyfriend in her drunken, jealous rage. Now this, fate has been good to Linda only once and that was just for a brief moment of imagined euphoria. She could only have a tiny fragment of the blessing that so many less deserving receive in abundance. And the only person she perhaps truly could have trusted and loved was locked up in jail and had to stay on the other side of a wire reinforced, thick glass panel. And ironically he delivered the brutal news that could break the last remnants of her spirit.

She looked back at Percy and could only moan in tormenting distress.

"Oh, no, not me."

"Don't panic. Get yourself tested. There is a good chance that you don't have it. After all you have been a virgin as late as thirty days ago. I can bear witness to that." And Percy cracked his first genuine smile he had after the day of his arrest.

"I have to fight back," she sobered up and her voice sounded stronger. "I'll kill the animal if he gave me the virus."

"Slow down. Don't overreact." He tried to sow resolve and strength into her. "Just make sure that you don't have any more intimate contact with him. No intercourse, no oral sex. Make sure he doesn't scratches you. Wear gloves when you are changing his bedpan, when you feeding him or when you have to have any close physical contact with him."

"I know, I'll handle it, but this news just gave me the shock of my life. I guess, as they say, I have to grin and bear. I hope I didn't give it to you."

"Don't worry about me. I'll rot over here anyway. And if I have to die, I'll happily die for you. For that one night we had together."

Linda wept silently and tried to stifle her horrible mental anguish. Fighting tiny drops of tear, forcing their way down from under her eyelids, she made an effort to retain her composure and not to show distress. Her mission to save Percy took priority. He came first. Her own problem should be handled later.

She waited for Percy to find Robert Schwechter's name and telephone number. She wrote it down and put it away.

She wiped off her tears and smiled at Percy, signaling hope and her will to persevere.

Their allowed visiting time ended. Linda couldn't and didn't want to hide her emotions. The female supervisor on the visitor side told her to leave and, as on the other side the guard was pulling Percy to his feet, she cried into the receiver.

"I love you, Percy. You wanted to protect me. Now it's my turn. I'll get you out from this hellhole. We will have our life and we will have children, together, I promise."

She couldn't hear him she just saw his lips move as two guards brutally dragged Percy away from the window.

"I love you too, Linda." His face twisted in agony and he cried but there was only silence and heartbreaking pantomime he could convey across the soundproof and wire reinforced safety glass.

Chapter Sixteen

On the way home Linda stopped at the Trumbull Mall and in a few hurried minutes purchased a bagful of clothing and household items. At home, as she carried the load inside, to her surprise, she found Spencer up and in a delightedly upbeat mood.

"I feel much better and I'll go back to work. I really miss flying. Finally I've got rid of that vicious bug."

Discomposed by the brutal possibility she just learned, Linda's flustered gaze faltered under Spencer's unjustified exuberance. Condensed in a moment of quizzical silence, she contemplated if her husband had ever had the moral fortitude to consider the possibility of contacting a serious disease. She reflected on his lifestyle, all the free time he had for himself, about those bachelor and swinging years and all the casual partners. If only one of them had the virus, Spencer might have been harboring it for years. He could have been infectious, for all the time during their marriage and did not have to have symptoms. Marriage license and blood test, meaningless if the virus or antibodies fighting the virus cannot be detected for months after contamination. She wished to be back at the airport cafeteria and waiting on people again, living in the YWCA and be healthy. She envied people having their health and being so unappreciative about it. *Abstinence,* she thought, *what a small price to pay for good health.*

Spencer's continuing happiness and incessant trivial twaddle didn't give much time for her to brood about her predicament.

"Linda, honey, don't get me wrong. I'm not happy to leave you alone, but flying is my life. Feeling that power, all under the control of my fingertips, looking at the clouds, high above the world, I think it is the closest thing to being an angel, silly me I shouldn't say something like that but that is how I feel. And I'm so happy to come home and find you here waiting for me." He paused for a second and a dark cloud of concern seemed passing across his forehead. "Have you heard about that Grimsby boy, how is he doing?"

"He," Linda spoke slowly and pretended absentminded unconcern. "He is in jail. I think he is facing first degree murder charges, thirty years if he's lucky or he may even get the death penalty if they prove malicious premeditated intent."

"Too bad," a gloating remembrance of his triumph lighted up Spencer's face, "I hope we had nothing to do with his motives to commit such a heinous brutality."

Linda had to keep her opinion to herself. She wasn't about to start a confrontation, she needed time to get her thoughts in order and decide what to do and how to proceed. She wanted Spencer out of the house so she could have some free time to act. Right now it seemed wise to remain nice and show complacency.

Two days later a dark, a hearse like limousine picked up Spencer and reporting for duty he was back at the airport. As soon as he left, Linda dialed Doctor Richard Lindberg's office.

"This is Linda Shrewsbury. I'd like to make an appointment with Dr. Lindberg?"

The receptionist silently scanned her appointment ledger and assuming a voice of haughty importance asked Linda. "I could fit you in," she paused, "let's see, I have a cancellation, at two o'clock, this afternoon."

"That's perfect. I appreciate it, thanks."

"What seems to be the problem?"

"Nothing, I hope, just a consultation."

"Very well, we'll see you then."

Linda sat down in the functionally well-arranged examination room. Meticulous and clean it reflected cold practicality. She looked at the drawings, displaying correct anatomical body parts on the walls, and tried to calm her heart that relentlessly pounded the walls of her carotid arteries.

After a near eternal waiting time, Dr. Lindberg knocked on the door and entered. He extended his clean, cold and sterile feeling hands to Linda; pressed it slightly against her sweaty palm and asked. "How are you? What brings you here?"

Linda had no reason to beat around the bush. She trusted this thin and tall, Yale educated, superbly intelligent and professional doctor.

"I want to have a blood test."

"I see," said the doctor without raising his eyes up from her chart, "regular lipid and metabolic panel."

"No, it should be more than that."

The doctor looked up, "Anything special?"

"Yes, I want to be tested for HIV virus."

Silence followed, even the have seen it all and experienced everything doctor couldn't believe what he heard; his facial expression changed to abhorrence and he involuntarily winced away from Linda. Even he, the doctor, feared the dead sentence implied by a possible positive result.

"Any particular reason for it," he asked. "Any risk factors, I mean," and he uttered his words with deliberate delay, "any risky behavior?"

"It's not me. It's my husband."

"How long have you been married?"

"One year."

"What makes you think that your husband is infected?"

"He is an airline pilot, he spends a lot of time away from home and he has been very sick for the last few weeks."

"It doesn't necessary mean that he is HIV positive, but if it makes you feel better I'll have the test done. I'll call you in a couple of days about the results. In the meantime your husband should see a doctor. Talk to him about you concerns."

Sure, Linda thought, *ask him anything like that and he'll beat you up for sure. Bloody good deal, he'd beaten me up for lot less than suspecting him of infidelity. I just want to make sure that I don't have it.* She kept her disturbing thoughts to herself and her agreeing voice projected willing assent.

"Yes, I'll talk to him. He is away though and he'll be back in about a weak, at the earliest.

A young colored nurse took her blood; she wore rubber gloves and handled the vials with extreme professionalism.

Next Linda called Robert Schwechter. Automated telephone machines transferred her call to his voice mail. She would have preferred to talk to him in person, as the news about contradicting the state evidence were so important and great, but there was no way to get through and Linda had to contend with the indifferent machine voice and keep listening to menus and selecting options. She hung up, wrote down what she wanted to say and dialed again.

He left a message on the tape. "This call is about the Percy Grimsby case. My name is Linda Shrewsbury and I live on Red Rose Circle, two houses away from the Grimsby residence. My number is 656 0769. I've found evidence that could be important for Percy's defense. Please give me a call. Please talk to me only. Do not leave a massage on my answering machine and make sure that at this number you don't talk to anyone else but me."

The timer of the voice mail machine cut her off. She slowly put the handset back to its cradle and felt disappointed. *It's not going to be easy,* she thought, *two young people against the world and without help and money.* She needed a breath of fresh air, remembered Percy's advice on benefits of outdoor activities and decided to take a walk. She put on her tight black stretch jeans and a matching navy stripe colored polo shirt. She eased her breasts into a padded push up bra and glanced at her image in the mirror.

Protruding proudly and ready to burst to bouncy freedom, her boobs resembled two cream-colored cantaloupes carried in a handbasket made of silk.

She walked out to Raymond Street and headed down toward the railroad underpass. She walked like a sleepwalker, looked down, kicking pinecones and constantly ruminating about her life and undeserved miseries.

She missed the coming of a small Pomeranian dog jumping up on her legs and trying to lick her hand. She touched the little fur ball and in excitement the animal wiggled his tail. Then she saw the owner. He was an elderly man. Perhaps eighty, gray hair and an eclectic collection of thinning bones and wiry tendons, his wrinkled skin had the texture of pickled prunes preserved in a jar of vinegar.

Smiling at her, with open friendliness and eagerness to chat, he began, "Don't afraid of him, Miss—," he hesitated. "She just wants to play, looking for attention and love."

"Oh, it is quite all right." Linda patted the excited critter. "I'm Linda, Mrs. Shrewsbury."

"Spencer Shrewsbury's wife, I've heard he got married. But I didn't know he was that lucky."

"Luck or no luck, I'm his wife."

"Sorry for my clumsy manners, I didn't tell you my name. I'm George Walker. I live on Raymond Street, right there, in that house over there."

Linda glanced at the house, "Nice house, I guess your dog must be doing a good job protecting it."

"He is a sweetheart," the old man looked at the dog lovingly, "He is my companion, but he is getting older like I am and prefers to rest by my feet. You must be poor Pamela's neighbor, what a tragedy her death was."

"Yes, indeed, a terrible tragedy."

"And you know," he stepped closer to Linda and lowered his voice to an intimate sounding, well-informed tone of confidentiality. "They'd arrested the young Grimsby boy, Percy for it, but I don't think he did all by himself."

The revelation jolted Linda out from her sleepy reveries. She became all ears and eyes. She tumbled upon somebody who possibly knew something, something that the police didn't or didn't care to know. She needed to maintain calm and pretend no interest beyond the levels of neighborhood gossiping. Her tone projected only mild curiosity as she asked him cautiously.

"Really, what makes you to think that?"

"I'm a poor sleeper, so is Maxi, and we always walk late at night. I was out and I saw a car. A car that didn't belong here was parked right over there. It had New York license plates.

"Did you write the number down?"

"No, but I remember it was a big and fancy new model car. That's why I noticed it. Not as if Darienates don't have their fair share of expensive cars, but over here everyone has foreign cars, Jaguars, BMW-s, Lexus models. Why would someone leave a Chevrolet parked on Raymond Street for overnight? If he were visiting someone he should have parked on his driveway. Don't you think so?"

"What model, do you remember?"

"Yes. It was a Chevrolet, a fancy one, an Avalanche. I used to like Chevrolet cars. I've had a 1966 Impala, what a car that was, 350 horsepower eight cylinder engine, and big wide seats, comfortable, powerful. I loved that machine.

"Anything else you have seen on that night."

"Yes. I saw the owner coming back to his car. A big husky chap, he drove away and didn't turn on his lights until he was out on Tokeneke Road."

Linda wanted to hug and kiss the old gentleman. He provided the missing link, the possible witness she needed to get Percy out of jail. She took a deep breath, pushed her already prominently displayed provocative chest an inch further out and asked him in a sweet, cajoling voice. "Would you be so kind and have coffee with me. I'd like to talk with you a few more words."

The aged ladies' man hasn't failed to notice her sexy breasts, her tight jeans on her wide and young derriere and hasn't failed to observe that she didn't mind him looking at her treasures and he replied honestly, although not with a totally impeccable and exactly proper tone.

"I talk to you, honey, anytime and as long as you want me to."

Chapter Seventeen

Late in the evening, Robert Schwechter came back to his tiny, overcrowded and messy law office. He sat down behind his desk, shuffled a few papers around and with a frustrated frown stared at his answering machine. The blinking red number showed ten calls.

Letting out a deep sigh and with a tired and uninterested expression on his face he began checking them. One after the other, he began pressing the play and delete buttons. They were mostly about old cases, people asking for references, threatening calls, solicitations and so on. Speeding through the process he almost missed Linda's message.

Hearing her name he stopped. Like getting an extra dose of adrenalin he made an attempt to focus. He replayed it, twice.

Wrote down her telephone number and played the message again to check the number one more time. Then he opened the wrapper of his tuna-fish salad on the bun sandwich, took a sip from his coke, pressed the speaker button and dialed.

Hoping it was Percy's lawyer Linda rushed to the phone. But she never knew, sometimes Spencer called unexpectedly, from an airplane thirty-five thousand feet above the earth or from a Hotel in Jakarta, or somewhere else on the other side of the globe.

She picked up and answered cautiously. "Hello, Shrewsbury residence."

"Linda?"

"Yes."

"This is Robert Schwechter; you wanted to talk to me."

"Yes, indeed," she didn't want to waste a second and got on the subject right away. "I've found a receipt for the purchase of that nylon rope used as evidence against Percy Grimsby."

"Yes?"

"It shows; it had been purchased on May 28, 2004, 11:40 in the New Rochelle Home Depot."

"So?"

"Percy was with me, we were walking together in Mianus Park on that day and at that exact time. He couldn't have possibly purchased the rope. The rope belongs to somebody else."

Schwechter was an intelligent and sharp lawyer with good, altruistic motives and intentions. Practice makes perfect, he trusted his instincts to tell the difference between the truth and a lie. He had become a public defender because he truly believed that injustice was being served to the poor just too many times. Overzealous prosecutors, negligent police work and clever entrapments and manipulations of evidence by the truly guilty, he had seen it all and he really pitied Percy, as he thought that he wasn't capable of hurting a human being, let alone committing premeditated murder. What he'd heard sounded welcome news to him but he had to handle it with professional reserve and cautiousness.

He said, "It certainly provides reasonable doubt on the part that he acted alone."

"Wait, there is more," Linda continued. "I have an eyewitness who had seen a strange car parked around the corner and he saw a person entering the car and leaving without his headlights on, around midnight on the night of the murder."

"That's very good, young lady." Schwechter sighed impatiently as if he had no time to discuss trivial details on the phone. "Could you stop in my office tomorrow at nine and bring me that sales slip? I must admit, your findings sound like good news for Percy and we should talk about it, but it's getting too late and I have other things to take care before I can call it quits for the day."

He quickly read Linda the address of his office and without saying good bye abruptly hung up.

Exactly on the minute Linda showed up at Schwechter's office. He noted with pleasant surprise how young and how attractive she looked in her lovely lavender floral dress and matching short-sleeved jacket. Her skirt flared out at the bottom and allowed her to move with ease and with dignified stealth.

He asked the young woman to sit down and be relaxed and comfortable. Sitting down she crossed her legs, fished the slip out of her purse, gave it to Schwechter and said. "I've found this in a wood stack piled up at the side of my house."

Schwechter looked at the weather parched paper and confirmed. "It has the VISA authorization code; it shouldn't be a problem to find who made this purchase."

"How is that going to help Percy?"

"Well, the State isn't going to drop the charges unless they have caught this accomplice and he confessed he acted alone. Percy still would have a hard time to explain what he was doing in Mrs. Leicester's house on the night of the murder. Especially considering that he doesn't remember or not willing to remember how he got there on the first place. The State is pushing for an arraignment as soon as possible, maybe two weeks from today. So we don't have much time."

"What is an arraignment?"

"The arraignment is when the court reads the formal charges against him and Percy must enter a guilty or not guilty plea. We haven't waived our right yet to have a preliminary hearing and the prosecutor hasn't yet filed the trial information papers. At least they haven't sent me a copy. Based on this information what you've just presented us, we'll insist on having a preliminary hearing, and possibly reduce the charges and reduce the size of his bail."

"Or drop the charges."

"I doubt it."

"But he didn't do the crime he's charged with."

"How can you be so sure?" Schwechter looked up, "What's your involvement in the case?"

Linda couldn't help her reaction; she blushed deep red and had to break away from Schwechter's sharp stare. She studied her knees for a long minute and slowly raised her tears moistened eyes. Having regained her composure she bravely dared into Schwechter's inquisitive and steady gaze and began to talk.

"Percy and I, we are in love. I must save him. He didn't kill Pamela. He had a fight with my husband over me. He beat him unconscious and threw him out of the door to the front yard. He was in no condition to subdue big and strong Pamela. Somebody else murdered her. Somebody, who carried Percy into Pamela's the house and left him there."

"Who would have had a motive to do something like that, if we knew maybe we could start from there, any ideas?"

"Pamela's ex husband, maybe?

Schwechter looked at Linda with serious disapproval. "That is a far fetched idea. It is far too much for the court, you are married to Spencer Shrewsbury but in love with Percy Grimsby, you are accusing the ex-husband of your murdered former rival for the attentions of a young gigolo, now a murder suspect. They'll rip you testimony into pieces in court. Your line of thinking is far too wishful and biased toward trying to establish innocence for your lover."

"Let me try to talk to Mr. Leicester anyway. I might be able to get something out of him."

"It's your prerogative. But I must warn you. You never know what you are getting involved with. Leave it to the professionals."

"But the professional won't do a thing. It's more convenient to assume guilt than disturb a hornets' nest."

"You are exactly correct. It could be a hornets' nest."

"I'm willing to go through considerable trouble to prove his innocence."

"Ok," Schwechter agreed, but as a married man he couldn't help the judgmental feelings he was developing against the young and possibly adulterous wife and added. "I surely wouldn't like to be your wedded husband."

Linda heard the rough insult. She thought to snap back at him but she held her anger. In a way Schwechter was right, although he didn't know anything about her marriage and had no right to cast the first stone at her. But it would have been too much to explain Spencer, Percy and her relationship. She swallowed the insult and let it go unanswered.

Hearing no defensive reply Schwechter continued. "If you need a good divorce attorney I could recommend one."

"No thank you, I don't want to divorce my husband."

Schwechter shook his head in disbelief. He thought. *Women, men never will be able to figure women out.* Still shaking his head he wrote down Mr. Dwight Leicester's office and home address with telephone numbers and gave it to Linda. "Good luck, you have about a week to get something substantial for me. If you do that, I'll make sure it gets included in the preliminary hearing papers."

The day just started and Linda had no reason or desire to waste a minute more of it. Still overcharged with adrenalin she drove to the Noroton Heights Shopping Center and went straight to the public phone next to the small doughnut shop. She punched in Leicester's office number and heard the secretary picking up.

She asked the woman. "Mr. Dwight Leicester, please."

"Who is calling?" The voice asked.

Linda decided to use an alias for safety and said as calmly as she could.

"Rosalie Malon."

"What is this in reference to?"

"Is he there?"

"No, he is not available, he is in conference."

"Look, don't play hide and seek game with me," surprising even herself Linda used a shockingly assertive tone. "Tell him that this call is about his ex wife and he'd better pick up. Interrupt whatever he is doing."

"Ok," the secretary said sulkily and rung the extension in Dwight's office.

Dwight had the New York Times sport section with the horserace results in front of him but he wasn't reading it. With a blank and satisfied look on his face he stared dreamily out his favorite southern exposure window.

The secretary announced through the line, "A woman wants talk to you about Pamela. Should I get rid of her?"

Dwight already considered Pamela ancient history, he had buried her weeks ago and he really preferred completely forgetting her. He couldn't have cared less if someone else was in jail for her murder. He developed an absolute denial about the case and hasn't even been thinking about any more that he had ordered the murder of his only son devoted mother.

"I'll talk to her," he said and looking annoyed moved his hand to push the speaker button. Then leaned back in his chair, arrogantly far away from the phone and announced.

"Leicester."

Linda took a deep breath. She had to give the best acting performance of her life if she wanted to have any chance to succeed in getting any useful information out of this shrewd and unscrupulous lawyer.

"Mr. Leicester, or can I call you Dwight; I have a message for you."

"From who, who is this? Is this a joke?" He glanced at the

caller I.D. and noted the unknown Connecticut number. He wrote it down while continued, "What do you want?"

"I want to congratulate you."

"On what?"

"The job you had have done on your ex wife."

"Are you out of your mind? Do you know who I am?"

"I know exactly who you are. And I have evidence to prove it, unless."

Now he leaned forward and picked up the receiver. He was far too long on the speaker line. Looking around, nervous like a schoolboy caught on cheating he lowered his voice and talked directly into the phone.

"Unless?"

This was a good start for Linda. She showed him the back door and he took it. Like a mindless fish he was nibbling at the bait. She hasn't yet hooked him but she dangled something interesting and tempting in front of his gaping mouth.

"Unless, you are willing to help me."

"In what way, I am a good lawyer. Do you need a lawyer and you want me to work pro bono? Is that it?"

"Oh no, sugar. May I call you, sugar?" She cooed into the receiver and released a tiny sexy moan to sweeten her voice. "It's much more personal than that."

"Talk!"

"Anybody listening to us?

"No."

"Well, I trust you. I know something about you, something bad what you did, so I thought, why shouldn't I let you in on a little dirty secret of my own?"

"What is it, Rosalie?" Dwight relaxed his posture. Now he had the reassuring feeling that he was talking to a riff-raff floozy. She was an amateur racketeer and she was ridiculously clumsy about it. *What the heck,* he figured. *This chitchat might grow into an interesting flirt.* More personal, huh, Dwight mumbled and he began to like the adventure.

It was Linda's turn to pretend. She had to be a vamp, a true-life fame fatale. She remembered the old TV shows with Zsazsa Gabor and imitated her.

"Dwight, dharling," she tried to entrap Leicester with a voice that was sugarcoated with promises and honey. "I want the same thing what was done to Pamela done to my husband."

Dwight has seen his share of conniving criminal and white collar crooks in his lifetime and law practice, he wasn't a dope to trust anybody over an unsolicited telephone call. He had to find out who she really was and how much she knew.

He said tersely, "I don't know what you are talking about."

"Of course you don't, sweetie. But I can explain and you will understand. Can we meet? You know, a get acquainted sort of thing. Then we can talk about the fine details, you know, the substance hidden between the lines."

Dwight thought he knew what to do. He figured that he was obviously dealing with a stupid blackmailing bimbo, who knew something about Pamela and wanted to shake him down for a packet of money. But perhaps she was for real, in that case why should he have bothered to help her out? But she sounded young and sexy. Why not? He can fuck her and kick her out afterwards. She sounded so naïve.

"Ok. We can meet. I guess. No harm." He agreed.

"But Dwight dharling," Zsazsa went on again, "could you get somebody who does a better job. The one who you hired for Pamela was a dope. He lost the receipt he purchased the murder weapon with. That was really dumb. Wasn't it?"

Now Dwight realized what was that she came upon, something potentially damaging. He had to meet her, not to bang her between the buns but to get rid of her. And that had to be done fast. Now it was more important to meet her than he thought on the first place. And Dwight knew he had better not to meet her alone. He needed Sal Sclafani's help to deal with her.

He agreed, "I meet you tonight."

"Could you come up to Connecticut and meet me at the Black Goose Grille and Bar in Darien, around eight o'clock? I'll be wearing a lavender dress with a black jacket, I'm young and sexy." And for added measure, to entice the old badger out of his burrow, she added an enticing, coquettish giggle.

"Done deal, will see you there." He said in a slightly flustered, disconcerted voice. The implications rattled his belief that he already put the final dot at the end of Pamela's story.

Dwight hung up on Linda, alias Rosalie and dialed Sal Sclafani. His shaky hands trembled with anger; he missed the number and had to redial the digits.

Hyperventilating with hate he venomously sizzled into the phone.

"Your hit man is dumb ass idiot. He lost the receipt for the rope he purchased to strangle Pamela. Furthermore he purchased it with his credit card. Some bimbo called and claimed she found the ticket. She wants to blackmail me. This is not what you've promised me, untraceable crime, the perfect murder, my ass. Now I'm in deep trouble."

"Don't panic, Dwight." Feeling insulted by his criticism,

Sal snapped back at him. "Obviously she hasn't yet gone to the police. It's better to get a call from a dumb broad than from a detective lieutenant. We can handle her. Do you know who she is?"

"Not yet. But I'm going to meet her tonight in Darien, in a bar."

"That's excellent." Sal answered calmly and his placid tone projected renewed confidence. "We shall see how stupid she is. Calm down, everything is under control."

"By the grace of God," not exactly feeling at ease and filled with trust, Dwight muttered discontentedly, "she is a bigger imbecile than your idiot hit man."

"I'll be there and I'll be watching the two of you talking. I observe and she wouldn't know who I am. Let's see first what she really wants."

"Do you think she gave the information to anyone else?"

"Most likely not, but you should be able to find that out, after all you are a trial lawyer."

"She wants me to put out a contract on her husband."

"Does she have money?"

"I don't think so; she wants me to do it pro bono for her silence."

"Got it," Sal muttered wryly, "she is going to be silent all right."

"The two us will take care of her." Dwight raised his voice, guffawed a little and continued disdainfully, "If she is young, we may have some fun with her before we dump her mutilated body into the East River, a free whack job, not on my watch and not out of my budget."

Chapter Eighteen

Most morning commuters are gone; the station platform seemed to stretch into deserted emptiness. Four pair of shiny rails in front of her Linda sat down on a bench to sort out her thoughts.

The telephone call, the pretend that she was someone else was a life libido depleting experience. The ascending sun was still far from its zenith and the high heavens had not yet flooded the earth with the scorching rays of noontime heat. She felt cold and yet her clothes were soaked with sweat and her hyped up neurons refused to slow and return to normalcy.

She pondered if she was way over her head into this matter of saving a man who wasn't her husband or by blood related to her. A disturbing realization of dire implications dawned on her and an unwelcome notion of predestination to crash and burn weakened her physically. But she felt she had no choice; she couldn't let Percy rot in jail, the only person who ever, perhaps too idealistically, cared about her, the only person who truly loved her and admired her as if he were an idol worshipper, and in whose innocent eyes she saw the depths of youthful devotion and the promise of eternal life. She had to take her chances, she thought about Spencer, the possibility of a deadly infection, his reckless infidelity and the brutal abuse and the beatings she had to endure at his hand. She needed Percy on her side; otherwise she had to stand utterly alone in this world and she already had far too much of those feelings in orphanages and in foster homes.

A nearly noiseless electric train passed by at high speed and rattled the catenary wires that kept making an eerie techno song long after the train was gone. The desolate platform was a spooky place but she had no strength to move.

Later she felt hungry and trundled over to the nearby Palmer's Supermarket. There she bought a turkey breast sandwich with mustard and lettuce at the deli counter. Exiting the store Linda walked by a few happily gossiping Darien housewives surrounded by their spoiled brats and thought about her destiny that lay somewhere between a husband infected with a deadly virus and a lover accused of murder and locked up in jail.

She drove home in Spencer's BMW. At home he ate the sandwich and gradually regained her composure. She figured if she brazenly dared into act one then she might as well try act two, the real danger, the challenge of a face-to-face meeting with Dwight Leicester.

Linda decided to go on with her scheme as planned and called up Detective Sean Doherty. At the end of the second ring he picked up and she heard his rough and raucous voice.

"Doherty?

"This is Linda Shrewsbury."

"Mrs. Shrewsbury," he miraculously remembered her, "how may I help you?"

"I need to wear a wire."

There was a long silence at the other end of the line. Doherty couldn't comprehend why anyone would have wanted to wear a wire unless was asked to do so by the police. Annoyed at her meddling into matters that should not be her concern he demanded tersely.

"Why?"

"I'm going to talk to someone and I need the police to make a record of it."

"Regarding what?"

"The Pamela Leicester murder case."

"What's your involvement in that? I thought that case was cut and clear. Percy Grimsby did it."

"I had a telephone conversation with Pamela's ex husband and he said a few things what makes me think that he had it done. I'm meeting him tonight and I'll try to make him admit his involvement."

"Just talk to him and come to the trial as a witness. It's the defense prerogative."

"Not good enough. I need police protection tonight. I have enough experience in what people capable of doing to cover their tracks."

"How so?"

"I grew up in orphanages. I look innocent but inside I'm a tough girl."

"I see," perusing the papers in front of him he paused thoughtfully. She did not convince him; he rather regarded her as a pesky nuisance that piqued his curiosity. Wary of her motives he continued cautiously. "Come down to the police station and we'll see what we can do. How did you make him agree to come to Darien and talk to you?"

"I asked him to do the same thing he did to Pamela to my husband."

Detective Doherty suddenly felt snappy. Her impertinence was too much. He didn't like amateurs interfering with police matters. This was a threat against one of his old high school friends and he had to take it seriously. He told her in a clipped and coldly assertive voice. "You definitely must come down and talk to us before you do anything foolish."

Twenty minutes later Linda was sitting at Detective Sean Doherty's desk. As if ready to swallow her sideways he looked at her.

"What do you want to do to your husband?"

"Nothing, I'm just pretending that I want to do something to Spencer to trap Mr. Leicester to admit that he had a contract to kill Pamela."

"That is very dangerous. Besides it's entrapment. Not legal. It may not be used in court as evidence."

"I didn't give him my real name. He doesn't know who I am. He has never seen me before."

"Casual encounter, I see. You just happen to have a wire on you." He wagged a forefinger at her, "All right, we're going to work with you. But you'd better watch what you are telling this man or we may have to arrest you for trying to kill your husband."

Hours later Linda returned to the police station. She had to undress, down to her panties and a policewoman fitted her with a tiny microphone right between her breasts, deep inside her cleavage. She put back on her bra and the policewoman carefully treaded the wire under the straps of the garment and down to a flat transmitter box wrapped around and high up on her right thigh. When ready and done, Linda drove to the Black Goose restaurant and sat down at the bar. Doherty followed her with his partner and parked in the back parking lot of the next-door pharmacy. A plainclothes detective sat down in the main dinning room, from where he could observe the bar. He had kept Linda in his peripheral vision but other than that, like a myopic wine connoisseur, he appeared only studying the beverage menu.

Linda ordered a coke, as she couldn't order any drink with alcohol, for she hasn't reached legal drinking age, smiled at the bartender and waited for Mr. Leicester to show up. Table-by-table the dining room filled up with elegantly dressed well to do Darienates having family dinners and wealthy country dandies courting refined, white, protestant and so obviously Anglo-Saxon ladies.

Shortly after eight o'clock a tall, broad shouldered and distinguished looking gentleman sat down next to Linda and greeted her. "Hello, Rosalie?"

She put on her sweetest smile, extended her hand and, speaking softly like a caroling hermit thrush, she wheedled to him.

"Yes. It is I," she paused and took a sip from her coke to moisten her lips, "Dwight?"

He nodded.

The man looked elegantly dressed, relaxed, confident, and appeared to be a finely polished decent person, the furthest thing away from a wife killer criminal. With butterflies dancing in her stomach and her heart pumping thousand beats per minute Linda pretended to possess cool composure and uncaring attitude.

She asked him. "Would you mind sitting in a booth. It would be better for privacy."

They walked to the back corner of the dinning room and sat down in a booth closest to the parking lot on the other side of the solid brick, outside wall. He gave her the first choice to select her seat. She sat down so she could see the plainclothes detective sitting at a table, not more than fifteen feet away.

After sitting down she put her hands on the table, drummed her fingers hastily, paused for a minute and came straight out with her first well-practiced line. "Don't get me wrong. I'm not here to judge you. I desperately need your help. That's why I'm here."

He played with his drink and gave her a mental rundown. She was indeed attractive, abundant red bronze hair and attractive eyes that could raise the dead if they set sight on them. Not a stupid bimbo or a melancholic basket case, *maybe it's a trap*, he thought, *she could be a policewoman.* Unsure and circumspect, he just glared at her silently.

"I'm so lonely." Linda sighed and extended a hand to Dwight and let it rest next to his. Under the table, stepping out of her right shoe she played footsy with his left leg and, as if nothing was going on, continued her silly pattering. "Nobody knows me in this parish and after we have done our business I'll skip town. You don't need to worry about me. This is a big country and I'll disappear like a gray donkey in the fog."

"A gray what?" The odd metaphor distracted Dwight and riding on his perceived male superiority he felt at ease. "Where did you get that expression?"

The initial tension seemed to disappear. Linda pressed her knees against his and kept cajoling in her best confidence gaining feminine tone.

"To me, you look someone who is feeling low. It seems that you are in dire need of being cured."

"Feeling low, cured, what do you mean?" He asked and grinned and there was a lecherous spark in his eye.

"Drink up, Dwight, a well mixed cordial should provide some of the remedy."

He finished his scotch and Linda immediately waived to the waiter. "Double it up, please."

He brought the drinks and she watched Dwight gulping down his second. Now she pressed her knees together and trapped Dwight's legs in between. With his face blushing Dwight's judgment became blurred under the double effect of alcohol and the extra dosage of sex hormones that his middle-age body unexpectedly produced.

Linda put her right hand under the table and touched Dwight's right thigh on the inside. She lingered on to measure his reaction and then began her inquiry with unselfish trust and condescending care.

"What made you do it?"

"Do what?" Dwight moaned and wouldn't have traded the promise of underage sex for anything. Linda reached further up, and, using her loose and nimble fingers she opened his belt and unbuttoned his pants.

"You know," she continued and pulled his zipper down,

"to have Pamela killed. You must have a lot of money. You couldn't have done it for the money. You must have had a much loftier motive than financial. Tell me, dear," she continued and pinched the head of Dwight's penis between her index finger and thumb, "have you done it for the almighty kicks?"

Dwight moaned. He was caught between the ugly devil of self-implication and the deep sea of reckless carnality. He forgot about caution, she only saw a young and willing female and trusted his friend, Sclafani, sitting a few tables away. He had to snatch her and give it to her between her so appetizingly delectable buns. Later on Sal is going to whack her anyway.

He blurted out his secret. "For the house, for the alimony, I had to get rid of her. She was a heavy albatross pecking on my neck."

Linda bent her fingers around Dwight's now fully erect penis and slowly started moving her fist. She said. "How did you do it, dear?" She kept stroking him and the touch of her silky fingertips made him throb and hard as stone.

Pleasure inundating his groin area Dwight mumbled. "I hired somebody;" a few more strokes and he nearly confessed all his sins; "A nameless mobster, he and his henchman did it for me."

"Not that stupid loser, Percy?"

"Not him, come on. They were supposed to make it like he did it."

Dwight whined with sexual bliss and had to stifle the sounds of heavenly joy bellowing from his guts He ejaculated into his pants. Linda felt the twitching movements and her fingers became wet. It was over. She withdrew her hand and smiled at the now spent and embarrassed Dwight.

"Did you enjoy it as much as I did?" With a reticent grin in the corner of her mouth she gave him a hackneyed, forked tongued complement.

"Yes, I did."

Stepping back into her shoes she stood half way up and with an awkward and innocently bashful smile excused herself. "Dwight. If you don't mind I have to wash up." She showed him her wet hand like a proof of decency. "I'll be back in a minute." She walked to the bathroom and didn't fail to notice a big bulky, swarthy looking fellow following her. She closed the door, headed straight to the window and climbed out. On the ground she rushed to Doherty's car, jumped in and yelled at him. "Let's get out of here."

Back at the police station, Doherty was so excited that he forgot about the proper etiquette and watched the microphone being removed from Linda's bra. She didn't mind him seeing her underwear and asked the detective with pride of accomplishment.

"Did you hear all the fine details?"

Doherty and all the other loitering station personnel laughed with hearty and raucous police laughs. The detective answered in the name of all. "Yes indeed, we've heard everything; it was superb, better than a porno flick."

They made a copy of the tape, gave it to Linda and advised her to get it over to Schwechter.

Doherty had his final comment. "You are one brave of a woman, Mrs. Shrewsbury, congratulations on mission accomplished."

Linda flicked him a reserved smile. "Detective Doherty, you don't know the half of what I had and possibly will have to do to overcome my handicaps."

He shook his head in admiring disbelief and said. "If you ever need a job, just come to us and we'll hire you as an undercover lady detective."

Leaving the police station Linda braved one more question and asked Doherty. "What's going to happen to Mr. Leicester?"

"We'll have write up the charges and will have him extradited to Connecticut. He will stand trial for the murder of his ex."

Chapter Nineteen

When Linda got home she saw two messages on her answering machine. Both of them were from Spencer. First he only informed her that he was cutting short his flight schedule, he didn't feel good and was coming home this evening.

On the second call, obviously upset by Linda not being home he yelled into the machine. "Where in the hell are you when I need you? I want you to pick me up at eleven o'clock tonight at JFK. I'm coming in from Johannesburg and I don't feel good at all. Make sure you are there with my BMW."

Linda looked at her watch. It was ten o'clock. She had a fighting chance to get there, but she had to hurry. In an instant she dropped her dress and rushed to the bathroom. She plopped her bottom down on the padded toilet seat and while sighed with great relief, decided on what to wear. Still dripping, she hurriedly plucked her panties back on, slipped into her blue jeans and put on a red poplin shirt. Buttoning the shirt she ran to the garage and within ten seconds she was pulling out and on her way to JFK, New York.

Fortunately the drive wasn't too bad and she didn't get tied up in any traffic jams. She parked her car at the Delta Airlines terminal and doubled up on the steps to meet Spencer at the arrival gate.

She saw him just coming out. Still handsome in his captain's uniform he looked rather tired, pale and seemed having lost substantial weight. He didn't fail to notice that Linda was out of breath. Her face abloom with roses of overheat and forehead profusely moist with beads of sweat she obviously just came in after a hasty rush.

Annoyed and suspicious he spoke gruffly to her. "Where on the earth have you been all day?"

"I've been working out at the YMCA and stayed on for the evening adult swim."

"I didn't know you were a member."

"I am now."

"Make sure to remind me to get you a cellular, I want to be able to reach you wherever you are and whenever I need you."

Yeah, Linda thought, *that's all what I need, an electronic leash.* She didn't answer and Spencer concentrated on the traffic. Tense and unhappy with everything, he cursed at the other drivers but stopped questioning Linda. Outside of a few ugly words he didn't talk at all.

Linda hasn't eaten since noon, awfully hungry she had a difficult time to control her impulsive snap backs. She knew better, she could provoke an irate retaliation and she would end up be beaten tonight. She hinged her hopes on, that at least, Spencer hasn't been drinking yet. She was hopeful; playing her cards right, tonight perhaps she could avoid the usual abuse.

At home Linda couldn't wait any more. She had to eat. Rushing to the refrigerator she asked Spencer. "Do you want to grab a bite?"

"No."

"I do."

"How come, didn't you have plenty time to eat before?"

"Of course, I just have a craving for a tasty bite."

"Then eat if you must. I hope you are not pregnant."

"Pregnant, from what?"

Spencer face darkened, he took the offhand reply as an intentional insult and retorted peevishly. "How should I know what you're doing while I'm gone?"

Ignoring the provocation she searched the shelves. She always had frozen leftovers, put the first plastic box she picked into the microwave and turned back to face Spencer. "I hope you not starting one of your unjustified jealous rages tonight. Let me give you a relaxing rubdown in the bathtub and you're going to feel better."

"Ok." He cracked an awkward smile and the tense ambiance he brought home seemed cooling off. He still refrained from turning to his main remedy; the booze and the drunken swaggering that always followed it.

She went to the master bathroom and opened the hot water faucet of the oversized Jacuzzi bath. She let the water running and returned to the kitchen.

In a minute she heard Spencer turning off the spigot and yelling to her. "Not in the tub. Let's take a shower together."

Bad news, she thought, and remembered the HIV test, an

unwanted possibility of getting forced into a life-threatening situation of exchanging body fluids. Spencer might be infectious. He may get aroused in the shower and will try to enter her, plus the other thing. Also, it didn't seem the most opportune time to let him discover that she wasn't a virgin any more. She had to avoid physical contact with him, she would handle the consequences of the rejection the best way she could.

She couldn't even claim that she had her period for she already said that she just swam at the YMCA. Under pressure she had to lie and she lied with aptitude. She yelled back to him.

"Sorry, dear. No can do. I must have picked up a bad case of yeast infection. Down south I'm all burning itches. I couldn't even take a shower at the Y. It feels awful. I had to cut my swimming short. Any more water would cause me terrible pain. But as I said I'll give you a good rubdown if you want."

In the meantime she finished devouring her freshly defrosted vegetarian lasagna, gulped down a little red wine after the spicy meal and felt the hunger pains subside in her belly.

She yelled to Spencer, "In a minute, I'll meet you in the bathroom."

With her mouth full and still chewing on her food, she rushed into her bedroom, undressed and put on a pair of elastic bicycle pants. She heard the shower running and burst into the bathroom, naked on the top but safely sheltered at the lower half.

Already naked, Spencer was testing the shower water temperature. In the strong bathroom lights Linda saw her husband's nude body and he had hundreds of various sizes, sick and frightening looking spots covering good portions of his sides and back.

She stopped dead in her tracks and fearing the worst, demanded.

"Spencer, what are those?"

He looked at the red violet to brown patches and said. "I don't know. They just came out a couple of days ago."

"Do they itch?"

"No."

"Spencer, I think you'd better see a doctor about that. That is not normal."

"I have no pains."

"It could be cancer and the sooner you get it treated is the better."

"They will go away."

Linda had to take a stand. For her own safety and life she had to tell Spencer about her concerns. He was obviously in denial and she had to wake him up.

"Spencer," she said, "I think you'd better have yourself tested. It looks you have symptoms."

"Symptoms of what," he snapped back violently.

"AIDS."

Spencer didn't want to hear any possibilities this horrible. Linda's accusation felt a lightning bolt striking him, down and out from a blue, cloudless sky. He had only one reaction, the only way he knew to deal with a domestic problem, violence. He would have never hit a coworker or his boss or not even a stranger, but hitting his wife was a different matter. In his subconscious he thought he owned her, she shouldn't have had her own opinion, her own will; she was supposed to be his own indentured slave. And a rebellious slave must be punished. That much he knew.

Spencer turned around and slapped Linda in the face. Not hard, just to put her into her place, where she belonged. She ducked and the hit missed her face and mouth but with a big smacking sound the blow slid down onto her naked shoulders and neck. She lost her balance and staggered back to the vanity counter. She grabbed the edge behind her and lifted her foot to fend off her enraged husband.

Rushing toward her he bellowed with insulted pride. "I do not have AIDS."

"Maybe not, but we should be better off safe than sorry."

"Take those panties off."

"No."

He moved in to rip Linda's bicycle shorts off; she pulled back, raised her left knee to her chest and aiming with her foot kicked Spencer right in the balls. He cringed, buckled forward and hissed in aching agony.

"Fucking bitch," the hurt man roared after he regained his voice. With one hand he clenched his crushed manhood and with the other grabbed Linda's throat. "You have sex with me right now," the insulted husband kept hollering and his neck and face turned flaming red, "prove it that you don't think I'm infected."

"Over my dead body, you selfish bastard," she yelled back and picked up the porcelain soap dispenser behind her and hit Spencer on the head with the hard, ceramic piece. The heavy porcelain material broke and the biting liquid flooded into Spencer's eyes.

He squealed, couldn't see and let her go. "I'll get you for this," he yelled and groped at the thin air, "you lousy cunt. Instead of being a good wife you always fight with me. You don't want to give me sex when I want it? I'll teach you respect if that is the last thing I do."

She slid out from under his arms, ran out and yelled back from the relative safety of the adjacent bedroom. "No sex until you have yourself tested and you are HIV negative."

"You test yourself, you whore. You've been the one fucking around."

"I've had myself already tested today."

"And?"

"I don't know the results. Maybe tomorrow I'll know it."

Spencer remained in denial. He denied his promiscuity, his double life and his carelessness. His pride couldn't let him comprehend, let alone accept his own responsibility. He had to blame somebody weaker and smaller than him. His ability to lie to himself, and eradicate his misdeeds from his mind, was strong enough to believe in his own innocence and non-culpability.

He washed his eyes, calmed down and lowered his voice a notch. Insisting on having the last word he offered a truce and stated with self serving magnanimity. "See, maybe you'd infected me. You don't get sick, but you carry the bug and infect others."

To calm down her beast of a mate Linda had to bury the hatchet for the moment. She replied with traces of courage and dim hope in her voice. "Maybe so, but until we know for sure we have no more physical contacts. It doesn't mean that we cannot live in peace and respect each other. We have to get through this together. We are married and we must have love for one another. In sickness and in health, isn't that what we've pledged?"

She cautiously extended her hands toward Spencer and he accepted it saying.

"Peace. Sorry I've got so upset and I hit you."

"Never mind," she smiled awkwardly, "You've missed

me. No problem. Anyway, it would not have been the first time."

Spencer put on his bathrobe and watched Linda to clean up the floor. They both had a long day and had enough. Without having consumed any alcohol but exhausted to the limit, Linda couldn't concentrate and like a dry drunk she staggered around while making the motions.

Spencer had the jet-leg effect, by Johannesburg time it was already six o'clock in the morning, and he had it. Outward, he pretended to be unconcerned and confident but inside he began to feel the deadly fright growing and chewing away his haughty intrepidity. Afraid to touch his own skin he loathed looking at his own naked body. For the first time, he realized the importance of having someone healthy and devoted around to take care of him. He had to acquiesce to that he might have a serious sickness and he needed all the help he could muster from his surroundings. He wanted Linda to be strong and vigorous but in the same time he abhorred the thought that he was dying and she would remain un-infected and survive.

He had to get a drink; he stood up and tried to walk to the liqueur cabinet. Half way across the living room he lost his balance; his head went into a spin, lost his vision and fell down on the living room carpet.

Linda couldn't move him; she put a pillow under his head and covered him with a blanket. Hours later he woke up and crawled into his bed. Week, pitiful and vulnerable, he shivered and catatonic convulsions were jerking his body apart. He couldn't see Linda next to him, called for her to come and make his sickness to go away, but she slept exhausted in her own room and the door remained locked for security.

Next morning Spencer slept late, Linda prepared his breakfast, put it next to his bed, took the audiotape and rushed out to give it to Robert Schwechter.

At barely past eight o'clock in the morning Schwechter was still in his office. Linda fast-forwarded the tape to the part where Leicester admitted that he had hired someone to kill his wife and it wasn't Percy. Schwechter listened carefully, cracked a taut smile and complemented Linda on her accomplishment.

"Good job. I'll take it together with the sales receipt to the prosecutor's office this afternoon and will push for an accelerated preliminary hearing and hopefully, based on that motion they will reduce the charges and reduce his bail."

"Can he be released now?"

"No. Only a judge can do it."

"Why wouldn't they drop the charges at least on the preliminary hearing?"

"Usual procedure is that they reduce the bail, then he can bail himself out and they consider the available motions. They are not known to make hasty on the spot decisions."

"But he is innocent."

"The procedure, low bail and the state will take its time to make a decision. Nothing we can do."

"But…"

"Young lady," Schwechter cut Linda short. "I think you have done enough. You should go back to your husband. Otherwise the state may look at you as a coconspirator and you could get into a lot of trouble. It is highly unusual that a married woman takes so much interest in a celibate inmate."

"But I am only seeking justice."

"Please," Schwechter said and stood up to show Linda to the door. "Enough is enough. You have to follow the rules."

Linda rushed home but on her way back she stopped at the supermarket and in minutes filled up her shopping cart. She drove into the garage and was carrying a number of bulky plastic bags into the kitchen when Spencer came down from upstairs. He eased up when he saw Linda dragging in the groceries and, in an almost relaxed manner, asked her. "Have you heard from Doctor Lindberg?"

"Not yet, but I think we're going to pay him a visit this afternoon. Together."

They sat down for a coffee and toasted fresh bagels. Linda spread low sugar apricot on hers and when she saw Spencer enjoying his second coffee he collected her courage and came out with a sensible suggestion.

"Spencer. I would like to make a deal with you."

He swallowed the bite of bagel he was chewing and sipped a swig of coffee after it and said questioningly, "What deal?"

"Spencer," She took a deliberate pause, "I don't want you to beat me any more. I've had enough of physical abuse in my life. I'll be a good wife if you treat me with respect. Don't curse at me, don't yell at me, don't threaten me and I'll take good care of you in return. If you are truly sick, and I mean if, I'll be at your side and I'll nurse you, make sure you get the best care and will be comfortable until you get better. But in the meantime you must stop abusing me."

"I've never abused you."

"Spencer, be real, you have abused me a lot. And I don't want to start a fight with you about it. What's the past is the past. Now you need me and I need you. We are adults and we can make it work."

"Why do you need me?" He squinted and gave her a wan smile.

"Silly question, I don't want to move back to the YWCA. Even that was too expensive for my income. I don't want to go to a bettered women shelter either. You have no idea how those places look like. I spent my teenage years in foster homes and orphanages. I didn't deserve that, I didn't ask for it. If my parents agreed and made a deal I would have grown up just like any other American teenager. Spoiled and pampered. But I had it rough and raw. I married you because you were my best chance to get a life, a better life than I had so far. I don't want too much. I just don't want you to hit me. You are not a bad person. You can do it. Look at me. Do I look like someone you have to hit? I'm not a nagging, ill willed bitch. I you have a problem with me, talk to me. Wouldn't you prefer me around smiling and happy instead of crying and scratching your eyes out like I was a crazy feral cat?"

Her intelligent approach overwhelmed Spencer. When sober he was truly a good person. Thousands of people trusted their lives to his steady hands and good judgment. He looked a well-respected member of society, at least in his outward appearance. He now realized how wrong was to have a double life, a secret, dirty double life. Now he was sick, he was vulnerable and he was scared. He couldn't deny any longer the possibility of having a life threatening sickness due to his own fault and now he had this wonderful person next to him, sitting in his house and being on his side. The shame and embarrassment broke his rigid concept of self-eminence.

He began to cry, took Linda's hand into his and asked for her forgiveness, "I'm sorry. I solemnly promise that I'll not hit you any more. Thank you for being my wife. Thank you for staying with me when I'm in need, when I'm down and sick."

"Spencer. I knew you would come around. But as a first step we have to see doctor Lindberg this afternoon."

"Well said. I'll go with you and I'll be willing to take that test if that makes you happy."

"It does. You have no idea how happy that makes me."

She called doctor Lindberg's office and made the appointment. She cooked wonderful roast pork, boiled potatoes and vegetables meal and they both ate heartily and were happy just being together. Linda didn't let Spencer drink and he obliged. It looked that peace had been restored; at least until the time when a new calamity would shatter the fragile truce.

Chapter Twenty

Sitting with Spencer in Doctor Lindberg's examination room, Linda watched the doctor looking through her medical records. When finished, he closed the folder, put it down on the table and turned to Spencer.

"Mr. Shrewsbury. The good news is that your wife tests came out negative. The tests should be repeated in six months and provided she stayed away from any risky," Lindberg paused, he didn't want to use the word, behavior, for he hasn't thought that lovely innocent angel faced Linda could misbehave at all. The doctor cleared his throat and braved the continuum, "I mean from any unprotected sexual contact and I'm sorry to say that includes you too," he paused again to make sure that Spencer wasn't going to erupt in protest, "until it had been established that both of you are HIV virus free." He stopped there and waited for Spencer to say something.

The doctor well-meaning caution made Spencer feeling most uncomfortable. Confronted with the need to admit; now in front of a doctor that he had unprotected casual sex, he should have stopped pretending. But his wife sat right next to him and he still had episodes that he wouldn't tell her under any circumstances. Lacking honesty and spine to owe up to what he did, he procrastinated, remained secretive and kept on lying.

He asked cautiously, "What do you mean, doctor?"

Doctor Lindberg had years of professional experience to tell news, sometimes very bad news to patients, sick, perhaps terminally ill or dying people. He knew he shouldn't tell bad news to anyone until he was one hundred percent sure. He knew what to say. He knew how to approach Spencer.

He assumed an official and detached tone and threw the mystifying cloak of medical jargon at Spencer. "I recommend testing you too, Mr. Leicester. We need to perform three tests, first we perform the ELISA test, if that comes out positive we repeat it and if it comes out again positive than we do something what's called the Western Blot test. If all three tests come out positive than we can be sure that the person is infected."

Linda interjected the doctor professionally trained and emotionless explanation. "What about my husbands' symptoms? What do you think of the bad flue he had, the lesions on his skin and the swollen lymph nodes?"

The doctor carefully put his rubber gloves on and touched under Spencer arms.

"We cannot be sure without the test." The doctor wavered

away from making a direct statement. "Each and all of those symptoms could be attributed to independent disorders. But be on the safe side, I'll give you a prescription of acyclovir tablets. Those are good virus killers and should protect you, Mr. Leicester until we can be sure of what you have."

He took out his prescription pad, wrote out the medication, stood up and explained the regimen to Spencer. "Take it five times a day for seven days. Wait for the nurse to take your blood and I'll call you with the results in two days, at the latest. In the meantime, after a day or two on the medication you should start feeling significantly better."

The doctor flashed an encouraging grin to Linda, nodded a goodbye and left the room.

Spencer whispered to his wife, "See, I told you I may not have it either. It might be just a vicious bug; a bird flue perhaps that I contracted on the Far East."

They filled the prescription at Walgreen Pharmacy and went home.

Spencer took the first pill and Linda told him. "Take a rest, honey, I make you tea and you try to get better. We'll handle your sickness whatever it is."

Later she asked him if she could go down to the YMCA, for the last time she liked the swimming so much. Of course she lied, at least grossly misrepresented the truth, for the last time she swam at the Y was at least two years ago. Deceptive as she was, she lied that she did not upset her sick husband. A noble pretend to assure his recovery and preserve her strength she needed to maintain peace and tranquility. But in a way she also embarked on developing a double life, the first step on a dark, unpredictable and slippery path. She had love in her heart, outside of her marriage, although its subject resided far away, locked up in jail. She never intended to make friends with strangers, like her husband did, or have sex with anyone whom she didn't love and couldn't trust in a long lasting and exclusive commitment. She handled her situation and emotions the best way she could and made the best use of her limited life experiences and parentless upbringing.

A badly needed, appreciative trust inundating his basic psyche, Spencer approved. "All right, Linda, go if you wish, at least one of us has to stay strong and healthy."

Linda took her backpack out of the closet; put freshly washed white towels, soap and shampoo in it and inspected her bathing suits. She had only two, they were both two pieces style, she selected the larger one, a satin black bikini not as small as the other one she wore at the beach, but still tiny enough to reveal her feminine contours and curvatures.

She drove to the YMCA on Post Road. At the front desk she purchased a yearly pass and entered the facility. The upscale Darien YMCA had a large cold-water pool, a total of eight lanes for doing swimming laps and a diving board at its deep end. From a large hot water Jacuzzi tub, patrons could enjoy a wide panoramic view of Long Island Sound. In the adjacent room there was a big size heated pool with 92 degrees water for elderly people and children to swim or walk in the water or practice water gymnastics.

She changed into her bathing suit, put her clothes in a locker cabinet and entered the main pool area. In use by the high school swim team, two coaches were instructing and ordering around young and lively vigorous groups of teenagers, not much younger than Linda herself. They all wore one-piece black, rather conservative swimsuits that made Linda feel uncomfortable in her small two pieces bikini.

To hide her provocative attire she went to the next room, quickly submerged into the warm pool and began walking back and forth. There were not many people and for Linda's relief nobody paid attention to her. Around nine o'clock the teenagers left and Linda had the big pool almost to herself.

She put on goggles and lowered her body into the cold water. First it made her shudder but soon she got used to it and in a minute she was swimming back and forth like a playful mermaid in high glee. She swam twenty-five laps; the exercise reinvigorated and exhausted her, in a most pleasant and satisfying way. It was twenty to ten and the YMCA closed at ten. It was about time to get out of the water.

She rushed into the ladies locker, threw her bathing suit off and turned open the handle of a showerhead in the middle of six available on each side. She adjusted the water to high temperature that almost scorched her skin. Soaking and pampering herself she enjoyed standing under the massaging and soothing stream. *Blessed to be nude,* she thought, *and being hot is sublime,* she smiled and held her face into the strong flood of the warm delight. Soaped her body and shampooed her hair until, from her naked figure that she was purifying so thoroughly, thick layers of foam cascaded into the drainage trough.

Then turning around toward the wall, she lingered with her fingers, around her pubic parts, washed and massaged her breast, spread her legs a fraction apart and cleansed herself in between, perhaps a moment longer than needed for an adequate job. In plentiful sprays she spit water in and out of her mouth, closed her eyes and imagined spending time, alone, in a tropical paradise.

With her eyes closed against the massive amount of soap

she didn't see the tall, middle-aged, shorthaired brunette taking a long shower next to her. Preoccupied with her own pleasures, Linda didn't notice her showering companion watching with intent and peculiar interest, every move she made.

When minutes later their eyes met, she asked Linda with the welcoming smile of a health-spa hostess, "You are an excellent swimmer. Are you new? I've never seen you here before."

Linda glared back. She didn't like her watery frolicking being interrupted and was in no mood to make new friends. Rather impolitely she retorted.

"Sorry, I have to wash the soap out of my ear," and turning around she showed her derriere to the uninvited and imposing stranger who was making her uncomfortable.

But the older woman, obviously enchanted by Linda's well formed youthful and desirably forms, didn't give up. She became impertinent and tried one more time when Linda turned and faced her again.

"Would you wash my back?" The stranger said and extended a soap to Linda.

Linda stared back at her. Now she was angry and she exactly knew what the unsolicited companion was after. She had experienced enough lesbian advancement directed at her in her orphanage years and she hated it.

She snapped back. "I don't wash anybody's back. And please, would you stop looking at me."

Linda rushed to wash the soap off her body and abruptly terminated the showering. She walked out the shower area, grabbed her towel and hurriedly rushed back to the locker room.

But to Linda's misfortune the older woman had her locker right next to hers. She came closer again and apologized.

"Sorry. I didn't mean to scare you. My name is Barbara Doherty. I meant no harm."

Linda's mouth dropped and showing startling surprise she forgot to close them.

"Doherty," she asked, "Detective Doherty."

"That's right. Why?"

Both still standing naked, inches away from each other, Linda told the older woman. "I know him. Tell him I said hello."

"You do, really?"

"Linda, Mrs. Linda Shrewsbury. He knows who I am."

"I see."

Linda couldn't resist and giving in to the nudging of the little devil sitting on her shoulder revealed. "And he knows that I'm happily married to my airline pilot husband, Spencer Shrewsbury."

Now it was Barbara's turn to drop her mouth. "Very well, indeed, I'll ask him about you."

Linda already had her shorts and blouse on. Walking out from the warm locker room she told Mrs. Doherty. "I hope that you are not too disappointed."

"What do you mean?"

"That I'm married."

Mrs. Doherty grinned like a Cheshire cat. "Don't take me wrong. I'm married too. That doesn't mean that I cannot admire your beauty."

"And be friends."

"Yes, friends, what else?"

Almost out of the door, Linda turned back and handed a symbolic olive oil branch, an offer of peace to Mrs. Doherty.

"We girls could a have a secret or two, couldn't we? Will be seeing you around."

Chapter Twenty-One

Giacomo Pugliese nervously waited for the arrival of his boss. He sounded awfully upset over the phone and that made Giacomo uncomfortable and concerned.

Sal Sclafani rarely contacted Pugliese in person. Unless the job he had in mind required information that was not suitable for discussions over the phone. Sal's visits to his house on Decatur Avenue in the Bronx never have been a friendly, social event to begin with. Giacomo worked for Sal and that was the end of their relationship. Sal never considered him an equal partner and in spite of all their commonly shared secrets and illegal activities, treated him as a low level subordinate.

Subordinate or not, Pugliese thought, he had got it made.

He never noticed the smell of permanent mildew in his old Bronx house. He didn't mind the narrow corridors and the small bathrooms with the archaic toilet fixtures. He lived there alone and he had to make no mortgage payments to anyone. Never married, he had his particular ways and he didn't want anybody, not even a wife to poke her nose into his business. Except the first ten childhood years, Giacomo spent his life in this house. The house originally belonged to his uncle who took him in after Giacomo's parents were killed in Caltanissetta, Sicily. Their neighbors killed them, thirty years ago, over a minor land dispute that pestered over two centuries and finally eradicated one of the opposing sides. Giacomo survived only because, luckily, he's been visiting his uncle in America. Reading the news in the Il Progresso, the uncle wisely advised him, 'do not ever return to your native land'.

The benevolent uncle raised him as his own son.

Giacomo never finished high school. When the young Sicilian turned fifteen, the school guidance counselor told his uncle, expressing her deep professional concern that his beloved nephew was perceptually impaired, or in more mundane terms was too dumb to learn anything. Giacomo dropped out of high school and spent his days and nights hanging out in the neighborhood. He never bothered learning a trade and never could hold onto any kind of job for more than two weeks. But he happily existed and for pocket change, in his own words, bummed money off from his uncle.

His uncle proved to be the worst educator that could ever possibly have existed. He kept giving him money, moderately of course, for at least two sensitive, although careless and pressure free years. Only when Giacomo turned seventeen his uncle thought that it was about time to find him a useful and profitable occupation. He arranged to have Giacomo drive cars for his friends and business partners. The excellent position came with a prestigious aura of power that Giacomo haughtily projected down to his peers. It was good and reliable income and Giacomo willingly did anything he was asked.

Sometimes the drives went uneventful, he had to pick up a small package here and deliver it there; some other times he heard gunshots and his passengers came back walking rather briskly and still packing away their guns into holsters under their high fashion cut, woolen blazers and jackets.

When Giacomo turned twenty-two, his uncle disappeared, and he never saw him again. Initially Giacomo didn't touch his mail but when after a few weeks they began to pile up he began opening them. He pried his uncle's desk open, found his checkbooks and paid the overdue bills. Forging his signature he signed his uncle's name on bank drafts, checked the balances on his accounts, and pretended on the phone that he was he. The deftly dexterous concept worked flawlessly and without a glitch. He assumed his uncle's identity, he figured if he ever came back he would have just returned him to himself and would have accepted his thanks for keeping things in good order while he had to be away, jailed, kidnapped or otherwise incapacitated.

The uncle never bothered to file the American citizenship application for Giacomo and the Sicilian nephew resided in this country on a long ago expired visitor's visa.

Maintaining a low profile, Giacomo kept doing his chauffeur assignments until he met Sal Sclafani. Then his fortunes changed for much better. Sclafani offered more serious and steady work. Giacomo became the enforcer and collector for Sclafani's loan sharking business. Giacomo never questioned Sal and always faithfully executed his assignments. Sal liked him, for he had a complete lack of curiosity and had no feelings, not even minimum compassion or understanding for any pleas and begging he ever heard. Over the years his perception became more impaired and that suited very well Sclafani's business needs and practices.

Giacomo trusted Sal and in his childish, never grown up mind he replaced his uncle and now Giacomo couldn't imagine what could have made Sal so upset. When the doorbell rung he let Sal enter and they sat down in the living room. It looked messy, for Giacomo never believed in hard work, especially concerning housekeeping, but for now he swept off all loose clothes, trash and papers from two armchairs and offered a drink to his guest.

However, Sal instead of being nice, outright attacked him with a rank, verbal tirade. "I told you to leave no traces in that Connecticut job."

"I didn't," he protested, "I've done a clean job. They even arrested the kid for it."

"The hell you did. Why did you have to purchase a rope and why did you have to use your credit card?"

"Anybody can buy a rope and use a credit card. It's not against the law."

"I wish stupidity was against the law."

Giacomo never had a good handle on understanding irony, didn't foresee the coming fury and replied with a guffaw that reflected confidence.

"Ha-ha." He said, "That would be very funny."

"You imbecile, you left the receipt at the crime scene."

"The police didn't find it; otherwise they wouldn't have arrested the kid."

"Somebody found it and she is blackmailing us with it."

"Shall I whack off her too?"

"It's too late. She met with my client and she tricked him telling her that he hired us to kill his wife."

"So, I still can kill her. Just give me the address."

"She wasn't as stupid as you are. She had been wired and as soon as she got the information she ran out. I couldn't catch her but I saw her getting into an unmarked police car with two detectives already in it."

"Shit."

"Shit for you, my boy. This time you've fucked up big. The police are tracking you down as we speak. They might be here as soon as tomorrow. I bet they already traced all your accounts."

"The credit card was my uncle's and as you know I don't exist. I've been using his identity for years. At least until he comes back."

"You right, you don't exist."

Sal quickly jerked out a steel hammer from his inside coat pocket, lunged forward, twisted the handle in his hand and brought down the flat, nailing end of the steel with full force on Giacomo's head. He plucked it out with a twist, raised it up and hit Giacomo for the second time. This time with the sharp end, the spiky wedge penetrated his skull and opened up a big gushing wound. For a split second Giacomo brain showed up gray and bloodless, a little gooey piece spilled out of his cracked skull, but a second later blood spurted out of his head like a red fountain in a gruesome display of colorful waterworks. Sal pressed a palm on the wound; stopped the bleeding and drag Giacomo heavy and lifeless body to the bathroom. There he dumped the body into the bathtub and let the blood flow into the drain.

Sclafani loved classical music; especially he loved Italian operas. He knew that Giacomo's uncle had a great collection of old long player records; he went to the stereo cabinet, flipped through the albums and picked out Cavalleria Rusticana with Benjamino Gigli. He looked lovingly at the picture of the famed tenor and with gentle care put the vinyl album on the record player.

The prelude began softly, the mesmerizing music swelled and Santuzza's pleading soprano filled the room. Hearing the beautiful melody, Giacomo smiled with great joy and, as Turridu's Siciliana emerged from the background, he adjusted the volume to maximum and returned to the bathroom. He needed to concentrate on the task he had at hand.

First he undressed the body; made a bundle of the clothes he removed and took them to the basement. He cranked up the gas burner in the small cast iron heating boiler, opened the front door and piece by piece fed the bloody clothing into the fire. He intently watched each lump burning first red hot then disintegrating into white ash and finally, through the chimney, into ethereal smoky nothing.

He walked up on the stairs, leisurely smoked a cigarette, rolled up his sleeves and commenced on his morbid butchery work.

By this time the wonderful and yet simple musical love story, so elegantly presented by Gigli's tenor, overpowered the empty house. In his eternally classic voice Turiddu castigated Santuzza's overbearing jealousy.

"Bada, Santuzza, schiavo non sono
Di questa vana tua gelosia!"

The music transformed Sal's mindset into a perfectly happy and elevated mood. No interruption could have stopped his pleasure. With the biggest serrated kitchen knife, the sharpest cutlery he could find in the kitchen draw, he proceeded to saw off Giacomo's head. He carefully directed the flow of blood, down in the drain and made sure that he didn't spurt any on his clothes or onto the bathroom floor or splashed a drop on the plasterboard walls. He worked slowly and meticulously, he cut through all the tendons, all the muscles and then cut the spinal cord. He lifted up the severed head and held it until the last drip of blood plopped out from the cut. He put the lifeless, grayish pale and hairy cranium into the sink and started to work on the hands. He sawed through the thick bones and did the same thing for the feet.

Turiddu was singing good-by to his mother.

"Mamma, quell vino e generosom e certo
Oggi troppi bicchier ne ho tracannati…
Vado fuori all'aperto"

Listening to Mama Lucia's last shrilling cries he collected the head, the legs and the arms, as a butcher does it after successfully dissecting a pig, into a large washbasin and carried it to the kitchen. There he turned on the food grinder, pried the bloody and morbid mass into smaller pieces, using paring knives and bone cutters, and one by one the pieces disappeared between the cutting blades. He ran the water for a long time; took ice cubes out of the refrigerator and fed them into the grinder to clean the cutting mechanism. He kept working hard, at least for one more hours until he was one hundred percent satisfied that all traces of human blood and flesh were cleared out and gone without a trace.

Then he returned to the bathroom. In the bathtub, most blood from Giacomo's body had already drained out. He took out a black plastic lawn and leaf size garbage bag and stuffed Giacomo's remains inside. Tied the bag tightly and placed it neatly outside, near the front door. Then Sal washed the bathtub, wiped his fingerprints off from every shiny surface and moved the plastic bag with Giacomo's headless and limbless torso into the trunk of his car.

Then gangster-businessman, Sclafani went inside, filled up the bathtub one more time with clean water and let it drain to clean the pipes. *I am a perfectionist,* he mumbled with an ugly grin on his face. *Not like stupid, inattentive Giacomo who had no knack for fine details.*

Having done the cleanup job Sclafani drove to Darien Connecticut, up to Pamela's house. He already had the keys and the garage door opener. Opened the garage and parked his car next to Pamela's car, standing unused in her garage.

The police removed the yellow crime scene tape last week, the closing papers have been signed and he, Sal Sclafani owned this house. The ownership of Pamela's car, as part of her estate was still tied up in probate court but the vehicle had a legitimate license plate and a valid garbage dump sticker.

He transferred the body to Pamela's trunk and went upstairs to take a rest. It was late and he worked hard all afternoon. He needed his batteries recharged. He poured a glass of fine wine, his first in his new house and enjoyed the serenity of the upscale and exclusive Connecticut suburbia, one of the last remaining safe and decent places in the universe.

Early next morning, at seven o'clock he waited at the

dump gate as the grumpy, bearded and overweight attendant pushed the rusty barrier apart. He drove up on the hill, effortlessly carried the big plastic bag out of the trunk and discarded it down into the big cavernous bin below. He looked down after it and thought with malicious forebode, one down and two more to go.

He lingered around for few minutes and soon he saw a large private sanitation truck coming up and dumping its load on top of Giacomo's remains. Sal knew, the bin, after getting filled up to its full capacity, would be soon emptied and a huge state transfer truck would transport the black plastic bag with Darien's daily garbage to the always-working solid waste incinerator in Bridgeport.

Three days later an alert conveyor belt sorter picked out the awkwardly shaped and unusually large black plastic bag. Opened it to check and separate its contents for incineration or landfill and saw the naked, decomposing, badly stinking human remains. He stopped the belt, called his supervisor and they filled out the proper report.

Two contract workers transferred the body to the Bridgeport Police morgue. As an anonymous person the mutilated corpse lay unclaimed and uninvestigated for a few weeks and eventually the State had, whoever it was, buried the body at the Connecticut Potter Field. No one ever made any calls to claim the body and no law enforcement agency attempted or made any connection to the Pamela Leicester murder case.

The New York City Police Department staked out Giacomo's or rather his uncle's house for a full week and when nobody showed up they obtained a search warrant and went in. Inside they found traces of recent occupation, but they found no evidence of any crime committed and reported back to Connecticut.

"Suspect, sixty years old male, appears to have left the area and have not used his credit card or checking account for the last two weeks. If anything new turns up, this report will be updated."

Chapter Twenty-Two

Spencer condition turned worse. His tests came back and all three were positive. The results confirmed that he had HIV. The news depressed him. He slouched down in the largest armchair in the house and stayed motionless for hours. His enervate hands dangling by the side he stretched his legs and stared into thin air with a lost, empty expression of total apathy on his face. He completely lost interest in his surroundings and didn't remember things very well.

His HIV strain seemed to be resistant to standard anti-retroviral drugs and his infection rapidly transformed into full-blown AIDS. Dr. Lindberg prescribed a cocktail of drugs including Enfuvirtide, it slowed down the progression of the disease but Spencer wasn't getting better.

Linda had to make sure that her sick husband ate regular times and took his medications as prescribed. She always wore rubber gloves and Spencer didn't seem being insulted by her carefulness any more. Bitter and deeply depressed, he wished his sickness wasn't happening and somehow this nightmare would go away. He was angry at the world, abhorred Linda condescending attention, but being too weak he lost his will and energies to fight. Linda kept busy, she did the shopping, the cleaning, the cooking and she waited in the pharmacies to fill her husband prescriptions. Amongst the multitudes of her nurse-marital duties she found time to take care of herself. She made sure she didn't neglect her body and face and she looked as beautiful as ever in sharp contrast to Spencer's frightening decline.

Linda brought in and checked the mail. She separated the bills, all addressed to Spencer; she organized them and tried to show it to Spencer when he had his better moments.

"What are we going to do with these, dear?" She asked politely and softly touched his hand.

Spencer had difficulties to move his arms and fingers. He really had to make an effort to understand what Linda wanted him to do.

"Write them out and I'll sign them, please." He insisted but he could do not much more than blink his eyes and nod his head.

Linda tried that method for a few week but Spencer handwriting become too shaky to be legible. His AZT regiment helped to slow his dementia progress but couldn't reverse it. He tried to sign but ruined the checks; the pen ran off and made long streaks and unrecognizable markings.

Linda tried to suggest something more practical. "Why don't you let me sign the checks? You trust me as your wife, as your nurse, you've put your life into my hands, you should trust me with your money, shouldn't you, love."

She called him love and addressed him as dear and he didn't fail to notice it. She developed a nurse to patient compassion for him, he needed her and she was better able to transfer her feelings to a sick person than to his former self, the abusing and wife-beating tyrant. She didn't use frivolously the most delicate and most misused word of mankind, love, but in the context of this strange relationship, she meant every nuance of its concept. Now Spencer presented safety for her, as long as he lived she didn't have to go back to the YWCA, she didn't have to search for a room to share with a strange roommate or not able to pay the rent and face the danger of being homeless. Spencer turned into her father image, and who would blame a devout daughter, taking care of her sick father and calling her father love. Spencer liked the asexual love radiating from Linda. She became a true replacement of his mother. A person who loved him without attaching complicated sexual strings.

He appreciated her dedication and reciprocated.

"Anything you say, my love," he whispered and there was kindness in his voice as he squeezed her hand.

Linda brushed Spencer's hair out of his forehead and bent down to kiss his pallid skin. "Let me take you to People's Bank and let's transfer the money into a joint account so at least I can pay the bills."

Spencer pondered about her request. He should have done the transfer a long time ago. His wife shouldn't have begged him to have their money in a joint account. It should have been done when they've got married, but he was a bastard control monster and didn't trust her. Untrusting and selfish, he inevitably ended up losing her. Now he needed to give up this final vestige of independence. He was sick and he couldn't start a fight over money. Nevertheless it was a big and painful decision. For a long time he couldn't say anything. Only later, after Linda almost left his room, for she thought that her husband had fallen asleep, he spoke up. His voice was barely audible. "Get me dressed. We're going to People's Bank. I'm going to convert all my accounts into joint ownership with you. I should have done that eons ago. I'll make sure that you are my sole beneficiary on my 401K-retirement account. I'll take care of you."

"Thank you, Spencer." She pressed his sick head close to her bosom. "I'll not disappoint you."

"About the house," he said and it seemed he was making an effort to concentrate.

"What about the house?" She adjusted the pillow under his neck and spoke unhurriedly. "No need to rush. One step at a time should suffice."

"Call my lawyer and get him over here." He fondled her waist and caressed her hand trustingly. "We'll change the deed. Tomorrow we'll go to the motor vehicle and reregister the BMW and would you call Allstate and have the agent change the insurance policy both on the car and the house to both of our names."

He had done it all. He lay back exhausted, physically and emotionally. Now he tied all his assets and money together with his lawfully wedded wife. *I've done the right thing,* he thought and pondered wistfully, with AZT treatment and maybe after chemotherapy, he'll pull out from the opportunistic infections, stop the disease and will live a normal life. Maybe even have sex again with Linda, safe sex that is, he wished and a dash of cheeriness flashed across his face, they could do it after all, his virus level may be drastically reduced, he could wear a condom and she would feel safe and will agree to the intimacy. He had hopes and he had to have them to get better and nourish his will to keep on living.

The money, the house, retirement accounts and beneficiary designations were transferred to Linda's name. She ran Spencer's financial affairs, she paid the bills, signed her name on the checks, and to keep track of the various accounts set up an Excel spreadsheet on the computer. She neatly organized their finances and it was necessary indeed. Drug expenses and medical costs were out of control, insurance paid most but not everything, she had large co-payments and huge deductibles. Spencer was on short-term medical disability and it was Linda's responsibility to make sure that the COBRA insurance payments were always paid in time. Spencer had adequate funds, he inherited plenty old money from his mother, and he earned good salary and benefits at Delta, the house had no mortgage obligations, but the expenses exceeded their income and with passing time the once large nest egg rapidly dwindled away.

It remained out of the question for Linda to get a job; she had to be a full time nurse and companion to her seriously sick husband.

Percy stayed in jail. The state was not in much of a hurry and scheduled the preliminary hearing for early September, after Labor Day, still three months away. Linda frequently visited Percy and tried to keep up his spirit and hopes. He came to the visiting room in his orange prison issued overall, seemed being well taken care of and seemed coming to terms with his unjust incarceration. Linda told him what she has been doing, she talked to him about Spencer's serious condition, his moods, the successful sting to trick Mr. Leicester to admit the hiring a contract killer, she even told Percy that she met detective Doherty's wife at the YMCA.

Percy and Linda developed a close bond and understanding of each other. Percy didn't feel resentful of his family not risking their assets for him and hasn't even discussed their ill disposed negligence to post five thousand dollars deposit and put up the house as collateral for his bail. He looked almost content with his situation, the warden allowed to have his laptop computer returned and Percy spent not less than six hours writing each day. He wrote undisturbed and uninterrupted, his cellmate respected his privacy and only talked to Percy if he asked him a question. He proved to be well informed and highly educated. Certainly knew a lot about philosophy, including Voltaire, Hegel, Nietzsche and Freud. Percy wrote ten pages a day and frequently recited paragraphs and discussed thoughts and details with Linda.

Since there was a reasonable doubt about his culpability, the guards treated him differently. They gave him an office assignment in the prison library and generally tried to separate him from the rest of the much tougher, hardened criminals.

Now, Percy and Linda were allowed to sit at the same table when Linda visited him, a guard watched them closely, although he usually kept his eyes glued on Linda's breasts.

When escorting Percy back to his cell the curious natured but otherwise rough and gruff guard with his pock marked face never failed to inform him. "You are one lucky bastard, Grimsby."

Mrs. Doherty hasn't given up on Linda. She scheduled her YMCA visits to match Linda's. She swam in the same lane with her, followed her into the warmer pool or the Jacuzzi and most of all she made sure that they always showered together, although she never made any passes or any references for a possible closer, maybe intimate relationship between the two.

They talked at length in the warm pool while walked back and forth or stretched their weightless legs and swayed their hips under the wavy surface. Relaxed and comfortable in the soothing water they talked to each other in confidence. Linda told her that how bad of a mistake her husband did arresting Percy and that mistake hasn't been corrected to this date. Barbara couldn't justify or defend her husband's actions but promised she would talk to him and a few days later brought back his response.

"Sean says." She said slowly. "The main problem is that Percy is not telling what he did while he was in Pamela's house and failed to explain how he got there, especially considering that there were no signs of forced entry."

Linda suggested a solution, which should have been tried much earlier and would have been tried for anybody under the protection of a private and unbiased lawyer.

"Maybe Percy really can't remember without professional help. And for his credit he doesn't want to invent a story. He doesn't want to lie. He might remember more under hypnosis."

"True," Barbara agreed and the glint in her eyes showed genuine interest.

"Is there a police psychiatrist," Linda insisted, "Who possibly could put him under and get the information that way? That would be legally admissible in the court of law. Wouldn't it?"

"Yes, there is someone, a doctor he does that on outside

contractual bases. He does lie detector tests for most police departments in Connecticut."

"Could you ask Sean, I'm sorry, Detective Doherty to arrange for the procedure?"

"I certainly could."

"Thank you." Linda said and putting her lips on the other woman's mouth she pushed her upper body closer to Barbara. She tilted her head back and with eyes closed and lips parting, accepted the kiss. Pulsating electrical currents charged her body with desires and flames of lust boiled the blood in her veins. The heavenly encounter lasted for fractions of a second; perhaps not even for that long of a time, but it meant passion and a promise of eternal paradise to Barbara.

Linda gently pulled away and softly whispered to her. "I knew you would come through for me."

She stayed back and stared into Barbara's eyes. Linda's troubled glaze, looking blurred and with twinkling layers of tears covering her eyes, radiated serious telling. I know what you want but you are not going to get it until I get what I want from you.

They both paused in disbelief that they've crossed this border erected by centuries of conventions, forced upon women by jealous men and they retracted in fright and fear of their own actions.

Linda spoke again only much later and reiterated her request. "When can you talk to your husband? Can I tell Percy to get prepared?"

"Tonight, I'll talk to Sean tonight. He'll need Percy's consent."

"No problem there," Linda promised.

Later in the shower room Linda washed Barbara's back.

She moved the soap in circles around her shoulder blades, taking her time as she descended slowly down, slightly caressing her buttocks and turning around to let Barbara do the same for her. It was late; there were only the two of them and under the warm rushing water they lingered on testing forbidden delight.

Encouraged, Barbara turned Linda around and pulled her closer. She squeezed Linda's touchy cheeks with both hands and pressed her breasts against hers. Her lips twitched and trembled with desire and she desperately searched for Linda's mouth but she stepped back.

"No, please, Barbara, I can't, not yet at least."

Barbara stopped, she was happy as is; she advanced million miles this evening and that satisfied her; she retreated back and whispered with true love and care. "I understand."

Chapter Twenty-Three

To recover his lost memories Percy agreed to undergo hypnotherapy. The trained professional, Doctor Bard set up an examination room within the medical ward of the prison. Robert Schwechter, Sean Doherty and the assistant warden were seated in an adjacent room and through a one-way glass window could observe the procedure and could hear everything via microphones.

Fearful of inconclusive findings, Percy only acquiesced doing it at Linda's strong urging. He still couldn't recall details on how did he ended up in Pamela's house on the night of the murder and what he has been doing there for almost five hours after the murder. Now both the prosecution and the defense agreed that there must have been a second perpetrator but Percy didn't remember any and couldn't explain his relationship to him and nobody could find his partner if had one indeed. A thorough search of this second perpetrator's credit card records and transactions only lead to a missing person, to someone who disappeared years ago. A mysterious third party obviously used his credit card but without establishing his identity, Percy remained the prime suspect.

Linda was the only one who truly believed Percy's innocence and insisted on bringing all unexplainable details to the surface. So sure of her intuition she accepted any methods or means to achieve her goal. Under her persistent persuasion Percy agreed to cooperate and seemed interested to experience the psychogenic preternatural.

Doctor Bard asked Percy to lie down on a cot, told him to relax and began putting him asleep. It took several attempts spreading over days before he successfully induced Percy into a profound trance he deemed adequate to affect psycho-neuro-physiological responses needed for a meaningful recollection of subconscious memories.

The doctor hoped that, Percy, in his deep hypnotic state, will make an uncritical effort and will become free from all inhibitions and preformed judgments to vividly remember his repressed and forgotten experiences in extensive detail and will recover his lost memory.

Initially the doctor tested Percy's state of trance with a few simple questions and when satisfied he indicated to the witnesses on the other side of the mirror to begin paying close attention. A steno typist readied her fingers to make notes and all concentrated with great interest and listened carefully.

Doctor Bard looked into Percy's eyes and asked gently,

"Percy, what did you do after Captain Shrewsbury threw you out of his house?"

Percy seemed to be awake, he acted normally and yet he looked a different person, he transcended onto a different plateau of existence and submerged into his subconscious to bring up what he couldn't remember before.

Percy slowly began. "A big husky guy appeared from the dark and hit me hard on the head."

Doctor Bard patiently waited to see if Percy had anything more to say and continued. He spoke clearly and emphasized his words. "What is the next thing you remember?"

"I came back from the blackness and I was at Pamela's front door."

"And what happened?"

"I couldn't stand on my own, that big guy held me up and he pushed the doorbell."

"Go on; tell us every detail you can."

"He hid behind me and when Pamela opened the door he shoved me inside and grabbed Pamela."

"What did you after he let you go?"

"I stumbled a few steps then I collapsed."

Doherty tapped on the one-way glass and Doctor Bard stopped the questioning. The detective came into the examination room and whispered to the doctor. "Ask him what made him to collapse and why he didn't defend Pamela."

The doctor pulled out a kerchief from the side pocket of his white gown and wiped off the sweat from Percy's forehead. "Percy, try harder. This is important. You're a strong, young man. Why didn't you try to fight the big man?"

"I don't know. It happened fast. I was weak. I had no feeling in my legs. I could not react fast enough; it seemed that I lost my own will. I remember I was trying to hold onto the banister but my hands slipped."

Doherty bobbed his head. "Good, ask him what happened next?"

"Yes, of course, but you must leave the room." The doctor seemed turning impatient with the intrusive policeman. "Your presence might distract him."

Doherty returned to the observation side of the one-way glass and Bard turned back to Percy. "Do you remember what the man did next?"

"He hit Pamela with his fist. She collapsed and lay motionless on the floor."

"What else?"

"He pinched my nose, forced my mouth open and put a pill into my mouth. He was choking me until I swallowed. Then he hit me again and I fell down next to Pamela and couldn't see much, except the man's legs."

"Explain, what were you thinking? Did you have any idea what was going on?"

"I felt losing my vision. Everything turned into a blur. But I remember I wanted to crawl on my hands and knees to help Pamela. But my limbs became heavy and I couldn't even lift a finger. I couldn't move. I tried to focus but barely could make out what he was doing."

"Go on, very important, describe it to me, the best way you can. What was he doing?"

"He got a kitchen knife from the drawer, ripped open a plastic bag, took out a rope and cut off a piece, about five feet long. He made a big knot at each end, put the rope around her neck and tried to strangle her. She woke up and she fought him for her life. Pamela was a strong and big woman and she fought bravely, but she lost, she couldn't breath any more her tongue came out, she kept spitting and biting but he held her tight and soon she stopped struggling and became quiet."

"Do you have anything else that you want to tell us?"

"It became dark, I recall of being dragged into the living room and him forcing something into my pocket. After that all went blank and silent."

"What is the next thing you remember?"

"I woke up in the morning and I was curled up on the living room carpet, I've got up and I saw Pamela in the kitchen, I checked her pulse, she had none and I called the police."

The doctor left the room to check with the witnesses. "Do you have any further questions," he asked them, "while the medium is still in trance?"

"Yes," Sean Doherty answered, "Can he recall the man's face, any special features that this alleged assassin had?"

Doctor Bard went back to the examination room and asked Percy thee same question. Percy answered clearly as if he were fully awake.

"Yes, swarthy face, big prominent nose, plenty of dark hair, black blazing eyes, about two hundred pounds, as tall as I am."

Schwechter indicated that he had no questions and Doctor Bard snapped his fingers to wake up Percy.

Percy rubbed his eyes and shook his head. He didn't seem to remember a word he said and asked cheerfully. "How did I do? Good or bad."

Coming through the door Doherty heard Percy. For the first time since his arrest he talked to his former prisoner with traces of sympathy.

"You did well, son; you should be walking out from

here as a free man soon enough. From here on we should concentrate on the real killer."

The NYPD took its time to arrest Dwight Leicester. He was a senior partner in a prominent firm of trial attorneys and the police were familiar with his face and name. He frequently defended criminals and he got off the hook many individuals for whose arrest and conviction NYPD put in a lot of effort and endured considerable risks to apprehend.

After receiving the request from Connecticut, NYPD undercover agents followed Leicester moves for two weeks. Three plainclothes officer were assigned to observe his daily routines, took pictures of the people he talked to and tried to identify the presence of bodyguards or weapons. At the end they reasonably ascertained that Dwight was not armed, had no bodyguards and kept a fairly predictable schedule.

After the second and now more pressing request from the Nutmeg State, police captain, John Wilson issued the arrest order.

Two uniformed officers stayed down in the elaborately decorated shiny bronze colored lobby of the Fred F. French Building and watched the elevators and doors with instructions to stop Leicester if he tried to sneak out through the back entrance.

Shortly after noon two uniformed and two plainclothes men rode the elevator up to the fourteenth floor. The two uniformed stayed in the corridor and watched the men's room and the other doors leading in and out. The other two officers entered through the double width front door of the law firm.

"We need to talk to Dwight Leicester." They demanded.

The young and attractive receptionist picked up the phone

to call in but one of the visitors put a finger on the pin and stopped her.

He flashed his badge and announced, "NYPD, show us the way to his office."

She considered, for less than a split second, to object and warn her boss but seeing serious threat in the eyes of the intruders she changed her mind and stood up.

"Follow me."

She took a turn and there was Dwight in his room, sitting in his huge leather chair, alternatively reading the paper or looking out the window to rest his drooping eyelids.

"Mr. Leicester."

He turned around unsuspecting and seeing his secretary assumed no problems and automatically offered his visitors to take a seat.

The first cop pulled out his badge again, flashed it and said in an assertive and intimidating voice, "You are under the arrest."

The other cop took out a piece of paper and read Dwight his Miranda rights.

"Please stand up, turn around and put your hands behind your back."

Dwight obsequiously complied with the request and they handcuffed him. His partner, Joyce's father, came in; cast an accusing and questioning stare at Dwight and asked the cops. "What's the charge?"

"Conspiracy to commit murder, based on the extradition request from Connecticut."

The serious charge caught Dwight's partner and friend by surprise. He could never assume that Dwight would be guilty of anything but he knew better than fight two armed men with police badges.

Trying to help and reassure Dwight he said. "Don't worry, buddy. I'll get you out before they reach the precinct with you."

The two uniformed policemen led Dwight into the elevator, descended to street level and escorted him out to the lobby. Dozens of acquaintances and small talk friends, returning from lunch and hanging out downstairs for one more minute, have seen him and with impertinent curiosity and patronizing sympathy looked on while the blue uniforms ushered Leicester into an unmarked police car waiting on 45th street.

The two plainclothes detectives mingled in unnoticed with the rest of the spectators.

After making multitudes of urgent telephone calls, his partner dispatched the firm's brightest junior partner to the local precinct to bail out Dwight regardless expenses involved.

It would have gone flawlessly fine, except NYPD wasn't taking Dwight Leicester to any New York City precinct. First they drove with him to the Bronx and then into Westchester County on Interstate I 95. After crossing the state line they transferred him into a Connecticut State Police car, waiting at the first rest stop and only a few feet away from the border. By late afternoon the Connecticut State Police checked him in at the Bridgeport correctional facility. He had to trade in his three pieces suit, wallet, keys and anything he got on him for a bright-orange prison overall.

A prison guard led Dwight to the holding pen and he heard the first scary, far too friendly, welcome greetings.

"New man coming in."

The warden allowed Dwight to make one telephone call. He called Sclafani.

"I've been arrested."

"Charge?"

"Conspiracy to commit murder."

"Don't talk to anyone unless you have your lawyer present."

"I am a lawyer and a damn good one."

"Don't talk anyway and I mean it. One word about me and you are dead, I can promise you that."

"I don't know how much they know, but everything is your fault, your guy screwed it up."

"No. Blame yourself. You fell for that broad."

"You were supposed to silence her."

An automatic message interrupted their conversation, "This is a prison phone and you have thirty seconds left to finish before cut off time."

Sclafani hurriedly wrapped up the discussion. "I'll come over and we'll talk. Where are you?"

"Bridgeport State Correctional Institute."

"See you there. Remember do not talk to anybody and don't believe anybody. I'll get you out faster than any team of best lawyers."

"Hurry up. I don't like this place at all."

The prison switchboard terminated the phone connection. Sclafani hung up and went into action without wasting time. He knew somebody who had been in the Bridgeport jail for years. He knew he could trust him; he could ask him to do anything and he would do it better than anybody else from outside. He deemed him the best for any inside job especially if it had to be done within the secure and most protected prison walls. *The sooner I reach him,* he drummed his fingers nervously on the tabletop, *the safer will be how matters might turn out.*

Took his car from the parking lot on Parkside Place and drove directly to Bridgeport. He went to the visitor's center but didn't ask for Leicester. He asked for his friend and in the cavernous meeting hall talked to him unsupervised.

"New guy, he is a weakling and cannot be trusted. He'll talk and all of us will be in deep shit. You must get rid of him."

"When?" His jail-mate friend seemed to be another one lacking curiosity.

"As soon as possible, the sooner is the better."

"Ok. Let me find out where he is and what activity schedule they assigned him to, might take a day or two."

"Hurry up."

Sclafani left the jail. He never attempted to talk to Leicester. He wrote him off. Leicester didn't exist any more. He became a marked man.

Frank Collins Supervisory Senior Resident Agent at the FBI satellite office in Bridgeport picked up Detective Sean Doherty's report. He read it and immediately called his boss, Squad Supervisor Steve Sullivan at the Hartford Field Office.

"Steve, we've got a possible federal witness for your organized crime and loan sharking investigation. He probably could tell you a few names and interesting particulars and help you a great deal. Would you like to talk to him?"

"Is he still alive?"

"I believe so; he was just brought in hours ago to

Bridgeport. They didn't get to him yet. Let's see if he knows something usable."

"What is he in for?"

"Murder, he ordered the murder of his ex-wife."

"What makes you think he would talk?"

"We could offer him a special deal; promise him a reduced sentence for his cooperation. He will be singing like a canary on methadone. Instead of life behind bars we could offer him maybe fifteen years and parole for good behavior after six years."

"How much he knows?"

"He must know a lot. He had used an organized crime hit man to strangle his ex. As much we know about him he is a very good trial lawyer. He got many career criminals off the hook. He seems to have compulsive gambling problems. That's from where the mob connection angle comes."

"It sounds a good opportunity to get some information." Sullivan took a sip from his black, sugarless coffee. "Meet you at the jail, in an hour."

Frank Collins and Steve Sullivan were talking to Dwight Leicester in less than an hour in a private interview room at the jail. They offered him coffee and doughnuts and tried to make him feel comfortable talking to the two FBI men in civilian clothes.

Frank Collins took the lead. "Leicester, do you have any idea who killed your ex-wife?"

Feeling still confident he said, "As far as I know it that young thug, Percy Grimsby did it."

"Then why are you here?"

"It's a mistake. They have a hard time to prove Grimsby's

guilt and now they're targeting me. They've got the wrong man."

Collins didn't need to be polite. He gave the bad news to Leicester straightforward.

"We have a tape where your voice clearly says that you've ordered her killing and it wasn't the Grimsby kid whom you've hired. He was supposed to be the scapegoat. Your guy was supposed to make the murder look like Grimsby did it."

"It's all hearsay. It has to be proven in the court of law. You cannot hold up as evidence something that I told a broad when I was drunk and she was playing with my dick."

"The district attorney doesn't think so," Sullivan interrupted, "you're facing life in prison. But we can help you. We can get you back to your lucrative law practice faster than you think."

Time passed and after some hesitation Leicester grumbled under his breath, "I was afraid that you would offer your help."

"Wait. Don't jump to conclusions. If you tell us a few names, not just the man's whom you hired to kill your ex, but a few names you've come across as a criminal lawyer."

"That would be unethical. I would be disbarred before I can blink an eye."

"If you don't, you're going to be disbarred as a convicted felon anyway."

"I can't. I trust my skills to get me out of here. I have the best criminal lawyers in the country as personal friends. My partner is on his way to bail me out."

"Don't count on it. We can persuade the judge to hold you here without bail. You are a very dangerous man, Leicester, a real danger to society. Hiring the mob to kill your ex, whom else do you want to have killed?"

Leicester tried to take a sip from his coffee and reached for a tasty chocolate doughnut but Sullivan pulled it away from him, "You have to earn that first."

Dwight laughed. "Do you think I'm a kid? You want to buy me off with a doughnut."

"Name you price."

"Freedom tomorrow, charges dropped and an official apology."

"That depends how much do you know and how much are you willing to spill."

"I know more than you think."

"Give us a sample."

"You've got to be kidding me? A free sample, get me out of here right now and I'll talk."

Collins signaled Sullivan. He had enough of this bargaining. He wasn't used to be being nice to criminals. Near his retirement he didn't want to jeopardize his pension after thirty-five years of hard and dangerous work by making a mistake and letting an important potential witness go free and disappear forever. They had to teach Dwight a lesson.

Agent Collins told his boss. "Steve, I had enough of this shyster, let him spend a couple of days here and we'll see if he still thinks that he has any bargaining leverage left in him."

They both stood up, signaled the guard to take Leicester away. Leaving through the door, Sullivan turned back and casually told inmate Leicester. "Give us a call when you think you are ready for a little honest man to man talk."

The late afternoon turned into dinnertime. The guard let Dwight through a number of doors, alternatively signaling the locking system operator or opening them up with his set of jangling keys. They passed through the laundry and the license plate workshop and at each place curious glances from utterly bored inmate eyes followed them looking for any kind of excitement to break their monotonous routine.

At the eating hall the guard let Dwight in and told him with contempt. "Find a seat anywhere you want. From here forward, you are on your own."

Dwight felt hungry and badly wanted to eat. The two FBI men didn't let him have the doughnut. The obnoxious NYPD arrested him minutes before he planned to go out for lunch. He hasn't eaten in at least ten hours. His blood sugar level dropped low and made him irritable. Mad about his arrest, the FBI's arrogance of trying to use him for their purposes, angry about everything and everyone except himself. He had to eat but he had to stand in line with a bunch of young riff-raff. Mostly black and Hispanic but some white, people with whom he never would have associated with, seen in the same room and let alone to have dinner with.

He filled up his tray with food and headed to the nearest table where he saw only a few, less frightening looking, inmates sitting. Walked around the first few tables all occupied with huge muscled black body builder type men or white bicycle gang member types with large and colorful tattoos. He tripped on something and a tall blond kid with shaved head stepped in front of him. He blocked his way and bumping into him knocked Dwight's tray out of his hands.

Dwight cursed and grabbed after his dinner, then something penetrated into his stomach, a blade sliced into him and the attacker brought it upward with such a force that his belly opened up like a can of sardines. He pressed both of his hands on his stomach and tried to push the bursting intestines back when the second knife pushed into his back. A sharp pain pierced his heart and he fell forward. Everything went blank and dark and Dwight didn't see the inmate crowd that closed in over him and surrounded his lifelessly crumpled up body lying on the floor. He didn't feel he was kicked and shoved under a table. People sat around him, rested their legs on his back and finished their meals, calmly as if nothing happened.

Dwight lay dead, he died without having a chance to scream, yell for help or fight back and he didn't even see his murderer. He died like a stray dog, outcast and despised by all his peers and even by his fellow inmates.

At the end of the dinner period, the guards emptied the eating hall and the cleaning crew found Dwight's body, lying in the sticky puddle of his own, ghoulishly red blood. His intestines gushed out and snaked around the vinyl floor tiles, as in his final death throws he shit all over and stank up the place.

The inmate cleaning crew assigned to remove him, cursed at the bastard whose death caused such a disgusting mess and forced them to work overtime.

The investigation ordered by the warden led nowhere. He questioned Percy, but Percy was organizing books in the library at the time of the murder and he had no idea that Dwight Leicester had been arrested and been brought to the Bridgeport Jail. The State never considered Percy's culpability in connection with Leicester's death and it did not have any effect on his pretrial hearing schedule.

Chapter Twenty-Four

The Stamford Superior Court scheduled Percy's preliminary hearing for September 8, 2004, Tuesday morning. On Sunday afternoon Rosemary, his mother, brought him his best and only dark colored suite, a freshly pressed white shirt, matching shiny shoes and a black tie to dress him up properly and make him look at his best. The prison barber cropped his hair and that made him look like a young business manager, trustworthy and acceptable by standards of middle class decency.

Two guards transported him from Bridgeport to Stamford the day before and he spent the night in a solitary room next to the general holding pen at the Stamford Police Station, near the courthouse.

The hearing took place in one of the smaller courtrooms. When the guard brought Percy in, he saw his mother, his lawyer Robert Schwechter, detective Doherty and two lawyers from the District Attorney's office. Sitting and waiting, Linda and an unknown middle aged, shorthaired brunette woman were also there.

At exactly ten o'clock, Honorable Judge Martinez walked in. All rose and the judge sat down. For the first minute he intently studied Percy's file and looking up, almost like a jovial grandfather, asked Percy a question off the record, "How does someone become a writer?"

Percy was caught off guard with this unusual opening and replied with a spontaneous reflex, "One has to be born that way. It all comes from within."

"The wife of a friend of mine was born that way," the judge eased up and his facial muscles relaxed, an incipient move that never made it to be a smile and continued. "She wrote a lot of poems that nobody could understand. But when she needed to write a letter her husband had to help her out." His honor sighed. "But anyhow, I'll not hold that against you. Let's begin."

The judge hit the desktop with his gavel and announced. "The criminal preliminary hearing for case number 2752S2004 is open."

The elderly woman steno typist positioned her back and shoulders, started to move her fingers and one of the District Attorney lawyers read the charges against Percy.

"First degree murder and conspiracy to commit murder."

Arthur Schwechter stood up and addressing directly the judge courteously requested, "Your honor. May I approach the bench?"

Martinez motioned both lawyers to come nearer to his desk and glared at them. "What is it?"

Schwechter leaned an inch closer to the judge and with elegant articulation, pressing intelligibly each word that left his mouth, he announced. "The evidence, the state is basing the charges on, were subsequently investigated and turned out to be false and untrue. We respectfully request that the state consider dropping the charges."

Martinez glared at Schwechter. The judge's face was cold and noncommittal. "Explain." He demanded tersely.

"Someone planted the murder weapon on the accused. Evidence had been found and was presented to the District Attorney's Office for examination proved that the rope used to murder Pamela Leicester had been purchased by someone else and could not have been possible purchased by the accused."

The prosecutor cut in. "That doesn't mean that he didn't use it to murder the victim. It only means that he possibly had not acted alone, that's why we have the conspiracy to commit murder charges added."

Undisturbed by the interruption, Schwechter continued. "We have an audio tape where Dwight Leicester admits he hired someone to kill his wife and that someone was not Percy Grimsby and the true perpetrator was supposed to make it look like that Percy Grimsby did the killing. The defense also properly submitted the tape to the District Attorney's office for evaluation."

The judge turned to the representative of the prosecution, "Do you still want to press charges?"

He answered indignantly. "The state must assume guilt. The accused was in the house at the time of the murder and he couldn't explain what he was doing there and how did he get there. He should be indicted and he will have his chance to defend himself and prove his innocence in the court of law and a proper trial jury should decide on his innocence and guilt based on all the evidence presented."

Schwechter interjected, using a dry and emotionless voice. "There is no need to drag a completely innocent person through a trial procedure. The accused does remember and in a legal deposition he already explained everything in details."

"Let me see that deposition," the judge demanded. Visibly annoyed and angry he reached for it. Taking his time, he read it and turned to the District Attorney's office lawyer. "Did you read this?"

"Yes, your honor. We did."

"Than what are you doing in my court with this case?"

The young but very ambitious assistant district attorney looked nervous. If he let this case go, he thought, it would not look good on his record of accomplishments. He had to try one more time.

With paying close attention to the unfolding debate Percy tried to eavesdrop. He had perfect hearing but still missed at least two third of the conversation. He only could guess that the prosecution seemed to have problems maintaining their case against him. He knew he was innocent; he wanted to get out of jail, regain his freedom, get on with his life and erase this arrest from his records. He had to fight his urge to get up and shout, I'm innocent you bastards, I didn't do it. He nervously fidgeted in his seat, looked at Linda for help and happily acknowledged when she returned his glances. He had new hopes, new reasons to live and have a life instead of suffering and withering away, locked up in a terrible place.

Linda sat much further away from the judge's podium than Percy and she couldn't even guess what was going on. But sitting on pins and needles of thousand agitated nerves she could see that Schwechter and the prosecution argued and fought hard. Barbara sat right next to her. Her presence annoyed Linda; she didn't feel absolutely sure about her. Linda thought that Barbara had strange motives and at best she was unpredictable. Perhaps if she insulted Barbara or rebuked her in a wrong way she could turn from a friend to foe and influence detective Doherty in an erroneous direction. But for now Linda had to give Barbara the benefit of doubt and had to assume that she hasn't gone insane and remained in control of her female-to-female attractions.

The assistant district attorney eyeballed the judge and spoke loudly. "We are positive that we'll prove his guilt beyond the reasonable doubt in a full criminal trial. He'll be found guilty as charged."

The judge face turned serious and offended. He raised his voice even higher than the prosecutor did. "Do you have any other evidence that you would like to present in this case to prove his guilt?"

"No. What we already have is adequate."

Letting out his rage and dissatisfaction with this young man's interpretation of the law the judge bellowed with rage. "Listen to me, young man. Do not ever bring into my court again a case without supportable evidence. Do not let yourself carried away by your emotions and misguided ambitions. Insist on the facts and do not engage in wishful thinking. Get out of my court." He brought his gavel down with full force and almost broke the oak plate that received the blow and yelled in a deep stentorian voice.

"Case dismissed"

He turned to the flabbergasted and motionless Percy. "Mr. Grimsby, you are free to go. The state expresses its sincere apologies and sorry for your unjust incarceration. All you records will be cleared and you will not have any criminal or arrest records in connection with this case. We owe you that much. Good luck with your writing endeavors. Don't let me see you in my court ever again."

The judge stood up and ponderously walked out to have his break.

Everyone in the courtroom stood up, left their seats and mingled about. The two district attorney lawyers packed their papers and silently disappeared through a side door. Nobody cared about them. They were the necessary but occasionally despised servants of the system. They had to do what they had to do. They done their work and fortunately in this case they proved to be wrong and couldn't succeed.

Rosemary hugged Percy and told him with an awkward but still motherly smile. "I knew you were innocent, son. We are so happy for you."

Percy hugged his mother. He leaned down to reach her face and gave her a light kiss on her forehead. "Yeah, mother. You all believed in my innocence. You just didn't want to lose the house and who could blame you for that. The three months in jail were good for me. Turned me into a man, the process almost killed me, but I luckily survived and now the whole mess is water under the bridge."

Almost imperceptibly he pushed her mother away and looked for Linda. Standing less than two feet away, projecting unreserved and unashamed happiness; her proud smile was sweetly healing elixir for him.

She jumped Percy's neck and embraced him, her long

and soft feminine arms hugging his neck, she pushed the silky warmth of her face against his jail time roughened skin. Percy inhaled her body fragrance, smelt her perfume and felt the rushing blood under her face. Her excited and aroused heart pounded in eager madness. Her arteries throbbed with wanting and the fine muscles under her skin trembled on both sides of her neck. He pushed his face into her soft bronze hair and searched for her rosy lips. She parted her honey-sugar mouth and accepted Percy's. They pressed together in a loving human vise. Squeezing and caressing in front of everybody they seemed shameless and oblivious to the baseless opinions of the indignant and the morals of the uninformed envious. She was there for him. She saved him and she saved his soul. She made him suffer, she tortured him with unfulfilled desires but she never abandoned him.

Interrupting the romantic scene, Rosemary ushered out her son and drove away with him. Barbara and Sean Doherty patiently waited to take Linda home but Robert Schwechter wanted to have a word with her.

"You've won, congratulation," he looked at her with a peculiar and doubting gaze and went on talking. "Are you sure that you don't need a divorce lawyer?"

"No thanks. I don't."

"All right with me, but can I give you a good advice, as a lawyer?"

"I'll take if it's free."

"Make sure that nothing unexpected happens to your husband. It would look very bad. They may not be this lenient on you."

"Is that a warning or a threat?"

"Both."

"I see. Don't worry," she said with confidence, "I'm taking very good care of my husband."

She left Schwechter and joined the Doherty couple. They stopped at Walgreen where Linda's got a month supply of AZT and acyclovir for Spencer and they went to Linda's place to visit and cheer up her husband.

Not healthy but doing better today, Spencer put on his heavy duty white terry cloth robe, tied the belt around his waist and came down to greet the visitors. True Irishman, Sean Doherty loved his drinks and immediately bonded with Spencer when he brought out his bottle of Chivas Regal. From their cordial glasses the ladies modestly licked tiny drops of Bailey's Irish Cream and the two couples seemed hitting it off with a good start.

Spencer stretched out in his armchair, swirled his drink around, took a sip and asked with his best easygoing and casual demeanor. "What's the occasion?"

Sean already gulped down his glass of the finest scotch there was; he loved the taste of it, it put him in a amicable, indulging state of mind and he blurred out the news.

"The judge threw out all the charges against Percy Grimsby."

Linda's eyes flashed at him. With a lightning burst of furious anger she had daggers in her eyes and tried to head off his unperceptive callous stupidity, but her warning came a second too late.

Spencer spoke up. "Is he out, free?

Doherty poured more scotch to himself and grinned as if he was telling great news to a concerned relative. "Aha, he is home free with his mother."

"No kidding, how come?"

"Somebody did a good job and collected enough evidence to repudiate the state's case."

"Who was that?"

"Linda," Sean turned toward Linda with pride and finished his saying, "your wife, she is the best when it comes searching out the truth."

Thin and long muscles twitched with dark, menacing shades on Spencer's sickly pale face. He needed all his self-discipline and military trained cool not to jump and start beating his wife. He grabbed the armrests of his seat and forced himself to back off.

He clenched his teeth but couldn't avoid sputtering his stifled wrath at her, "What business of yours was that?"

Linda knew the dangers of his jealous rages; she tried her best to defuse his anger and suspicious distrust. "Just a neighbor," she said cautiously, "I was simply a Good Samaritan."

"Well, don't be, not at my expense. I need you right here, right next to me. What about me? I'm sick and you'd better take care of me first."

The Doherty couple saw the gathering storm, mostly sowed by Sean's inadvertent verbal negligence and leaving Linda to deal with an upset and near demented Spencer, cowardly decided to leave.

As soon as they were out the front door Spencer turned to Linda. "Have you been fooling around with that Grimsby kid?"

"No. He'd just got out today. What do you think who I am?"

"I know who you are, bitch, take off your clothes."

"What?" His unexpected demand startled her. She jumped back and yelled. "No."

Spencer roared, suddenly all his energies concentrated and he didn't look sick any more. He became a raging lunatic, gulped down another glass of straight up scotch and roared. "Your clothes, take them off or I'll rip them off for you one by one, you fucking slut."

Young Linda had no strength or marshal arts experience to fight back. Her first impulse was to obey and hope that her obedience would tame the beast. She unbuttoned her red belted shirtdress, pulled her arms out of it, neatly folded the garment and placed it on the sofa.

Spencer watched her like a hungry lion watching a frightened gazelle trembling in front of him. His predatory lust froze her. Motionless and timid she looked weak and soft. Yet, she was beautiful in her fright. In her high-healed lanza sandals, wearing only a set of light pink lacey bra and miniature thong she was sexy and defenseless.

Spencer didn't see her fragile beauty. Out of control he thundered with mad rage, "All of it; take off everything. I want you totally naked."

She took off her underwear and stood shaking and shivering in the middle of the living room with her crazed and angry husband.

He pulled off the belt of his robe, grabbed it in the middle and hit Linda hard with it. "On your knees slut," he howled, "I'll teach you whom to associate with, who to help when you have to take care of your sick husband."

He hit her again and again, this time with brutal force and enraged fury. Linda fell on her knees and she crouched down trying to cover her head and neck. He hit her pink colored skin; he hit her buttocks, her back, her round and delicately feminine shoulders, repeatedly, many times, and striking harder each time.

Linda moaned with pain, she cried in shame and anger that Spencer was doing this to her again. She considered getting up and running to the kitchen, grabbing a knife and finishing him off, once and for all.

Then she remembered Schwechter's warning. She couldn't do it; she abhorred the thought spending her life in jail. She remembered her mother, visiting her, seeing her to deteriorate into a miserable, wasted wreck of humanity. She wanted to have a different life. If she had to be a martyr so be it, but she couldn't lower herself down to the level of Spencer's less than animalistic behavior. She felt sorry for him, he was sick with a deadly disease; but he still failed her as a husband and now he further degraded himself with beating the only asset he had left, his wife. She really took good care of him; anybody else would have fled in panic and not remembering any matrimonial oath, as like sickness and in health. She coiled up into a small lump and hoped for a miracle that his ire would subside before he kills her.

Spencer soon ran out of breath. Gasping for air he stopped and sweat rolled down on his forehead and dripped off his back. He began to shiver and he coughed. And he coughed with terrifying spasms. He couldn't breathe any more and fell back on the sofa. The air rattled into his throat with pain and bloody aches burnt his lungs. Spitting out red blood laden mucous he lost consciousness.

Linda stood up, collected her clothes, ran up to her room, locked the door and threw herself on the bed. She screamed and sobbed in desperation.

"Oh God, I just wanted to help. I thought I was doing the right thing. God, give me strength to endure this, I don't want to end up like my mother. Give me guidance. Show me the right way."

She cried on for hours on end and she didn't care what Spencer was doing, dying or living, she hated him now, irrevocably and forever. She had enough of him. Much later she stood up and looked at herself in the bathroom mirror. She ran her fingers down on the long, red-welted streaks covering her shoulders, buttocks and back. They were already swollen and painful to touch.

Later she took a long soaking bath and put on moisturizing cream to cover most of her skin. Wrapped her body in a bed-sheet, fought the burning pains of her wounds and tried to suppress the uncontrollable chattering of her teeth. After a long, hurting and lonely suffering, the lotion soaked into her skin and soothed her aching blisters, bloody lumps and contusions. Defeated and humiliated, she finally calmed down and fell into an exhausted sleep.

When Percy got home with Rosemary, he went to the second floor to check his room. His belongings weren't there. His father converted his son's room into a home office. He had his desk there, bookshelves with engineering books, his computer, a large drafting table and a leather revolving chair.

Surprised and predicting bad news Percy returned to downstairs and asked his mother. "Mom, what happened to my things?"

"Dad took them to the basement. You can have the basement for yourself. He needed an office. He has too much moonlighting work. We need more money."

Percy rushed to the basement. There he found his bed, his desk and his computer with his books, manuscripts disorganized and piled up in the corner. Down there, in the mushy windowless dungeon, smell of mildew permeated everything and air felt damp and cold.

He yelled back to his mother. "Ma, it's cold down her, no heating."

She answered. "Get the electric heater from the garage, but don't use it too much, our electric bill is way too high as is."

Percy had nothing to discuss with his family any more. He carried the electric heater to his new basement home, bought a thick carpet and pasted posters on the concrete walls. Next week he drove back to Bridgeport and retrieved his belongings from the jail's storage wing. He returned with two big cardboard boxes and his laptop computer. He plugged his computer in and commenced working. He had only one thing left, his book, and he worked on it nonstop, day and night.

Fall lingering just around the corner, Percy soon reestablished contacts with his former clients, raked their leaves, cut their grass and, still being near the end of the summer with pleasant temperatures, he began giving tennis lessons again. He didn't seem like talking about his jail experiences and most people had the decency not to ask him.

He used the basement service basin to shave and wash up, and joined the YMCA to take showers.

He had a life again that he considered almost bearable.

Chapter Twenty-Five

Weeks passed. Linda injuries healed and the red welts from her back and buttocks almost disappeared. Fearing Spencer, she threaded her ways around him carefully, with tense, ready to flee alert. Spencer's wild mood swings, going from complete calmness to tears and anger in seconds, terrified her. Spencer couldn't any more recollect recently happened episodes or events. He kept asking Linda, the same questions over and over and he couldn't remember he already asked the same before. Without Linda's help he couldn't have followed his medication regiment. He became irritable and distrustful and acted belligerent without cause. He became disruptive and for no reason threw things at Linda, he broke vases, lamps, decorations he could reach and yelled if Linda removed the broken pieces or he couldn't find the items any more.

At first Linda tried to reason with him. She asked him about the beatings, "Spencer, you hurt me. I didn't deserve that. I've been good to you and I'm trying to give you the best care I can."

Spencer's face showed a genuine surprise, "I've never beat you in my life. I cherish you, you are my beautiful flower, my little hummingbird, and I would never hurt you. Come on."

Linda tried to make peace and replied soothingly. "That's ok, past is past, just never do it any more. Please."

"Never do what?"

She had the patients of an angel and repeated her request. "Spencer you are still much stronger than I am. Just don't beat me, please. I know that you are sick and you are angry at the world but don't take it out on me. I'm the only one who really cares about you."

"I don't know what you are talking about. I don't feel well but I'm not seriously sick."

"Spencer you have full blown AIDS."

"No. I don't and would you leave me alone with your stupid paranoia."

She couldn't get through and reach him. The virus already damaged his brain beyond hopes of repair and it was the matter of time before he was getting progressively worse and totally demented. She had to be careful around him, she had to find his calm moments to bring in his food and medication and she had to be always alert to escape and get to safety when his unpredictable and spontaneous rages exploded.

Dr. Lindberg came out once a week, looked at Spencer

and tried to convince him to go to the hospital or at least check into one of the local HIV hospices.

Spencer didn't want to hear about any of that. "I don't want those queer fruitcakes around me. They make me sick. I'll fight off this infection at home, in my house. I spent my life here and I have no reason to move out."

Doctor Lindberg gave Linda prescriptions to calm down Spencer. He gave him Zolpidem and that put him deep asleep for eight to ten hours at a time. The extra rest made him regain some of his former strength and his dementia became tolerable. After two weeks of testing times, calmness returned to the Shrewsbury residence and Linda could think about herself again. She had to get out of the house and late in the evening, after she fed and cleaned Spencer and gave him his sleeping pill, she slipped out and went to the YMCA for a healthy swim, some company and a relaxing shower.

The Darien YMCA, just like its hometown, was small, clean and exclusive. Official policy naturally offered acceptance to anyone, regardless of color, creed and financial status, but under the pretext of overcrowding and restricted facility capacities, they basically limited membership to Darien residents and that meant well to do or at least upper middle class whites. Naturally other races came, but rarely and only as one time visitors, and were regarded with polite but curios attention, watched carefully and treated with assumed, although phony equality.

Linda arrived shortly before nine in the evening, quickly changed into her, now one-piece style-bathing suite and headed directly to the big pool. She swam in freestyle, splashing the water and making her laps like a high school varsity competitor. She finished fifty lengths, climbed out of the pool, took her towel and went to the large warm pool in the other room.

There she saw Percy. Standing with his back toward her he stared aimlessly away, obviously thinking hard and daydreaming about something interesting and important to him. Linda slid quietly into the water, stealthily sneaked up behind Percy and using both hands covered his eyes.

Percy felt the touch of fine feminine hands. Almost imperceptibly he sensed the closeness of her body against his. Didn't budge or move; just spoke out, softly and lovingly and only to the being holding him in sweet captivity.

"Linda?" he whispered.

"How did you know?"

"I'd recognize the tenderness of your hands, even if I am blindfolded and bound by ropes at the bottom of the darkest well on earth. I feel your warmth before you touch me, I see you before I open my eyes, I always see you, I always think about you."

Linda bobbled around to his front. Shoulders still submerged in the water and trying to catch her breath and face deep cherry-red from the swim and the hot water, her sparkling eyes revealed how elated she was finding him.

"Percy, Percy, you never change. See what you've made me to do. I blushed. I feel my face is burning, shame on you."

"Linda, your fire is my holly cleansing pyre; it purifies my soul and inspires me to reach to the furthest parts of the universe in search of you. You and I, we are together forever, we are against the world. I've lost all my dreams in your dreams. I was down in the gutter, besmeared in the mud and you've reached for me. You've picked me up and us together, we'll break down every concrete barrier and rigid stonewall and we'll break into pieces every chain keeping us apart. I'll never find another lip, another woman to quench my thirst for pleasure and fulfill my starving desire for love."

She loved his poetry. It gave her wistful weakness and evoked emotions that, she felt, would last into endless eternity. *No use of denying,* she thought, *I feel the same way about you. But our relationship is forbidden and easily could be frowned upon and disapproved just about everyone we know.*

She pondered for a second and then answered her admirer. "Percy, you know who I am. Why do you have to elevate me to so unreasonably heights all the time?"

"I know who you are. And I don't care. I want you to follow me to my grave; I want you to stand in front of me in the sizzling summer sun or in freezing arctic cold and tell me. I'm the one who you've been waiting for, I'm the one who you love, for I love you Linda and I'll love you forever because in this whole sinful and carnal dirty universe we are the only two who are true and innocent."

She'd heard him; she heard what she wanted to hear. He was the tropical island in the cold stormy seas of her life. He was the lighthouse in the dark she was aiming for. She just couldn't reach him yet. She whispered to him. "Percy I love you too. If you love me you'll wait for me. I'm coming and we'll be together for the rest of our lives, the two of us against everybody else."

They didn't have to kiss or touch. Their emotions and commitment sufficed for every physical touching and sensual pleasure. They were together for life now, no force in the universe was able to separate them, and no physical barrier remained insurmountable for their eventual glorious ascension to happiness and joining in heaven on earth.

Minutes passed; nobody else stayed in the pool. The wall clock indicated only a few minutes before closing time.

Linda wanted to talk more and suggested. "Percy, let's meet in the parking lot. I need to talk to you, seriously, no poetry this time, please."

"Done deal," he answered hastily, "I'll wait for you in front of the ladies' locker room and I'll walk you to your car. Better yet we should go somewhere and have a late night snack. What about Black Goose Restaurant?"

Linda smiled enigmatically, "Not that place. I have a much better idea. Let's go to Silvermine Tavern. The night is chilly and I'm sure that they have the fireplace going. We can sit by the crackling flames and talk."

"What an excellent idea," Percy exclaimed. "Why didn't I think of it? Let me drive. Leave the BMW in your garage. It's safer that way."

"Ok, but not in you father's pick up truck."

"Come on, I have my own car. I drove my Corolla over here."

"Good enough. Is it clean?"

"It's clean as a whistle. You should know by now that I'm a very neat person."

A half an hour later they were driving in the dark night on their way into the spooky and isolated New Canaan woods. Percy drove on a narrow country road, along the bubbling Silvermine River and soon they reached the rustic, old New England style, country inn. The dining room, embellished in charming colonial decor was dimly lit and seemed almost empty. They sat down in a private booth and listened to the sounds of the rustling waterfall coming in from the old millpond on the other side of the terrace.

A young waitress dressed up as a country maiden brought the menu and left them alone.

The building, almost two hundred years old but recently renovated, fixed up and repaired, stood on the same spot where at one time prospectors washed silver out from the river and traveling between New York and Boston, wealthy merchants stayed overnight. Being surrounded by old time grandeur, one could feel the presence of long gone souls and ghosts. The aging and moisture-laden walls and the antique furniture emanated mildew and old money provided a perfectly authentic New England place for the rich, old people and young lovers alike.

It was hard to talk business and be unromantic in a place like Silvermine Tavern.

Percy broke the silence. He turned to Linda, for few long seconds admired her pretty face, long, auburn bronze hair, rosy lips and delectably delicate shoulders. He was totally and head over hill in love with her.

He whispered to her. "No poetry this time. I'm very seriously in love with you."

Linda turned her innocent, baby face toward him. She saw somebody who looked completely different than anybody else she ever met. She pictured him as an idealist, who could put up his entire life for the love of a single woman, one who could never hit a woman for he admired her so much, one who could never raise his voice at her, one who would never look at another woman, one who could write and recite poetry to her, one who was young and had a future, a future with her, together and forever. He was her man whom she didn't have to tie down to earth by lust and carnal desires, loveless sex and yet whom she desired physically so strong that she ached with pain when at nights alone in her room she had her dreamy reveries. She knew that love like that happened only once in a lifetime and happened to only a privileged few.

She answered, "Yes. That is the problem. I love you too. I'll love you as long as I live and I'll never love anybody else. That's our curse. What are we going to do about it?"

The maiden came back, took their orders and very politely and wisely disappeared.

Percy continued, "Linda, I know it sounds unromantic, but trust me. I know I have talent an aptitude in me. I have finished my first real good novel in the jail. I had something to write about and it was just coming out of me. It's perfect. I've sent it to a literary agent and she liked it. She is trying to place it right now with publishers. One day, soon, I'll be rich and I'll be able to give you everything what you need and what you deserve."

"Percy. I know who you are. I see that you have a good head on your shoulders. In spite of all your romanticism and poetry you are a realist. Nobody can fool you. You clearly see things the way they are. Growing up in the orphanage and in foster homes taught me to face the truth and suffer the consequences of my mistakes and transgressions. The biggest shame if one deceives his or her spouse, lover or significant other and lives a double life. If you are deceiving your mate than you have nothing, you are deceiving yourself, you are lying to yourself."

"I'd never do anything like that. I promise."

"I know. Neither would I, but we have to overcome a few very serious obstacles before we can be together."

"I know."

"Spencer has AIDS."

"I thought so."

"I didn't know he had it before or he fooled around and contracted the virus while I was already his wife. His tests came back positive. I had myself tested too and mine came back negative but to make sure I have to take another test in six months. I have three more months waiting to do on that. It's a deadly disease and it's the price I'm paying for my ignorance, misjudgment of character and hasty decision. I'm staying away from him right now, he is too sick to do anything anyway. But we have done things before."

"You were still a virgin after a year of marriage to him."

"Yes, I was." She smiled and lovingly put her hands on Percy's. "But he had me to do unsafe things with him. There is chance that I have the virus too. And if I do, there is chance that I've given it to you too. I'm awfully sorry if I did."

She couldn't continue. It was too much for her nerves. She broke down, bowed her head and cried, silently but from deep inside, from the bottom of her sorry soul. Percy took her hand and wiped off her tears, gently, and with understanding and love.

"If you did, so be it. I'll die for you and we'll die together. I love you and I have no life without you. Don't worry about me."

He stopped and the waitress brought their dinner. He took a bite but she couldn't. He reached out, caressed her face and run his fingers through her hair. "Linda, stop crying. Most likely you don't have the virus. Be careful handling Spencer and you're going to be all right."

She ate a few forkfuls. That made her feel better and she told Percy. "See this is your muse, the one you put so high on the pedestal."

"I know and that's why I put you on the pedestal. But the question remains what are we going to with Spencer?"

"What do you mean?"

"How long do you want to stay with him?"

"Percy. I can't leave him. I took a marriage oath. I can't abandon him when he is sick."

"I admire your commitment and integrity but it hurts me. I know all about your commitment but nevertheless I would like to leave with you right now, rent a room here and disappear tomorrow morning, together and forever.

"Percy, you said that you would wait for me until I'm ready. Please be patient. He is very sick, he will not live for long, then I'll be free and I'll be yours. I'll marry you and we'll stay man and wife for the rest of our lives."

"Yes, I know. But it is so hard. I'm so much worried about you. He beats you, you're working all the time taking care of him, he abuses you and there is always a chance he'll infect you. And you don't even love him. You never did."

"He will die soon."

"He would die sooner if you didn't take such a good care of him."

"Percy, don't say such a thing. That would be murder. I couldn't do that. I'll do my best to keep him alive."

"That's a noble but very daunting pledge."

"Yes. And I need your help to fulfill it."

"How?"

"I'll hire you as a full time help. You'll have to take care of everything outside of the house. You'll have to help me sometimes with him, move him out of his bed and clean his room, anything that requires strength. I'm afraid to go alone inside his room. He is very unpredictable and his moods change so fast that sometimes I have no time to escape his wrath."

"Do you think that my presence would calm him down?"

"Not really, but under the circumstances that is the best what we can do to stay close to each other and still not accused of abandoning or murdering him."

"I'll do it for you. Not for him."

"Good, I'll pay you a salary. Minimum wage though."

Percy smiled. He almost finished his mahi-mahi fish-platter. *Wonderful,* he thought, *after all I am going to be together with her and that's the best news I could have ever heard.*

He answered jokingly, "I didn't know you had money."

"Yes, I have. I have all his money in joint accounts and I handle his accounts, his mind is too far-gone to do numbers and bills. And I have joint ownership of the house and the car."

"That's not bad." He said facetiously.

"That's true. He did that for me and I promised to take good care of him until he dies. I cannot rush his death. Honestly. Be happy to be my groundskeeper."

It was getting near closing time. The country maiden brought their check. Percy reached for it and wanted to pick up the bill but Linda took it away and said. "Let me pay for this, Mr. Groundskeeper, this is your sign on bonus from the Shrewsbury estate."

Percy let the check go and as she took out her credit card he couldn't resist the opportunity. "They have very nice rooms with private baths here. We could take one and enjoy breakfast in bed."

She smiled bashfully and reproached him. "Good try, Mr. Grimsby. But no thank you. No sex means, no sex. We must observe abstinence until the situation settles down. I have to be there in the morning when Spencer wakes up. Report for duty tomorrow at nine, my lawn needs to be raked and cut. Start helping me out with my household routines and chores."

"Routines, chores and what other needs?" Never willing to give up he cast a double meaning smirk at her.

Chapter Twenty-Six

Sclafani had respect for the dead. He directed his rage against the living if they had crossed him, betrayed him or couldn't pay their debts. Out of that reverence, deeply seated in his early childhood religious upbringing, he waited not less than four months before packing up his family and belongings and they moved, en masse, into Pamela Leicester's house, next door to Linda and Spencer.

The oversized moving van, freshly arriving in from the Bronx, backed up against the front door and four muscle-bound movers labored for hours, until after darkness fell. They brought in over hundred boxes and expensive although not exactly elegant furniture, reflecting his wife rather trashy than refined taste.

Sclafani didn't bother to show up for the moving, he trusted his wife as the best homemaker there ever was and excused himself on the account of an Atlantic City business trip where he sought out and met new high roller gamblers, checked their social and financial status and arranged for large, approved on the spot loans for the wealthy ones.

His wife, Luisa was in her late thirties; she looked like and acted like a fattened, colorful cockatoo. Tied up in a beehive her dark hair towered at least eighteen inches high on the top of her head. She had more than abundant greasy makeup covering her face and her body shape compared to a doubled up question mark with bulging breast, wide hips and enormously protruding derriere. Her feminine qualities made her extremely proud and self-conscious. She loved her body and in her careless manners reflected a conceited, innately shallow attitude.

Her two boys, fifteen years old Dennis and fourteen years old Brian looked already obese but in spite of their oversized bellies and fat arses they run around with glee and, no hesitation or modesty, assumed control of the neighborhood.

When Linda went out to check the mail, a rainbow colored feminine parrot greeted her with a great, exuberant smile.

My name is Luisa," the creature blabbermouthed. "It's such a nice street. We're so happy to move here." She looked with a curious and condescending glare at Linda, "Do you live here? You are an au pair, right?" Glancing at the name on a large envelope she continued, "For the Shrewsburies."

Linda didn't want to start the neighborly relationship with regrettable repartee and discordant exchange of misunderstandings. She had no intentions to make an issue out of a perhaps unintended insult.

"Thank you for the compliment," she smiled with friendly sociability, "but I'm Mrs. Linda Shrewsbury."

"Oh," she paused dumbfounded. "Sorry sweetie, you looked so young. I thought, never mind my manners. This moving is so bothersome and my husband is terribly busy with his business and these two boys, they don't let me have a moment for myself. My name is Luisa. But I already told you that, right?"

"Call me Linda. It's a pleasure of meeting you. Welcome to the neighborhood."

By now the two boys noticed their mother talking to Linda and, nosy and questing like two young hunting and gathering baboons on the dry plateaus of Ethiopia, they approached.

Mrs. Sclafani kept up her chattering. Loud and mindless she introduced her boys with an avalanche of verbal incontinence. "This is Dennis and that one is Brian. They are my two little angels, the hopes of our future and the pride of their father. They are such a good boys. I wouldn't give them up for the world. Come on boys, meet Linda from next door."

Prime examples of impertinent adolescent male intrusiveness, the two good boys, getting impertinently too close, approached Linda. They noted her young age; her sexy and delicately feminine figure, her pretty face and they saw a subject for their lecherous fantasies and an easy target for their practical jokes. For now they just stared at her with bold arrogance and rude curiosity.

Linda, irritated by their intruding insolence, tried to maintain her distance and dignity.

She reiterated, "Mrs. Shrewsbury. My name is Mrs. Shrewsbury."

The boys' audacity had no limits. They snapped back. "Ok. Mrs. Shrewsbury, if you insist." Laughing irreverently, the boys insolently exchanged doubled up furtive winks.

"Will see you around," they declared and thanks for merciful providence dashed off to play.

In a safe distance, out of sight and hearing distance they burst out in a boisterous guffaw. "Have you seen her?"

"What a sexy broad. I wish I would have her email address."

"I bet she could teach us a thing or two."

"Do you want to make out with her?"

"Anytime, and I will. Have you seen the way she looked at me?"

"Serious?"

"Do you want a bet? Ten bucks that within three months I plug her."

"You are on, Dennis. Three months from now."

"First I am getting her telephone number."

"Are you going to talk to her?"

"Yes. I'm going to ask her if we can have a date. I'm going to play with my dick and she is going to listen to me and she is going to play with herself. Just wait."

"Ask her to send us naked pictures of herself. I'm sure her husband takes nude pictures of her."

"That's enough of her, Brian. Let's play stickball in the cul-de-sac."

October soon came to its end. The days became shorter and with daylight savings time ending, it turned dark around five o'clock. Halloween fell on a Saturday, a spooky day, made gloomy with overcast skies, drizzling rain and with the falling leaves covering blacktop and lawns. Large groups of cheery children dressed up in fanciful customs and in the evening went from door to door, collected candy and threatened with tricks if not treated with proper respect.

Spencer didn't have a good day. He looked unusually irritable. He complained about sharp and stabbing chest pains and had chills combined with nonstop shaking. Linda forced him to eat a big bowl of hot chicken soup, gave him an extra aspirin and wanted him to stay in bed. But Spencer got up in every ten minutes and always found a reason to make Linda run upstairs to his room and yelled at her when she got there.

"Where is my remote?" he hollered, "How many times I have to ask you to put it right over here on the night table."

"It's there; you threw a used paper towel on top of it."

"Why can't you stay up here with me?"

"I have things to do."

"Like what? Who is that guy in the backyard?"

"Percy. He is blowing the leaves for us and cutting the grass."

"Percy who, who is he?"

"Our groundskeeper, I told you I needed someone to help out."

Spencer's mind wandered off. He forgot about Percy in a split second. He just saw Linda standing in front of him and yelled at her. "Get me the sports section."

He acted difficult. With darkness approaching Linda wanted to stay downstairs to open the door and make sure she wasn't going to offend potential goblins, gnomes and other underage monsters. She had a big bowl of candy ready by the entrance but she didn't like keep opening the door by herself all evening and especially after dark. She decided to give Spencer his Zolpidem pill earlier. Spencer took it and he soon calmed down and fell asleep.

Linda practically begged Percy. "Could you stay with me tonight? I would feel better not to be alone and keep opening the door."

"No problem." He agreed.

"Let's sit in the living room."

Watching the door throughout the evening they listened to the street noises and waited for the doorbell to ring.

The house sounded silent. They dimmed the lights inside and Linda turned on the entrance door lights outside. There was enough light outdoors, and with both pupils dilated wide, she could see in the dark, not far just passed the front, half way onto the driveway. Kids came and left, first little ones with parents, later on older ones in groups, and by ten o'clock all Halloween activity seemed winding down to a quiet end.

Linda and Percy stayed sitting, haven't talked too much and behaved like a married couple having a nice tranquil late fall evening in their own home.

At ten thirty, the doorbell rang again.

Linda stood up. Cautiously, Percy followed a step behind. They saw two shades outside, two young adolescent boys dressed up in dark suits, wearing dark glasses and looking like Jake and Elwood. They opened the door, first just smiling but when they saw their faces painted with dripping black streaks and noticed the funny hats, they burst into laughs and gave their remaining candy bars to the late visitors. Linda and Percy laughed, jeered, perhaps a notch too laud but had no malice or intent to mock and or denigrate the pair. They didn't recognize the late night callers, their new neighbor's sons, Dennis and Brian.

They were happy that Halloween night came to its end. It was a relaxing night with no trouble yet. Soon they kissed good-bye. Percy went home to his father's basement and Linda went upstairs to her bedroom with a street front dormer window.

She fell asleep and hours later she woke up to thumping sounds hitting against her wall and eggs cracking up and splashing all over her window. She jumped up and saw the two Sclafani boys taking eggs out from cartoons and aiming at her house.

She jerked the window open and yelled out. "I see you son of a bitches. I know who you are and I'll make you pay for the cleanup."

They saw her, leaning out in her lacey night slip they saw her exposed round shoulders shining in the rising moonlight, and they saw her long bronze hair cascading down and reaching her breasts. They saw the attractive female and they yelled back with impertinent teenage horniness.

"Come on out, slut and give us a blow job."

Frightened and shaking with sudden alarm she shut the window. But she couldn't shut it fast enough not hearing them again.

"Send us pictures, nympho. We want to see you your pussy." And pulling their zippers down, they waggled their erect penises with vigorous zeal.

Linda closed the venetian blinds and wished if she knew where Spencer's gun was. But he never showed it to her and she wouldn't have known how to use it.

The boys stood around for few more minutes and when they saw no more movements inside they left.

"Do you think she knows who we are?" Denis asked.

"I sure hope so." Brian answered.

"Is she going to go to the police?"

"No way, we were just getting acquainted. Come on, now that she knows how big dicks we have, she can't resist us any more."

Chapter Twenty-Seven

Next day was Monday. In the morning, at first chance, Linda called Sean Doherty and complained about the nighttime incident. Sean expressed his regrets and promised to send out a patrol car to investigate.

Soon a pair of officers arrived, the man stayed outside, searched around for clues, took pictures of the egg stained walls while his partner, an attractive young policewoman in full regalia, a gun holster dangling on her hips, fingers caressing a billy club, a crackling two way radio and a can of Mace, knocked on the door and when Linda opened it took out a writing pad and began interviewing Linda.

"I'm Officer Francis Dubois, Your name, please."

"Linda Shrewsbury."

"Do you live here?"

"Yes."

"What time had the reported incident occurred?"

"Around four o'clock at night."

"What did the alleged perpetrators exactly do?"

"They were throwing eggs at my house."

The officer smiled condescendingly and said. "It was Halloween Eve and we had many similar problems that went unreported throughout the night."

"But not like this one."

"Why. What makes this one different?"

"I opened my window, leaned out and yelled at them."

"So, I don't see anything special about that, was there something else?"

"They flashed me."

"Doing what?"

"They took their thing out."

"They took what thing out; please be more specific. This is why I'm interviewing you and not my partner."

Linda didn't like this policewoman. She was pretentious and coldly keeping her distance. Linda struggled telling her the details of the nighttime indecency. But she had to go on. "They took out their penises." She blurted out angrily.

"And what?"

"They were shaking their dicks at me. Is that specific enough for you?"

"Madam, I'm just doing my job. You called us. What did you do?"

"I got scared. They yelled obscenities at me."

"Be exact. What did they say?"

"I don't remember exactly. I shut my window and closed the venetian blinds."

"Do you know who they were?"

"I think so, the two boys next door."

"I see. But you are not sure. Are you?"

"No, I'm not. It was dark and they were far away."

"Then how did you see what they were doing?"

"I didn't see their faces but I saw clearly what they were doing."

"I see. How old are these boys?"

"Early teens."

"Juveniles."

"Maybe so, but at any rate we should go next door and talk to their parents."

"Leave that to us. Please stay inside your house and we'll talk to them. We'll be back."

She left and with her partner they rang the doorbell at the Sclafani house.

Sal Sclafani opened the door and with a wide gracious smile welcomed the two officers. "How can I be any help to Darien's finest?"

"We have received a complaint that your sons threw eggs at houses last night, used obscene languages and exposed their private parts."

"Them? They were sleeping at home in their beds all night long."

"How can you be so sure of that?"

Sclafani knew his boys were out last night. He saw them coming in shortly after four o'clock. He also noticed the missing egg crates from the refrigerator.

Deep inside in his psyche Sal Sclafani profoundly despised police or law enforcement but on the surface he was and always has been an outstanding benefactor of the local patrolmen benevolent association. He generously contributed to the different funds and always had stickers on his cars attesting to that fact. Supportive of her husband, Luisa came up behind him, put her chin on his shoulder and folded her arms around his belly.

Reinforced with the support of his mate, he repeated with conviction.

"As I said, but let me repeat it one more time. They were soundly sleeping in their beds."

"Can we talk to them?" The policeman asked.

"They are in school. But talk to us. They are underage juveniles anyway."

"How old?"

"Fifteen and fourteen."

"I see. How can you be so sure that they were not out earlier last night?"

Sclafani forced on his best smile, a broad and gummy grin that was more deceptive than convincing, and said charmingly. "My business makes me work long hours, sometimes way into the night. Last night I left my house just around eleven and I checked upon my boys or say good night if they were still up. I found them already sleeping in their beds, both of them. I came back at four; they were still sleeping like two babies."

Offering backup and giving weight to his words, Mrs. Sclafani grimaced, raised two of her pudgy fingers and nodded a heavy yes. *The truth, so help us God.*

The young officer flicked a doubtful glance at both and continued. "Can we look at their room?"

"Come on, please." Sclafani protested indignantly. "No. Haven't you heard me? They were home and sleeping. I'm sorry. We have things to do. Is there anything else we can do for you two or is that it?"

Francis looked at his partner. "You've heard them," she said, "they checked on them at eleven and at four. How many times do you expect a parent to peek into the rom of two teenage boys? Accept the fact, they were home."

Francis thought she had enough proof of the Sclafani boys' non-involvement. She figured their father couldn't possibly have known the time of the incident and he did not lie to protect his sons. He appeared to be a hard working decent guy and a true, law abiding, model citizen. Anyway she didn't like Mrs. Shrewsbury. She never liked redheads with long hairs and greenish-blue eyes. She was causing trouble and unnecessary work to the police. She shouldn't have opened her window at night and leaned out in her pajamas. She was asking for whatever she received.

"Thank you sir, madam, we're sorry for the inconvenience, thank you for your help," Officer Francis nodded to each and walked back with her partner, slowly, a demonstration of authoritative dignity, to Linda's house.

The patrolman told Linda. "Mr. Shrewsbury. The two boys from next were not involved in the last night incident."

"But, I thought…"

Officer Francis cut Linda short. "Next time, please, be more observant and perhaps take pictures if you are accusing anybody of offending or trespassing."

Sclafani asked his wife, Luisa. "Who in the hell is trying to incriminate us? What's the matter with this people already?"

"I think it was the bimbo, next door."

"Who the fuck she thinks she is? How does she look like? I've never seen her yet."

"You are not missing anything. She is a recluse. Very rarely comes out of her house. She is either timid or stupid, maybe both."

"Sounds like a real winner. She is going to have fun with my boys. They will practice their pranks on her all right."

Few days later Linda had to run an early morning errand. As she drove by the school bus stop, she saw the two Sclafani boys standing and watching her to let the cross traffic pass.

Their eyes met for a second and Linda saw their lips move. "We're going to get you and will rape you, you bitch."

Later in the day Linda asked Spencer, "Spencer, you have a gun, don't you?"

"Yes I do. What do you want with it?"

"Sometimes I afraid of being alone in this house, you know you're being deep asleep and I would feel better if I knew where it was."

"Ok. It's on the top of the dining room china cabinet. Get the stepping ladder, reach in and you'll find it. It's in a shoebox behind the front molding."

Linda went, got the gun and, leaving it inside the box took the weapon to Spencer. It was a Beretta P38 automatic pistol, a sleek masterpiece indeed. Spencer checked the magazine and noted with satisfaction that it was fully loaded with six bullets.

He caressed the cold metal and looked at it with gentle love and care.

"My good friend," he whispered, "it had been with me in the Gulf war. The best weapon I've ever had."

"Have you ever killed anyone with it?"

"At one time two insurgents attacked our base, they were from the local helps hired by the air force to work for us inside the base. They stormed into my tent and yelled, "*Allah Akbar! La illa il Allah. Asadu ana.*" They were so frigging busy yelling that I shot both in a jiffy. I didn't even have to reload. My Beretta was so accurate and fast that I could got them both before they got me."

"Gee," she exclaimed in admiration but shuddered, the frightening story gave her the chills.

Spencer aimed the gun at the door and said. "Bang, bang-bang. I want to have it with me all the time. I'll clean it and make sure it's in good working order."

"Where are you going to keep it?"

"Under my pillow, it's going to be a better cure than all the medicines they pushing on me. It will cure me for sure. Thanks, sweetie for reminding me of my forgotten friend."

Spencer looked happy, he thoroughly cleaned and oiled the gun and Linda; at least she knew where he kept the firearm in case she needed protection.

It only occurred to her much later that she had given a weapon to a person having a mind deteriorating with advanced dementia and if anything had happened, if Spencer killed somebody with that revolver, the law could have looked at her as an accessory to murder.

Chapter Twenty-Eight

Thanksgiving passed and came Christmas. Spencer had a difficult time to handle winter. He contracted pneumonia, spent a week in the Stamford hospital but had gotten better and insisted on returning to his house and his wife.

Linda maintained a busy schedule. She kept the house in order, made sure Spencer rested comfortable and gave him his medicines on time and exactly as prescribed. She had him getting up from bed and forced him walking around to maintain his muscle tensions. She washed his pajamas and made sure his bed sheets and towels were clean.

Spencer became accustomed seeing Percy around. He couldn't detect signs of an ongoing affair or even an intimate, nonphysical attraction between Percy and his wife. Spencer developed a profound respect for Linda, he saw how hard she tried to provide a secure home and how honestly she intended to make Spencer's sickness more bearable for all involved.

Percy helped Linda to set up the Christmas tree. Together they bought a freshly cut tree at the Weston Tree Farm. On his father's pick up truck he took home the handsome spruce for her and mounted it in the living room.

Linda took out Spencer's mother Christmas ornaments, decorated the tree and Percy hung the outdoor lights. The cheerful embellishments turned the house from gloomy dark to bright and festive. The sparkling and colorful lights, twinkling silently on frosty nights, made even the coldest the wintry scene majestic and heart warming.

The day before Christmas Percy brought over his mother, Rosemary's old world cooking book and showed Linda how to make the traditional Hungarian Christmas walnut and poppy seed strudel. It came out excellent and even Spencer enjoyed having a freshly baked big piece of it.

For Christmas evening dinner Linda grilled salmon steak with baked potatoes and vegetable garnishes. Percy bought a half a gallon bottle of fine, semi sweet Chablis and the three together enjoyed drinking it. Only Spencer had one too many and became obnoxious.

He raised his goblet and looked at Percy, "Percy, my boy. I thought for a while that you were in love with my wife."

Percy had a few drinks in him too but he remembered the promise he made to Linda and retained his common sense. He loved her more than to get her into trouble. He knew that Linda and Spencer haven't been practicing marital intimacy. Percy loved Linda without physical contact and they knew they loved each other forever and without need to talk about it.

He raised his silver chalice to Spencer and complemented. "Spencer, your wife is a saint. And who wouldn't love a saint. Look the way she is taking care of you. She hired me to help out around the house, when nobody wanted to hire me because I was in jail."

"Yeah, that figures. I wonder why she did that." Spencer mumbled and tried to overcome his growing inebriation. Suddenly he slammed the table with his fist. "I love her. You can't love her. I forbid you to love her."

Linda cut in, "Come on guys. It's Christmas. Let's have peace and love in our hearts." She went to the kitchen and got Spencer's sleeping pill. Came back, filled up a tall glass with water and demanded. "Take it."

Spencer pushed her hand away. "Not yet. I'm just getting into the good mood here."

He turned to Percy. "How come you are not with your family on Christmas night?"

"You two are my family. I live in my parents' basement and they no longer consider me part of their family. Linda helped me to get out of jail. Not them."

Percy said that, trying to help, but Linda wished he didn't. Linda remembered the severe beating she received from Spencer for getting involved. *Oh God,* she thought, *not on Christmas night. Not after all the work and effort I put into this to have a peaceful Christmas with the people closest to me.*

Spencer didn't miss Percy's blunder. He stood up, wobbled sideways and yelled contentiously, "I don't remember adopting you."

But his weak knees gave out. He couldn't stand straight without holding onto something. Dizzy and lightheaded, he staggered out of balance. Instead of fighting Percy and Linda, he needed their help just to stay on his feet. Resting on Percy's holding hand; Spencer looked at Linda with hate. Dementia destroying his mind, he couldn't appreciate Christmas and the time for peace. He thought, Linda, the devil's sorceress attacked him and he raised his arm to strike her.

Percy saw the move and let Spencer go. He lost his balance and fell between the dining room and the living room. He hit the floor like a sack of coal. Face down, he spit up bloody saliva, coughed and with awful spasms kept kicking his catatonic feet.

Linda put on rubber gloves, wiped Spencer's face with a paper napkin and soothed him with no anger in her voice. "Spencer, dear, you need to rest. Let's go upstairs to you room, take your medication and come down when you feel better."

Percy helped Linda to push Spencer up on the stairs. He got into his bed and willingly took his medications including the sleeping pill. In ten minutes the powerful chemical knocked him out and, like a giant baby, he slept peacefully. Except, instead having his favorite teddy bear with him, he cuddled his loaded gun under the pillow that he embraced for security and assurance.

Providence having moved Spencer out of the way, Linda and Percy stayed alone in the living room, just the two of them on Holly Christmas Night, a place and time for wonderful happenings.

An ice crackling bitterly cold night, true peace descending from above, a thick blanket of freshly fallen snow covered lawns, streets, roofs and tree branches with crisp, fluffy flakes. A cold northern wind blew in and piled the dry, downy drifts into six-foot snow walls in front of entrances and garage doors. Blocking exits and access, the winter locked the young lovers inside.

Percy adjusted the fireplace, sturdy maple logs burnt anew and next to one another in cozy comfort they sat on the sofa. Wide eyes of wondering souls, they stared into the flickering flames. The wind chimes twinkled on the porch and neither sounds of cars nor any alien signs of outside life disturbed the stillness of their magical micro universe.

The heat radiating from the burning wood reddened their faces. They sipped more sweet wine, attracted and irrevocably in love, their bodies, as if electrified magnets of opposing poles, inched closer and touched.

Overwhelmed by awe and not moving his eyes away from the blazing embers, Percy's trembling fingers caressed Linda face and he whispered to her, "Linda, can I play a song for you on the piano?"

With her skin too hot to touch and face looking feverish, the dancing flames reflected back and transformed her tired and overworked being into a young and mysterious gypsy woman sitting at the ancient bonfire of her tribe.

Softly whispering she leaned so close he could feel the soothing whiff of her breath. "I didn't know you could play."

Percy pulled her closer; their bodies touched and the energy from the fire warmed their blood. The magical rays penetrated deep inside and set ablaze the center of their cores that, as preordained to love they waited for their romance to unfold.

"I know enough to play this one, for you, and only for you."

"Sure, if you want to. I want you to play a song for me."

"I want to play and sing my heart out. I have to tell you how I feel. Words alone would be too weak and ineffective to tell you how much I love you."

"What kind of song is it?"

"It's an old, very old, I mean very old Hungarian love song."

"Where did you learn it?"

"From my dear grandmother, whom I loved awfully much."

They went to the piano, to Spencer's mother classical Baldwin upright. Ready and willing to convey joy under expert hands, the instrument stood against the wall in the living room. Linda had it recently tuned and it had beautiful quality and mellow sounding tone.

Percy sat down on the piano chair, opened the cover and run his fingers across the keyboard. First he ran a couple of F minor scales and he hit F minor cords and inversions and played softly the first two bars of an old melancholic, andante rhythm song. He had a pleasant, well-practiced tenor and he sang with passion and true yearning and expressing the sorrow of the unfulfilled love tormenting his heart.

There is frost on earth, freezing snow and ice,
There in secrecy, I search for your eyes,
There are no flowers, no songs from my lips,
It is forbidden, loving you and kiss,

Linda listened and smiled, the enchanting pleasure of the dreamy melody encompassed her soul and pearls of glistening tears moistened her eyes. She knew what Percy was singing about. How could he have found such a perfect song and such a perfectly befitting tune that reached the bottom of her tormented soul and touched the extremes of her affection starved heart? She listened and Percy continued with the second verse.

There be bright sunshine, balmy gentle breeze,
There be soul and heart, joyfully to please,
There be happiness, dancing day and night,
Then, my dear sweetheart, we will love and unite.

He sang with hope and trust in heavenly providence. His voice wavered with emotions and his heart constricted with longing and desire. Linda came closer, he turned his face to her and she kissed his lips. Her lips were wet from the wine and she pressed them hard on his. He let his lips slid apart and she pushed her sweet tongue deep inside his mouth. As they embraced an inferno of passionate lust exploded inside them. He rolled around his piano chair to face her and she lowered herself onto his lap. She pushed his back against the Baldwin, lifted her legs across and straddled above his throbbing groins. Her red jersey dress pulled up high and revealed her upper thighs; she pushed her bottom down and his strong erection pushed into her panties across all layers of clothing still separating them.

She wiggled and he inched further and deeper inside. With her mouth fully open she sucked his lips and let his tongue entangle and explore the taste of hers. There was no way of stopping the volcano forced to erupt by pressures compelled to build up by suppressed months of secret longings and aching desires.

He pushed and pulled and pressed harder against her and she moaned with forbidden delight.

Desperately lost in her emotion she begged him. "Percy my love, please stop, we can't do this, not yet at least. It's wrong and I can't stop unless you force me to stop. Please don't do it. I want you and I want you with all my desperate and fiery passion."

Percy implored to her. "Linda, please have mercy on me, don't ask me to stop. I can't. I must have you."

She kept kissing him, wiggled her bottom in little circles and pushed it up and down in her tortured lover's burning lap. "I shouldn't have kissed you. Why did you have to play that song? That made me to do it. I haven't yet got back results from my second test. I could be dangerous, deadly dangerous. We must wait until we are sure. Now we've been careless. You must have a test too. This is a terrible torment. Why do you have to love somebody who is married to an AIDS patient? Oh God, what a punishment, what a price to pay, and for what. What have we done to deserve this agony?"

He stopped kissing her and relaxed his trusting hips. He only caressed her face and rubbed his face into her hair. "Linda. I told you. I love you. Calm down. You are not HIV positive and even if you were I would still love you."

"You can't possibly mean that."

"I mean it. And I'll wait for you until you will be mine. There has to be a God who will reward us for our honesty and innocence."

She slid out from his lap and stood in front of him. He reached out and hugged her wide hips and sexy derriere; he buried his face into her bosoms and inhaled her feminine fragrance and youthfully sweaty smell. She caressed his sad and sorrow head, grasped his neck and playfully, spreading them wide, run her fingers on his shoulders. "Thank you, Percy. I promise I'll be yours. And from that day on it will be just the two of us, against the whole world. I promise."

"When?"

"Soon, with God's willing, soon."

The hour of midnight passed. Icicles and big puffs of fresh snow broke off from tree limbs and fell down with ethereal, unearthly sounds. The infant messiah swept across the wintry universe and had arrived promising salvation and forgiveness to sinners and righteous saints alike. He brought new hope that God wouldn't let his people to be possessed by evil powers. To liberate them, his son was willing to suffer for their sins and free them from their predicaments and let them fulfill their God sanctioned true destiny and make good use of their God given talents and strengths.

The snow made it impossible to leave the house. Percy slept on the living room sofa and Linda went up to her room upstairs. She locked her door, undressed and naked; and she kneeled down by the side of her bed. Her long hair covered her shoulders and barren back; her round buttocks shone in the bright moonlight. She bowed her head; put her hands together in pray and let her blessed and healthy hormones rip her body apart. The torture of unfulfilled desires, her raging passion, the yearning of her young womb shuddered with erotic hunger to conceive. She let her life force punish her with vengeance for denying herself the most fundamental and life-sustaining urge to procreate and multiply.

It would have been phony for her to try conventional prayers, especially not on Christmas night. She had to tell God what burdened her heart and she had to plead Him for salvation through Him and by Him.

"Oh God, let me follow my destiny. I'm not a saint, I was never meant to be a virgin. Don't turn me into a nun. I thank you for the holly passion you blessed me with. I thank you for the desire and the lust I feel inside of me. Please don't let my longing burn out before I can fulfill my destiny. Let me love be my lover without sinning, without any evil threatening me with punishment and sickness. I promise I'll use my burning desire for a good cause and I'll not waste it on promiscuous carnal fornications. Thank you for the true love of Percy and let me fulfill it for him and for me please."

She slid under the bed sheets and slept late next morning. By ten o'clock, when she finally woke up Percy already shoveled most of the snow away from the front door and cut a path to the street. Linda made fresh coffee and the three together had the delicious Hungarian pastry for breakfast.

Later they opened up the Christmas gifts. Percy gave Linda a bottle of Pure Poison by Christian Dior and twenty inches long, wide and heavy, gold Byzantine style necklace. She gave him a warm and fashionable ski parka from the Darien Sportshop. Percy gave Spencer a bottle of Chivas Regal and Linda gave him a brand new, 42" plasma TV. Spencer gave nothing to Percy but gave Linda a one carat diamond white gold solitaire ring and a one carat cluster diamond bracelet from her mother's collection as he couldn't go out and Christmas shop on his own.

Promising a new and hopeful beginning Christmas day stayed crisply cold and cleanly beautiful. Peace prevailed in Darien as the Sclafani family was spending the holidays on Marco Island, Florida in their plush vacation condominium.

Chapter Twenty-Nine

Months passed and warm spring days brought nature back to life. Laden with drooping bell-shaped white flowers and sending sweet fragrance along the old crumbling stonewall on the front, the Lilly of the Valley patch emerged from the ground. Pristinely white flowers, clustered on hundreds of green stems, grew anew and covered the decaying dry leaves of yesteryear. Colorful crocuses, daffodils and tulips, multiplying in densely crowded assemblages spread across vast patches of the emerald, springtime lawn. The days lasted long again and people no longer put on heavy boots and did not need bulky overcoats. Benevolent downpours washed away most winter dirt and the town sweeping truck sucked up the rest. Gravel dumped in winter on snow and ice that accumulated for months along street gutters and edges of street side properties, disappeared as if it were never there.

Huge maple trees flowered and dropped bushels and bushels of reddish flowers and filled up the air with abundant pollen promising rejuvenating growth for old, gnarled branches and young saplings alike.

On this colorful carpet of red flowers and yellow pollen covering the pavement and the grass and under the brightly green, freshly sprung leaves, life came back to Red Rose Circle. Children played on the lawns, bicycled on the streets and their tinkling voices filled up the air with youthful joy and sweet chimes of careless play.

The Sclafani boys, Dennis and Brian, came out and rode their bicycles around the neighborhood. They had no inclination to bury themselves indoors with books and homework, they didn't need to study, their father never did, and they had strong intentions to follow his footsteps.

Few days into their wild frolicking they ran out things to do and from places to go. On purpose maybe, but mostly subconsciously they stopped more and more frequently and for longer and longer periods at the end of Linda's driveway. They looked at each other and remembered her temptingly enticing feminine forms.

"Have you seen her lately?" Brian asked.

"No," Dennis guffawed, "I think she's afraid to come out."

"Afraid of coming out and showing us her boobs again."

"Maybe we should make her to come out." Dennis suggested and opening Linda's mailbox he looked inside.

"I bet she can't wait to renew our acquaintances."

"Let's get her out here," Dennis continued and slammed shut the thin metal door. Then casting a lustful glance at her window he finished his line of thought. "As if by mistake I'll rub my hand against her ass and you watch how she reacts."

But Linda didn't come out. She saw the boys playing around her mailbox but remembered how little of a help the police was and she chose doing nothing. Flustered and helpless she only stared in their direction.

She saw Brian twisting and trying to break her mailbox and she decided not to confront him. Perhaps the boys saw her silhouette behind the living room window curtain for, trying to get her attention, they became bold and obnoxious.

Dennis opened the mailbox again, took out her mail and read the name on it. "Linda Shrewsbury. Ha. I'll bet she is stupid enough to be in the phone book. I'm going to give her a call."

Later in the evening, past 10 o'clock, the phone rang. Already asleep, Spencer wheezed heavily and tried hard to get enough oxygen into his infections ravaged lungs. To avoid waking him up, Linda grabbed the phone.

Although annoyed at the late caller she kept her calm and talked into the receiver with a hushed down voice. "Hello."

"Hi."

She kept silent and she heard the heavy breathing at the other end.

"Who is this?" She asked cautiously.

"Do you know what I am doing?"

Surprised and not understanding she forgot to slam down the phone.

The caller thought she was giving him a chance and continued.

"I'm playing with my dick. What are you doing?"

Alone with her sick husband in the big house she panicked

and fear froze her voice. As Linda stayed silent the caller continued. "It's really big and thick, just the way you love to suck on it."

She came back to her senses and yelled at him with anger. "I know who you are and I'm going to get you."

"Yeah, come on and get me. Come on over and show me the pink inner folds of your juicy pussy. I want to fuck your brains out. I know you're not getting any and you have the hots for me."

Linda had enough. She recovered from her immobility and fright. And anger making her enraged she slammed down the phone. The phone rang again. She picked up and it was the same caller. She pushed the pin down and disconnected the call. She waited until she heard the dial tone again and left the receiver off the hook. It made terrible noises for annoying seconds but soon enough the phone company gave up and the line began sending constant busy signals to the late night caller trying persistently to call her over and over again.

She tried to guess who the caller might have been. It must have been one of the Sclafani boys next door. She looked at her caller identification screen but the display indicated unknown caller. Linda called up information and asked for the Sclafani's number. But she couldn't get it. They had an unlisted number.

Next day she called the phone company and tried to make a complaint. But the official in charge told her that the phone company couldn't do anything except give her a new and unlisted number. She did that and the obscene calls stopped. But she couldn't shake her well-founded suspicion that the Sclafani boys next door were after her. She anticipated trouble and that scared her but didn't want to get Percy involved. He would have been so overprotective that he would have done something to the boys and went back to jail right away. She didn't want to get Percy into trouble. He suffered enough as is.

She needed to handle it on her own. Thought about the gun and contemplated the possibilities to shoot the two boys and her chances of getting away with it.

Dennis' sixteenth birthday approached. Already six feet tall he weighed two hundred and twenty pounds. His blood testosterone content reached dangerous levels and he couldn't think about anything but sex. He constantly browsed the Internet for explicit sexual pictures, for all kinds, but preferred most of all, bondage and torture. His younger brother, not yet fifteen yet, was a few inches shorter, but being a better fast food junkie he weighed about the same. He developed the same Internet browsing habits and they overdid each other planning and bragging about what they would do if a real female came their way.

They had massive erections, nonstop, day and night. They constantly talked about raw erotica and the object of their dirty fantasies was Linda, their young and delicately feminine and vulnerable next-door neighbor.

On Red Rose Circle, houses had large properties and were widely separated and made private by dense and abundantly planted shrubbery and trees. Under normal circumstances it was safe and prudent for any attractive female to sunbathe in any style, small and provocative bikini or maybe topless and perhaps completely in the nude.

Linda loved to sunbathe, she liked the late May sun caressing her with warmth. She loved to stretch out on a lounge chair and tried to get the full effect of the invigorating rays. A double row of dense hemlocks separated her back porch from three sides from anything nearby and there was no way to see in unless someone hid in the bushes and shamelessly peeped in.

After lunch she came out in her white bathing robe. First she sat down and opened the front, letting the sides fall down showing her tiny bikini to the birds in the sky and to the squirrels on the trees. Feeling too warm she removed the robe and lay down on her back. The gently cooling breeze, showering her with millions of impregnating pollen particles, seemed to have mistaken her for a flowerbed and landed on her in abundance.

In the quiet afternoon she heard nobody, only the birds chirped and tree branches swung to and fro and provided soothing, silent serenity. Safe and alone she unbuttoned her top and let her round apples be massaged by the warm rays and let her large and erect nipples be kissed by the gaily playful swirls of the springtime air.

Later she checked around, saw nobody and removed her bottom. She spread her legs slightly apart and with amorous wind puffs drying the wetness and sweat off her pubis, she enjoyed the exciting sensation of being licked by ethereal and invisible fairies gathering and dancing all around her nudity. She dreamily revered that this sunbathing felt far more enjoyable than any kind of sex she knew, except of course the forbidden sex with Percy that she never forgot and so often longed to have again.

First Dennis made the discovery that Linda sunbathed outside. He climbed into the bushes, hid cautiously and enjoyed what he saw. He played with himself until his fist cramped. Then called Brian over and showed him what he found, the subject of their fantasies, their naked neighbor. They sneaked back to the bushes and watched her with hearts pounding wildly in their throats. Their excitement and desire reached near eruption levels and in anticipation they hyperventilated and arousal vibrated in their voices. They were ready for the fun, for the kind they so much wished to have.

First Brian formulated the idea. "Let's get her."

Equally willing and ready to go forward, Dennis seconded his brother's suggestion. "Yeah, let's get her into our basement. Maybe, at first she will play hard to get, but later on she is going to enjoy what we're going to do to her. The two of us, remember all those sites on the Internet, two bulky guys and one tiny woman."

"How are we going to do it, Dennis?"

"We have to sneak upon her. I grab her head and I'll keep her mouth shut. You hold onto her legs. Make sure you don't let it go otherwise she is going to kick you in the balls."

"Then what."

"We'll take her inside and we both going to mount her finally."

"Where?"

"In the basement. Mom is not home."

"Then what. Are we going to keep her?"

"Yeah. We're going to keep her."

"How long?"

"Long enough. When he had enough of her we're going to sell her on the international sex slave market."

"Do we know anybody who buys prostitutes?"

"No, but dad does. He has contacts everywhere."

Linda has fallen asleep and woke up only to Dennis

holding her mouth with his left hand and lifting her up by his right. Reaching under her arms and squeezing her back against his chest he had a firm hold of her. Brian grabbed her feet at the knees and held them so strong that she couldn't move them an inch. They lifted her up, dragged her through a narrow path between the interwoven branches of hemlocks, and carried her into their basement.

They shut and closed the hatch door and moved her into a secret concrete block compartment built by Dwight Leicester between the boiler room and the oil storage tank vault. Using duct tape Brian wrapped Linda ankles together but didn't have enough to secure her legs to the frame. Dennis threw her down on a mattress and using oily cleaning rags tied her hands down to the headboard made of steel pipe bars.

She was naked, didn't have a piece of cloth to cover herself, she was tied up and she was in the possession of her most vicious enemies, two teenage male animals or rather much less than animal level of evil doers.

Linda screamed at the top of her lungs but Dennis hit her across the face and pasted an ugly smelling duct tape on her mouth. She hardly could breathe.

"I'm first?" Dennis said. "Watch what I'm doing, you're next."

Linda wiggled, she tried to kick in Dennis' teeth but the attempt just made the teenager angrier. He threw his weight across her legs and yelled to Brian. "Tie her legs down with something."

"With what?"

"Get some rope."

Brian ran upstairs and frantically searched the kitchen for a bundle of rope but Mrs. Sclafani came home and caught him in the act. "Brian, what are you looking for?"

"The… I don't know."

"Come on. What is it? Where is Dennis?'

"In the basement."

"Get him up here right now. I need the both of you."

Brian couldn't find the rope and he had yell down to get his brother. "Come up, Dennis. Mom just came home and she wants us to go with her to the Nielsen Nursery. She needs us to load things on the truck. We must go; otherwise she is going to be down there in a minute."

Dennis glared menacingly at Linda, "Stay put, bitch. We're coming back and we'll take care of you when we return. Don't try to escape we'll find you and we'll kill you before you can get help."

He walked up and left Linda tied down on the dirty basement mattress. Her naked butt was forced to lie on ugly old stains of unknown and dubious origin. Her lovely arms, already desecrated with contusions, scratches and bruises were in pain and stretched above her head. She only could move her hips, she threw herself up and down and from side to side but with each throw she only increased the hurt in her shoulders and made the rags cut more into her flesh.

She fought on with the fury of a captured wildcat and kept thinking: *these son of a bitch low life bastards are not going to have me. I'll kill them first.* She wriggled, moaned, kicked until became exhausted, gave up and lay still.

Chapter Thirty

Linda lay motionless until her hyperventilation subsided and her breathing returned to near normal. Her arms ached and ugly black and purple bumps and welts disfigured her delicately pinkish skin. She searched for any means to get free, a blade to cut her loose, a rusty bar in the frame that she could break. But anger blurred her judgment. She couldn't act rationally. Had only one thought: *I have to get out of here; God gave me a chance and took them away. Now it is my duty to free myself and take revenge.*

Lips pressed tight and face red with effort she tried to loosen up her arms. She squeezed her fingers, and almost breaking the bones she tried to slip out from the knot tied around her wrist. She pulled and the oil soaked material seemed to slip.

She twisted on it and the frayed bind yielded. Linda wished, she could break the old cotton cloth apart. Clenched her teeth and jerked her arms with a force she thought she never had and heard the sound of ripping material. Her right arm was free.

She quickly untied her left, tore off the duct tape from her mouth, grabbed an old greasy work shirt off a hook on the wall, put it on and ran to the basement door. Pulled the sliding lock and she was out. She ran across the shrubs, back to her porch and in a second she was back in her house.

She didn't even wash, put on a jean and a shirt and drove like mad maniac to the police station.

Detective Doherty greeted her like an old friend. "Mrs. Shrewsbury, what brings you here?"

"Those bastard from next door."

"What is it now? What is your problem with them?"

"They tried to kidnap and rape me."

"Hold it. Slow down. They did what? How do you mean?"

"I was on my back porch. They came over and dragged me to their basement."

Detective Sean Doherty's face turned somberly grave. He took out his report pad and began making notes. "Please tell me exactly what happened. What were you doing on your back porch?"

"I was sunbathing."

"Did you wear provocative bathing attire?"

"No."

"What were you wearing?"

"Nothing."

Doherty stopped making notes. He took off his glasses and

with profound suspicion scrutinized Linda's face. "Nothing, do you mean you were naked?"

"Yes, I was naked. Nobody was supposed to peep at me."

"Sorry to say," The detective paused, "Mrs. Shrewsbury, it is against the law to sunbathe in the nude if anyone else from outside can see you. Have you been teasing those boys?"

"No. Never, not even in my dreams."

"Mrs. Shrewsbury, those boys are underage. Legally if you have sex," he paused again, "I mean any kind of sex, a sexual pass, even attempted sex or lewd behavior in their presence it would be against the law. It's a severely punishable felony and you could get into a ton of trouble. If their parents find out and press charges you may spend the rest of your life in jail."

"For the love of God, I wasn't having sex with them. I hate them."

"See there is the connection. Love and hate. They are very easily interchangeable emotions."

"You are not serious."

"I'm dead serious. If I were you I would drop the charges and I would hope they don't press charges."

Obfuscated by anger and frustration Linda could have strangled this obnoxious policeman. But he was right. She shouldn't have sunbathed in the nude when she knew two teenagers lived next door and they already had made explicit sexual passes at her. She made a mistake, the predators moved in and she paid the price. There seemed no remedial action available. She trapped herself.

Doherty stood up and showing her the way out he politely advised her. "I like you very much, Mrs. Shrewsbury. You did an excellent job of implicating Dwight Leicester. It's most unfortunate that some mob connected jail justice servers killed Mr. Leicester. If he lived and cooperated he would have been a useful witness. My wife has nothing else but praises and admiration for you. She likes you with all her heart. We're worried about you. Please don't get involved with underage kids. We like you socially but I don't want to see you again inside the police station."

He showed her out and Linda drove home in utter frustration. At home she took a bath, put lotion on her bruises, covered her arms and wrists with a long sleeved blouse and went to take care of Spencer. She gave him dinner, medication and fixed up his bed. She saw the gun under Spencer's pillow and took it.

Spencer saw her taking the gun and in his weak voice called after her.

"Linda, what are you doing with my gun?"

"Let me have it. I need it. People are after me and I have to protect myself. I'll bring it back tonight. You can sleep with it. I only need it for an hour. I need to scare someone."

"Be careful. Let me show you how to use it."

His sickness ravaged and ire tormented mind turned Spencer into a manic paranoid. He liked Linda taking action, fighting back and punishing all the people who tried to destroy them. Spencer felt that everyone became his enemy and welcomed the idea that his wife planned taking out a few or teach a couple of bad ones what the Shrewsbury family was capable of. He showed her the trigger, the magazine, the bullets, taught her how to unlock the safety and how to aim. He prepared Linda to fight.

The Sclafani boys rushed to the basement at the first chance they had after helping their mother unload the spring fertilizers, bag of limes, topsoil and mulch she purchased at the Gardeners' Center Nursery on Post Road.

They couldn't find Linda. The ripped rags lay strewn around the mattress and crumpled pieces of duct tape covered the floor. The basement door stood ajar. She disappeared, gone.

"Shit. Where did she go?" Brian asked, and there was a dumbfounded surprise on his dim-witted face.

"Home, you idiot," Dennis growled at his brother. "If you had gotten the rope in time she wouldn't have escaped."

"What are we going to do?"

"Nothing, she molested us. We're underage. Remember. She sunbathed in the buff. That's lewd behavior. She was corrupting the mind of innocent minors."

"You've got to be kidding me."

"No. Don't worry about a thing. She wouldn't go to the police. She knows she started it. Anything happened afterwards is her fault."

"Lets' go out and see what she is up to."

They took their bicycles out and pedaled back and forth on the street with arrogant audacity considering the crime they just committed.

Linda saw them and she couldn't control her anger. The police betrayed her. She thought she had an ally and a friend in Detective Doherty. She thought his wife liked her and she had friends who would back her up and would stand by her when she needed support and help. She checked the Beretta, stuck it into her pants and rushed out to confront the boys.

Calmly and with ugly, offending impertinence they waited for her. Looked provocatively into her eyes and tried to intimidate her. She almost choked on her words. The cold arrogance projecting from her attackers spooked and frightened her. But she couldn't show fear. She had to go on.

"You two," she jerked the gun out and pushed the cold metal against Dennis' temple. "I'll shoot both of you, like two repulsive filthy dogs if you ever again come near me. Is that clearly understood?"

Dennis cocked his head to the side. The gun didn't frighten him. He knew Linda had no guts to pull the trigger. And he knew bloody well that she was in trouble. She not only tried to corrupt a minor, but now she threatened them to cover her own criminal tracks. Too bad, Dennis grinned like an imbecile, she will have to pay for this. But Brian looked more nervous. Swallowing his saliva nervously, his Adam's apple jolted up and down and he didn't seem to be absolutely sure of the outcome.

The boys' audacity unnerved Linda. She withdrew the gun and retreating backwards slowly moved away. Her eyes blazed with hatred. She wasn't ready to snuff out two lives but she got very close to doing it. She reached her front door, but the boys remained standing at the end of her driveway and she heard them yelling at her. "Come back to our basement, anytime, bitch."

Sal Sclafani came home around eight o'clock. He was in the good mood. Things went well. People had been paying their installments, including huge usury interest and today he didn't need to hustle anyone.

Shortly after Sal came home and settled down, Dennis approached his father. Sitting comfortably in his armchair the connected man had a glass of wine in his heavy boned, large diamond rings adored hand. Seeing the agitated fluster on his son's face the worried father asked.

"What's up Dennis?"

"Dad, the woman next door, she threatened to kill us."

"What?"

"She pulled a gun and told us that she is going shoot us like two rabid dogs."

"Why?"

"I don't know. Ask her."

"She must have had a reason."

"You know she is crazy. Remember that egg throwing incident."

"Let's talk to her. Let's find out how did she mean?"

He went out with Dennis, Brian followed and the burly father pressed Linda's doorbell button.

Spencer was asleep in his upstairs bedroom. Sitting in the living room with Percy, Linda reiterated to him the afternoon story. The doorbell rang and they saw a big towering man and two oversized adolescent boys at the front door. Linda knew who they were and guessed why they were here.

She looked at Percy. "What shall we do?"

"Give me the gun," he said, "and open the door. I'll be behind you."

She opened the door. Sal Sclafani smiled. Polite like a debt collector on a social call he greeted Linda like a true gentleman. "Mrs. Shrewsbury, there seems to be a misunderstanding between you and my boys. Would you mind us coming in and talk about it?"

Linda looked at him in astonishment. His audacity and pretentiousness had no limits. She glanced back at Percy but the young man signaled her, that letting Sclafani in was ok.

She let them in and in the well lit living room Sal had the opportunity to view Linda's face. She offered seats to the visitors and the boys, spreading their knees wide apart, sat down with impertinent, cocky assuredness.

Without hesitation Sclafani stated the purpose of his visit. "You don't mean to kill my sons, do you?"

"I'll kill them if they ever touch or bother me again."

That surprised Sclafani but he kept pressing his point. "I don't want any misunderstandings here. I want to maintain good neighborly feeling between us, after all this is Darien, the best and most peaceful place in the country, but you shouldn't threaten them like that."

While he talked he tried to remember why she looked so familiar.

She protested indignantly, "Your sons tried to rape me. They kidnapped me and tied me down. Tell them, next time I'll shoot. I'll shoot to kill. I'm not joking."

"You seem unhurt. Make sure you don't associate with minors. You leave them alone and they will leave you alone."

"Good idea. Make sure they understand that."

Sal remembered now. She was the girl from the Black Goose Restaurant. The one he chased from the dining room to the parking lot. Who wore a wire and ran to an unmarked police car. The one who caused all the trouble. The missing link. The one he searched for. Right next door. Of course. Where else? And that clown behind her. He must be the one who went to jail for the murder of Pamela. And she got him out by betraying everyone else. This whore must have found that sales receipt. She caused the death of Giacomo and Dwight. Of course, they are lovers, he thought, but he needed to double check.

With his best confidence-gaining smile he extended his

hands to Percy and asked with phony presumptuousness, "Mr. Shrewsbury?"

Percy didn't take his hands. He repulsed him. His brats hurt Linda and he would never forget or forgive. He murmured reluctantly.

"No. I do grounds and cut grass. No speak English."

"Spanish

"No, Hungarian only."

"Hungry?"

"No, Hungarian, *Magyar.*"

"Ok, whatever, I don't speak that language."

Sclafani didn't want to waste more time. He knew what he had to do. He had to take out this woman before she could point a finger and find out who her new neighbor really was. She could easily turn into a damn ratfink, she is far too curious and inquisitive, and that guy, the groundskeeper, the one pretending he doesn't speak English? If he is trying to protect her, he too will have to go.

Sclafani retreated politely. He hasn't intended to raise suspicion, as that would have interfered with his plan and would have made his task more difficult by eliminating the element of surprise. He stood up and headed to the door with his boys.

At the door he said. "I trust it is all fair and square. I'm sorry if my boys misbehaved in any way. It will not happen again."

Outside he turned to Dennis and Brian. "Leave her alone. I have an unsettled matter with her of my own. I'll take care of her. She will not threaten you two again. I promise."

They walked the remaining steps home in silence. Inside the house he castigated his sons again. "Next time you're kidnapping her, don't let her escape. Make sure she's tied down securely. That was very dumb what you did. She's liable to press charges. And you two may have to spend your teenage years in a Juvenile Correction Institute, until you're twenty-one. We have a good reason to take her out, and we have to do it tonight.

Luisa came out of the bathroom where she just put on her facial packing. Except for her eyes, the thick cream covered her face and she bore close resemblance to a dim witted green owl.

"Where have you guys been?" She asked.

"We've been making friends with our next door neighbor."

"For what, don't we have enough friends already?" She shrugged and went back to apply more makeup on her face.

Chapter Thirty-One

After Sclafani left with his overprotected brats, Linda trembled and felt very nervous.

She mumbled angrily and scolded herself. "I shouldn't have been so nice to them. I shouldn't have let them into the house as guests. This is going to encourage them to harass me again. They will never leave us alone."

Percy held up his palms, moved them to indicate calm and tried to pacify and comfort Linda, "Nothing what you can do now. You already went to the police and that friend of yours, Doherty, gave you a condescending speech about morality. Contrary to his opinion, first thing tomorrow morning, we ought to find a good lawyer and press charges. Those boys belong inside an institute. They are dangerous."

Linda couldn't calm down. She kept fuming. "You've said it. We cannot let their aggressiveness go unchallenged."

Percy nodded concurringly. "I wouldn't trust that pretentious bastard father either. He has the looks of a mafia hit man. He talks nice to your face but stabs you in the back."

"I know that and I have to deal with the problem. I'm very busy with Spencer but I must find time to get ready for some defensive action."

"Linda, you know what." Percy's face lightened up and he wagged a forefinger at her. "Let's go down to the YMCA. Swim and relax and you are going to feel better and together, we will come up with a reasonable solution."

They went out together. They made a big loop through the back door and after cutting across the rear neighbor's yard took Percy's Corolla to the YMCA. Linda put on her tiny and sexy two pieces bathing suit. She thought: *it is my right to dress anyway I want without being molested. It's not my fault that I have a desirable and beautiful body.*

She swam and he watched, but soon they both went to the warm pool and talked. Not as agitated as before but still with anger and with an urging sense of revenge.

Barbara was in the warm pool and a young woman was talking to her. Also wearing a small, two pieces bathing suit the stranger had an attractive, although rather muscular body. They drifted closer and greeted Linda and Percy with a friendly smile.

Barbara carefully touched the black and blue marks on Linda arms with her fingers and asked. "Love, what happened to you?"

"Hasn't your husband told you yet?"

298

"No. He is still on duty. Who did this to you?"

Linda told her the story. Every detail, the way it happened.

Flustered and indignant, Barbara angrily berated her husband, "Sean is an idiot. He should have arrested those two. They're going to do it again no matter what their father promises."

"Yes, put the brats in a state institute and I'll have to live with the irate parents next door."

"What do you care? If they bother you they have to face the consequences. They will get into trouble with the law."

"It doesn't seem to work that way," Linda sighed resignedly. "They can do a lot of nasty deeds and the law wouldn't interfere. They can kill you first and the police just take pictures of your dead body, if they find your remains at all. But anyway, I'm going to get a lawyer tomorrow morning."

"I'll talk to Sean," Barbara reassured Linda. "Don't worry. You did nothing wrong."

The other woman, only listening in until now, came closer. Linda recognized her and said, "Francis, Officer Francis Dubois, I remember you."

"Yeah, that's me. I've heard your story. That's terrible. We should have done something when we went there for the first time. Don't worry about you being naked on the back porch. First of all, you made reasonable precautions that nobody could see you. Second they peeped in on you. Third if they saw you they should have complained to the police. They've committed the serious crime."

The clock showed quarter to ten. They went to the locker rooms. Showering and soaping the three women kept on talking. In their natural state, like three naked Greek nymphs under a waterfall, they gesticulated and chattered on nonstop.

Linda hasn't failed to notice Francis superbly developed muscular body. With each move and stretching arch, her fine muscles twitched playfully; her breasts were size of large muffins, tight and muscular. She lifted her arms to wash her armpits and her biceps bulged out, she stood on one leg to wash the other and her strong quadriceps expanded and swelled gracefully. Her round belly lay flat and her buttocks round, strong and prominent, she seemed to be a vigorous beauty of strong will and dynamic self esteem.

Linda saw the attraction between Barbara and Francis. She saw how happy they were to be naked next to each other and how much affection they displayed when they exchanged glances and their eyes lovingly locked.

Linda whispered to Barbara. "I'm very happy for you. I couldn't do it, but I'm happy that you've found her. Congratulations.

"Thank you," Barbara answered, her round face showed no shame.

Drying their bodies in the locker room, Francis suggested going to the police station to prepare a new report. All four, including Percy went and sat down in a conference room. Francis took out a notepad and began writing.

She asked Linda, "Have you encouraged the two Sclafani boys in any manner or way?"

"No, never."

"Have you been aware that they might be watching you undress?"

"No, absolutely not."

Francis asked few more question. When finished, she took

the completed report to a night court judge and returned in an hour.

"We have a search warrant. Let's go."

The dispatcher radioed the patrol car on night duty and Francis headed out with her partner to the Sclafani residence. Linda and Percy wanted to join but Francis said. "You two, you stay at the Police Station. Have coffee and doughnut with the boys."

Sclafani waited until Luisa fell asleep. Hearing her long deep, no eye movement dreamless breathing, he carefully slid out from under the comforter and dressed up. Put on black jeans, a crewneck sweatshirt, and a black cotton long sleeved pullover with a dark woolen cap. He put on his thin black cotton gloves and tucked his fully loaded magnum 45 under his belt. He had no intentions of using it. He followed his basic principle not to leave any traceable evidence of his presence at any crime scene he needed to get personally involved. He didn't want to fire his gun, unless he had to do it in self-defense. He wanted to work with weapons he could find at the Shrewsbury residence. He intended to make it look like a domestic fight, a violent conclusion of a sickening love-triangle. *An easy routine operation,* he figured, *I don't even have to be concerned with disposing any of the bodies; it will look like they've killed each other. And the police might do whatever they want with the carcasses.*

He waited until the clouds covered the moon and walked through the hemlocks and reached undetected the French door of Spencer Shrewsbury's dining room at the back of the house. Using his handy diamond cutter, he cut the small glass panel and carefully unlatched the lock from inside.

Making no noise he pushed the door open and entered.

Inside it was pitch black, nothing moved and apparently nobody was awake.

Perfect, he thought. His pupils dilated widely in the dim moonlight and gave him a perfect night vision. He could see what he needed to see. He took the biggest and sharpest kitchen knife off from the knife holder. Remembered Dennis talking about Linda's gun and touched his under his jacket. The cold feel of the metal reassured him as he proceeded to check out downstairs. He found nobody and figuring that everyone had to be sleeping in the bedrooms he approached the stairs. Moving stealthily up on the steps he made no noise, except the dull thumps of his heart that pounded wildly in his ears as the thrill of the battle stimulated his pleasures of having and enjoying a predatory kill.

He relished the ecstasy of the sadistic wrongdoing he embarked on to commit. An easy freebee; Luisa wouldn't even know her husband had gone out. No more witnesses, no more threats. He would have preferred if Linda had not escaped yesterday. It would have been less complicated but on the other had he would have been deprived of this blood-tingling sensation, a professional murderer on the prowl.

Spencer suffered miserably during the night. His stomach couldn't hold its contents. In the middle of his sleep he belched up his dinner. It blocked his windpipe and he couldn't get air into his lungs. Suffocating he jumped up and tried to breathe. He couldn't, his windpipe was blocked with acidic bile. The fear of dying overpowered him. His throat rattled and with a horrifying yowl he attempted to inhale. Finally life saving air, dragging binge-tasting particles deep into his bronchus, rushed into his oxygen starved lungs.

He sat down, feeling saved from the mows of death he

reached under his pillow for his faithful Beretta friend. It was there. He grabbed the weapon, he thought he heard noises and saw a shadow coming toward him. In his dementia-ravaged mind he was back at the airbase on the island of Diego Garcia and was fighting an armed assassin infiltrating his tent.

He cursed. "We just hired the bastard as a cook, only a few days ago. We gave the benefit of doubt to that son of a bitch. And see what he wants to do."

Then he saw the towering menace reaching for his gun and caught the glint reflecting off a blade as the assassin plunged a knife toward his chest. Spencer aimed and fired at the gray mass then he pulled the trigger twice more. This time he shot directly into the head of his assailant and pumped two more bullets after the first four. Red brain tissue splashed on his bed and blood spurted on the wall and all over the room. Floating down on the walls the gooey grime dirtied the upholstery of his favorite armchair.

Spencer still didn't know who his attacker was. The perpetrator lay on the floor but his body still seemed moving. Spencer fired his last two bullets into his head and reached under his pillow for a second magazine. He ejected the empty one and shoved in the new. He fired six of the eight bullets, all of them into the heart and above the shoulders of the man on the floor. When Spencer stopped the attacker had been reduced to a bloody pulp that only resembled in shape what it once was, a human being.

Like a wounded lion, Spencer roared in anger. On rampage, losing control, he went furiously berserk. Ran downstairs, saw nobody and went outside and bellowed into the night and his voice exploded with wrath. "You fucking son of a bitch. Come on and get me. Come and get Captain

Shrewsbury. I'm not dead yet and I'll kill you all you damned assassins. You want me to die. You will die before me."

The captain yelled, bloody saliva sputtered out of his mouth and he collapsed. He couldn't move any more, he ran out of oxygen, gasped for air and the rage suffocated his larynx.

"Linda, where are you? Where are you, my dear wife?"

He sobbed and pummeled the ground with his fists. "I'll kill everybody who wants to hurt you. I'm dying anyway and I'll kill the bastards."

He struggled and got up. With his last wind of strength walked over to the Sclafani house and yelled. "Come on out you son of a bitch Sicilian. I'll kill you and I'll kill both of your sons. I saw what they did to my wife, my love, the only person who cared about me. Where are you, Linda?"

He banged on the door and shot his last two bullets into the lock. Then he saw the flashing lights and heard the police sirens.

"Freeze, drop your weapon."

He stuck his arms up and dropped the gun. Two officers jumped him and wrestled him to the ground. He shivered with cold and his throat rattled and the air loudly wheezed in the top of his lungs.

Officer Francis Dubois rushed to reach him and yelled to the others. "Get a warm blanket. Now, that is Captain Shrewsbury. He was just trying to protect his wife. Take him inside, back into his house. He is very sick. He is going to get pneumonia. Put those damn handcuffs away."

Francis escorted Spencer back to his house. Upstairs she saw the mess. Sclafani's body was a bloody blob on the floor, his head blown into pieces, his chest wide open and his arms and legs frozen in a gnarly death twist of final agony. He was still holding onto his gun and the kitchen knife lay next to his side. Francis led Spencer into the guest room, made him to get in the bed and turned on the heat.

She radioed the Police Station and asked the dispatcher to send Linda and Percy back to Red Rose Circle.

When Linda saw Spencer she rushed over and could say nothing but thanks and praises to him for standing up for her. "Spencer, I've heard what happened. He intended to kill me and by taking him out you saved my life. He was after me and he wouldn't have stopped until he'd gotten me dead. Thank you for trusting me and caring about me."

The police allowed Linda to make hot tea for Spencer and let her give him his medication. When she came back up with a loaded tray in her hands, Spencer talked to her, "Linda, my sweet delicate Linda. I am the one who needs to thank you. You've been working so much and I have been so bad to you. I'm sorry that I ever hit you."

Standing next to Linda, Percy listened to Spencer. He remembered Spencer hitting her. When he was strong and healthy he was arrogant. When he had the power, he abused his wife. He never loved her with admiration. He never treated her as his equal. He used her as a slave, something what he owned and had the right to abuse and maltreat.

I, Percy thought, *I have seen Linda's true values. I have discovered her soul and reached out to her in her suffering. I've made a lifetime commitment to her. She had become my life and I would never look at anybody else any more. I am the one who truly loves her. She belongs to me and not him.*

But Percy kept quiet. He listened to Spencer crying his pathetic regrets.

"I've been bad and I've got sick. And instead of us enjoying our marriage look what I made you go through."

Spencer shivered with fever and his temperature climbed above 104 degrees. Francis called for an ambulance. Linda comforted him, rubbed his shaking body and offered him solace. "I forgive you, Spencer. You turned into a nice person. Your sickness brought out your better side. You were careless and over complacent. Now you are paying the price. But it is not over yet. Have hope and faith."

Percy looked on. He didn't feel the same sorrow for him but listened and admired Linda's moral strength.

Spencer tried to speak. He was determined to speak his mind, "Unfortunately it is not only I who has to suffer penitence. You have to pay the price too. And you have done nothing wrong."

Linda told him with magnanimous forgiving. "That is the past, nothing what we can do about it. Now I want you to go to the hospital and make sure that you'll get better. Your room is a terrible mess anyway. We have to hire professional cleaning team before you can come back home."

The ambulance arrived and they wrapped Spencer in thermal blankets and took him into the Stamford Hospital Intensive care unit. His temperature now hovered near 106 degrees and he became delirious.

Doherty also arrived and asked Linda and Percy to stay and make a statement. Two officers pulled a yellow crime scene tape around the house, took pictures, marked Sclafani's body position on the floor and collected glass samples at the French door where Sclafani broke in.

Doherty dictated his observations to a rookie, "Signs of forced entry. Intruder broke the window and approached the sleeping family with gun drawn and knife ready to kill.

Homeowner shot and killed him in a clear case of self-defense. Homeowner's wife has not been home. She has been at the police station reporting an earlier unrelated incident."

Francis Dubois heard his last statement and commented, "Unrelated, my stinky ass."

Chapter Thirty-Two

Luisa Sclafani heard the big commotion outside. Waking up from deep sleep she was groggy and confused and tried to understand what was happening. She felt to her left to wake up Sal but he wasn't there. Concerned, she kicked off the comforter and jumped out of the bed. In the spooky darkness of the house she clearly heard somebody yelling and there was banging at her front door.

"Sal!" she creamed at the top of her voice, "where the fuck are you?"

She reached for the light switch and flicked it on. The bright electric brilliance temporarily blinded her and she kicked her bare toes into the cold steel of the bed frame. She screamed like a pig in a sack, "Sal! What the hell is going on?"

Luisa was still frantically groping to get her gown when she heard shots. Peaked out the window and saw several police vehicles, arriving, brakes squealing and coming to screeching halts.

The flashing lights were blinding here and someone yelled, "Police, open up."

By the time she reached the bottom of the stairs two officers kicked in the front door and two others broke through the glass of the slider off the kitchen. Seeing her rushing forward, the first officer stopped and flipped open his badge, "Mrs. Sclafani." He asked.

"Yes. What's this all about? Why are you breaking into my house in the middle of the night?"

He shoved a sheet of paper in her face and replied, "We have a search warrant and we have an order to arrest your sons. Where are they?"

"What charges?"

"Kidnapping and indecent exposure."

"You have got to be kidding me. Nobody kidnapped anybody."

"Please, madam, stand aside and let us search the house."

He pushed her out of the way and six officers panned out to find the boys.

Dennis and Brian woke up to the noises and the shots. In their first gut reaction they wanted to run, get away first and figure out later what was happening. Then they thought, maybe it was just a false alarm. The police was coming to next door to investigate a domestic fight. Daddy should have everything under control anyway.

But then they saw the police banging on the front door of their house. They knew something was hot; they had better flee and explain things to daddy some other time. They grabbed their clothes. Dennis jerked open the window, jumped to the garage roof and Brian followed.

Outside, hidden in the hemlock hedge, they dressed up and ran toward Tulip Tree Road and within a minute reached the densely forested Seleck Woods Park. Once deep inside the trees they stopped to catch their breaths.

First Dennis got back his speech. "Something is fishy, it doesn't smell good. Maybe dad is in trouble. Let's hide here a little while." He checked his watch. "Damn it, it is three o'clock in the middle of the night."

"We wait here until dawn," Brian said and tried to suppress the chattering of his teeth, "and we'll take the first train back to the Bronx. We can call mom from Uncle George's house and find out what happened here."

Brian, always the practical half of the pair, asked Dennis. "Have you got money on you?"

He looked at his wallet and showed his brother that besides the loose change he had a couple of crisp hundred dollar bills stashed amongst the credit cards.

"We are safe." He said with a grin. "With that we can rent a room for a temporary hideout. Maybe taking a train is not that good of an idea. If they really looking for us the station will be the first place they search."

"We ought to keep off streets until daybreak. There are police cruisers everywhere. I heard Darien Police do thorough work when comes to capturing runners."

They sat in silence but soon they became bored and

restless. Dennis took out a joint from his sock and lit it up. He inhaled a big puff and gave it to his brother, "Here. This should make you feel better."

They smoked for ten minutes and broke into laughs.

"I bet Dad shot the bitch. This whole stupid fuss must be about that cunt."

"Do you think he fucked her first?"

"Probably."

"You would have fucked her afterwards."

"Shut up, you idiot."

The talking was macho but they soon ran out of composing braggingly brave and uselessly hackneyed clichés. Then they heard dogs barking in the distance. In their elevated state of chemically induced euphoria they found the proximity of the yelping bloodhounds funny.

"Imagine. The fuck-heads needed to bring out the dogs."

"They're never going to find us. Remember we'd crossed a brook, twice."

"Dennis, I'm hungry. Let's go to the McDonalds. It's right here at the highway rest stop."

"There? We have to watch out for all those faggots in the bathroom."

"Have you got any better idea? Like hitch a ride to Bridgeport and get on the train there."

"Good thinking, nobody is going to check the station at Bridgeport."

They listened. The distant barking seemed to subside.

"Let's go." Dennis said and they got up and headed straight toward the McDonald's arch, flickering between the trees in about hundred yards away.

Forming a single file they were trudging ahead on a dirt path when flashlights shone into their eyes.

"Stop right there," a man yelled and he was holding back three large, drooling dogs. The dogs were ugly and looked dangerous. They growled menacingly and snotty saliva hung from their big canine teeth. Stretching the leashes to snapping point, the animals kept snarling and sticky pieces of foamy goo reached down to the dirt.

The boys turned around and tried to run back into the woods, but two more police officers blocked their way. They both had their guns drawn and looked ready to fire.

"Stop," somebody hollered. "Lie down on the ground and put your hands on your back. You are under the arrest."

They knew the game ended. They ran out of options and they obeyed. They lay down and their faces rolled into the loamy soil. It smelled like putrid decay and the rotting mushrooms puffed spores into their flattened nostrils. Their nasal passages quickly clogged with slimy snot and they needed to breathe through their mouths. With cramped neck muscles they couldn't hold their heads and from the ground earthworm droppings smeared all over their lips. The spores tickled their noses. They sneezed and their faces became soiled with green mucus and brown dirt.

They heard an officer hastily reading their Miranda rights. Someone strong put the handcuffs on them and they were jerked up to stand on their feet. And a stern, deep voice ordered, "Let's go."

Brian cried, his handcuffed hand hurt badly but Dennis acted defiantly. He spit the dirt out of his mouth and, face darkening with irate threat, he said ominously, "You're going to be sorry you did that. You have no idea who we are and what are we capable of doing."

"I guess not," an officer retorted gruffly, "but we surely intend to find it out."

The police shoved them into the squad car and by five a.m. they were secured and checked in at the Darien Police station. Wearing their brand new orange colored prison overalls, they were sitting at unease on an uncomfortable steel bench, inside a wire mesh enclosed holding pen.

Luisa watched angrily as the police turned her house upside down. She tried to follow them around and went with them into the boys' bedroom and down to the basement. She still had her night robe on and indignantly tried to harass the searchers. "I told you, you're not going to find a thing. Wait until my husband gets back. He is going to have fun with you. He knows the best lawyers in New York."

The police made painstakingly measured efforts to keep within professional limits of search conduct. They didn't touch the master bedroom and the general living area. But they emptied out every drawer, scrutinized every piece of paper and flipped through every magazine in the boys' room. They turned to Luisa. She calmed down and looked almost uninterested. She thought the police wasn't getting anywhere.

They had to ask her twice, "Where is the basement? We want to see the basement."

The police knew what they were looking for; they just tested the limits of Luisa's defiance.

"Whatever," she shrugged, "Do whatever indulges your dreamy fancies."

They went down and stopped in the middle of the messy and mushy smelling place.

"What?" Luisa asked insolently.

"Is that it?" The eyes of two officers surveyed the area.

"Yes." Luisa put her hands akimbo. "Can we go back upstairs now?"

"Any other rooms?"

"No."

Francis Dubois came down and she knew exactly where to find the hidden door to the dungeons. She trusted Linda and believed, without doubt, her story. She scanned the walls with her piercing and no nonsense glaze; and she saw a slight, barely visible fissured chink in the wood panels that solidly covered the back wall.

"What's there?"

"Nothing," Luisa shrugged and rolled her eyes.

Francis stepped closer to the wall and ran her fingers on the panels. She picked a knotty grove and tried to move the section. It yielded.

"Stand back." She said and raised her Doc Martin clad right foot. She kicked the hairline crack and it broke open. She shined in her flashlight; saw the mattress and the torn pieces of rag still tied to the steel bars. Without turning back she glanced back above her shoulder and snapped at Luisa.

"What do you call this?"

She couldn't answer.

Francis turned on the lights and entered the secret room. A team of detectives followed her and panned out. Collecting evidence, hair samples and taking pictures they worked in silence, without making remarks or comments. Francis picked up a blood stained dirty white cloth and dropped it into a plastic evidence bag.

Then she turned to Luisa, "Did you know about this place?"

"No."

"I see," she said threateningly. "You are under the arrest."

314

"What for?"

"Obstructing justice and tempering with evidence."

"I did none of that."

"You will have your chance to plead your innocence to the judge."

"I want to talk to my husband."

Francis nodded, "That can be arranged," and signaled one of the officers. "Let's take her next door," and turning back to Luisa she grinned disdainfully, "You'd better, you ought to talk to him. He is at your next door neighbor's house and you can personally ask him what he was doing there."

Francis led Luisa up on the steps into Spencer's bedroom. Sal Sclafani's body lay on the floor in the same position, twisted gnarly and frighteningly dead.

Luisa saw her husband and collapsed onto his body. She opened her mouth, no sounds left her catatonic vocal cords, in muted horror her lungs were frantically sucking in the thin air and thirty seconds later she screamed with an ear-shattering howl.

Francis turned calmly to her partner and said with mocking irony. "Would you call this positive identification? I definitely would."

She hated Mrs. Sclafani. Didn't know it exactly why but her sons hurt Linda, and Linda was part of her clan. Her secret clan of women who would have cast no stone at her for what she was born to be.

She waited until Luisa couldn't cry any more and asked her in a sharp, clipped voice, "What was your husband doing in this house in the middle of the night?"

"I don't know."

"Did he brake in?"

"I don't know."

"Did he use force?"

"I don't know."

Her two-way radio came on. She listened, went to the next room and called Detective Doherty on her cell phone.

The detective reported to her, "They found evidence that Sclafani is connected. He is a well-known loan shark. And he has been suspect in several murder cases. No indictments though."

"Nice neighbors," she said. "What shall I do with her?"

"Bring her in. The conspiracy charges wouldn't stick. But we can keep her in protective custody as a potential witness and turn her over to the FBI."

"Good enough. Let's build our case on that."

Chapter Thirty-Three

A month later all remnant signs of the break in and the killing were erased from both houses. A professional crime scene cleanup team disinfected and repainted Spencer's room. He recovered from his double pneumonia and went home to recuperate. He lost forty pounds off from his regularly robust weight, and looked an emaciated, pale skinned skeleton of his old self. His eyes sunk into his skull and for hours, with sorrow and regret, he despondently stared at the uncaring walls. He saw his young wife and thought how good life could have been with her if he hasn't yielded to his lustful temptations and hasn't searched for instant gratification elsewhere. He knew now how good of a person she was and how much of a better life she would have deserved. But than he thought, if she didn't have such a hard life she wouldn't have turned out to be this good of a person. She would have been a Prima Donna spoiled princess just like the others he knew.

Percy received his first positive reply from his literary agent. He returned her call and she arranged a meeting at a West 54th Street coffeehouse on Manhattan.

"Excellent work, young man," she complimented Percy, "I like your plot. You have good complications, interesting conflicts that is properly connected to your protagonist and antagonist. Your characters are richly developed; they grow as the story unfolds. And you have a good sequence of interlocking and expertly sustained series of dramatic tensions. I marked up your manuscript. Please take a close look what I did and give me another draft. Say, in about a month."

Surprised by her praising comments Percy couldn't immediately reciprocate. He opened his mouth but no sounds came out.

She smiled at him encouragingly and asked, "Is that a problem?"

"No. Of course not," recovering from his pleasant, but nevertheless shocking surprise, Percy finally gathered his thoughts together, "I'll do it. Any weak points I should know about."

"You must have a good start. I almost put your work down after the first chapter. It didn't pique my interest. Try to start with some dazzling tension, forecast a drama. You have a good story but it doesn't unfold fast enough."

She pulled out her checkbook and continued, "Here is two thousand dollars to bring me a better second draft.

Deliver me a faster moving plot and sharper conclusions. I know you can do it. If I still like it I'll give you a lot more and we'll sign a contract."

With that she stood up, offered her right to Percy and asked.

"Do you have the time to work on this? You must concentrate your energies to accomplish your goals. This advance should provide the financial support you need. Stop whatever you're doing to make a living and start writing full time. Get yourself a clean, neat room where nobody bothers you. And work; work hard, talent is not enough. Writing requires more work than aptitude."

Percy rode the train back to Darien in understandable euphoria. He didn't go to his basement but went directly to Linda. She was doing the dishes in the kitchen and, scrubbing clean a large, black cast iron pot, she had both hands inside the foamy water. Percy went behind her and kissed the soft skin on her nape, above her long neck and under the curly tufts at the edge of her reddish coiffure.

She turned around and a glint of anticipation flashed up in her eyes.

"Good news?"

"Linda, I received money, two thousand dollars for my writing."

She put the pot down, turned around and threw her soapy arms around his neck, "Very happy for you. I knew you work was good."

She landed a soft kiss on his lips and he hugged her. They pushed their bellies closer and he touched the firm, resilient flesh under her flimsily thin cotton dress. Holding her soft shoulders he let the delicious sensation, a deluge of all encompassing arousal, engulf his trembling flesh and bones. She responded and lifting her waist rubbed her loins against his. He felt her pubis and blood rushing into his groins turned him hard. He pushed further in but he knew she wasn't going to let him go all the way. Her husband lay in bed with deadly illness and she was still married to him. And they had to respect that.

She finished the dishes, dried her hands and they sat down at the kitchen table.

Linda cocked her head and grimaced teasingly, "What's next, maestro?" She asked.

"I have to finish the second draft within a month. I have to incorporate her comments."

"It seems that you have your work cut out for you."

"I must make time for it."

"Let me suggest something. It may sound selfish but I think that's what we ought to do."

"I'm open to suggestions."

"I think you parents should find another groundskeeper. Move out from their basement. Move into our guestroom, next to mine and work. When you want to take a break you mow my lawn and keep the shrubbery neat outside. You don't even have to pay rent."

"Of course I do. I give you a thousand dollars for room and board. Plus I'll do all the work you need me to do. Then I can quit everything else and concentrate on my book."

"Sounds fair, move your belongings this afternoon and began working on your book tonight."

"What about Spencer?"

A dark cloud of sad worry floated across Linda's visage and shaded the pretty features of her melancholic face. "Spencer.

He is very sick. Most of the time he doesn't even know who he is, let alone who you are."

"Shouldn't we tell him?"

"Tell him what."

"That I've moved into his house."

"He wouldn't understand it. He is past being able to comprehend anything rational."

"Where is his gun?"

"Under his pillow, he wouldn't part with it."

"I see. Can't you remove the bullets at least?"

"No. He checks the magazine everyday and he would get mad if I did that."

"I guess I have to be double careful not to upset him."

"You bet."

Percy moved in and with great fervor commenced on rewriting his novel. He worked all night and slept during the day, except when he had to cut the grass or take the garbage to the town transfer station. He kept giving two hours long tennis lessons but only three times a weak. He made commendable progress in revising his writing and kept his distance from Linda. She remained adamant on not sleeping with Percy but now, trusting him, she left the door of her bedroom unlocked and at times slightly ajar.

On summer nights, the heat radiated down from the attic and there was no air conditioning to keep the house cool. She opened the windows but it was still far too hot. To get to his room Percy didn't need to pass by Linda's door. On rare occasions, late at night he dared to step closer to her door and in the darkness wondered, imagined the mystical contours of her body stretched out on her bed and under the flimsy sheets.

In the warm and humid nights Linda inadvertently kicked off the bed sheet and lying on her stomach she slept like a resting divinity from a Botticelli masterpiece. Her long auburn hair covered her shoulders and arms. Hugging a fluffy pillow she pulled one of her legs all the way to her chest. Lately Linda's body became more mature and feminine; the moonlight enhanced the image of her naked buttocks and the shiny luster of her golden skin seemed to invite Percy to come in and touch. She needed to be kissed and loved but she lay there off limits, for she had a wedded husband and her lover had to be satisfied with the sweet desire of only wanting her.

She turned on her back and her legs spread apart. Sleeping only in a short nightshirt top, she shamelessly exposed her naked bottom. The sight turned Percy into a statue of Sodom cast in stone and he didn't dare to move or make a sound.

Dark and dense hair covered her strongly developed lips and protected, with insane modesty, the gentle arch of her pubis rolling down gently into the valley of her abdomen. Sleepily she reached down and caressed herself. She rubbed with gentle circles, just above where her lips united and progressed into a single ravine leading to her love mound. She moaned with pleasure and slipped her middle finger inside.

Percy watched and forgot to breathe. Her hand inched a little forward and now two fingers disappeared. She played and rubbed, pressed down harder and shook her hands in a faster, insanely frenzied pace.

Percy stood there, mesmerized and bewildered by this heavenly gift of watching her. He stayed motionless at the sight of the most sacred vision of an earthly mortal man could ever experience.

It didn't take long. Her young hormones soon exploded and she wiggled, thrust her hips, up in pleasure and fell back, exhausted but satisfied. Her breathing soon turned into long sleepy rhythms and she went back to dream world and didn't remember in the morning except she had a good night rest and a gratifying and pleasing dream.

A weak later, Linda also had good news. She took her second HIV test and it came back negative. Now she knew she was infection free. Percy's first test also came back negative a week earlier and he was waiting to take the second one in six months.

Their perseverance, determined abstinence and honest morals were bringing in good results and a promise of good life, later, in a not too far distance down on the road.

Francis called and informed Linda that Dennis and Brian have been placed into the Bridgeport Juvenile Correctional Institute and, based on the judge's advice, planned to join the marines when they turned twenty-one. Francis also got news that Luisa Sclafani successfully testified against her husband's boss. The federal court had him locked up for life and without a chance of parole. Luisa received a new identity, a new Social Security number and assumed a different name. She moved to the Southwest under the witness protection relocation program and took a job in a beauty parlor as a hairdresser.

Chapter Thirty-Four

Spencer's health remained stable throughout the summer. Under Linda's devoted care he fought infection after infection but with the November winds and cold rains his struggle to survive turned into a Herculean effort.

Her husband's nonstop anger and bitter frustration turned Linda's days into twenty-four hours miserable servitude. Arrogant and supplicant simultaneously, riding on perpetual personal ambivalence, remorse and lost feeling of helplessness against an undefeatable enemy, Spencer's moods ebbed and flowed between violent and depressed. He couldn't take his rage out on anyone but Linda. He yelled at her for the slightest delays and threw objects at her when she offered an excuse.

Linda acted as if she were a saint. She realized his reactions weren't directed at her personally but his disease made him behave irrational and belligerent to the only one who was willing to take care of him.

She didn't hesitate to talk to Spencer about his sickness. She wasn't afraid to touch Spencer. He held his hand, gave him hugs and rubbed his ugly splotches covered back that gave him brief moments of forgiving relief.

Spencer couldn't get used to Percy's presence. In his paranoid state of mind Spencer was convinced, Percy brought in the viruses and the diseases that contaminated him. Spencer insisted on Percy wearing gloves and washing his hands before entering his room. In Percy, he saw a dark angel, a wicked demon and considered shooting him with his Berretta he kept under his pillow. He didn't see how much help Percy meant to Linda. He only saw his closeness and his good relationship with her. And he hated him for that.

Percy saw the bitter resentment in Spencer's eyes and threaded his ways around him with utmost care. Always ready to fight and on the lookout Percy frequently asked Linda.

"When are we going to take his gun away?"

She glanced at him, nodded or shrugged but remained weak on the issue. "First chance we have," she replied sometimes, but never did anything.

Percy's agent found him a publisher. Percy received his editorial review and correcting and polishing his novel, worked long hours at night. Linda asked him many times to show her his work but he remained secretive and refused to let her even reading a page.

"You'll read my novel when it's complete," he insisted. "It's going to be a surprise."

"Is it any good?"

"Of course, it's being published, isn't it?"

"Is it about me?"

"Of course, who else."

"Is it about us?"

"I plead the fifth Amendment."

She wanted to grab his manuscript but he didn't let her. She even sneaked into his room when he raked the leaves and tried to find his novel on his computer. But she couldn't get through his password. He was unforthcoming and inflexibly unbending beyond reason.

Toward Thanksgiving, Spencer contacted a serious flue. He blamed Percy for spreading the virus. He seriously contemplated to take him out for good. He checked his gun and waited. In his demented and fever ravaged mind he blamed Percy for his troubles and sickness.

Past midnight, after Thanksgiving Day, Spencer had a terrible coughing attack. Exhausted from the holiday work, Linda took a sleeping pill and slept like a log. Percy had to check on Spencer's coughing.

Interrupted in his work, he grudgingly left his computer, put on a pair of rubber gloves and a mask and, having preconceived notions of irritable fret, entered Spencer's room.

Turned the lights on and saw Spencer aiming the gun at him.

Spencer yelled, "Got you, you son of a bitch."

He fired, but in his weak condition he couldn't hold the gun straight and missed. He tried to fire again, at close range this time, but Percy, fast tennis player reflexes and coordination aiding him, hit his hand and knocked the gun out of his grip. It flew across the room and landed at Percy's feet.

He stepped on it and shouted. "No more guns. Do you understand that? You're the son of a bitch. Do you think you can do anything? Just because you are sick you don't have a license to abuse the both of us. She works so hard that she is always tired and exhausted. She is chancing deadly infection while attending to you. She needs me to help her out."

"This is my house. I do whatever I please."

"Be thankful that you are not in the hospital. Appreciate that we're taking care of you in your home."

"Sure. And you like the arrangement. You made my wife your lover. I know you are fucking her."

"I do not. She is a martyr and you are an animal. You've struck her many times before you've been sick. I saw what you were doing."

"It was none of your business."

"It was and is my business. I love her and I'll protect her from you."

"You are waiting for me to die. But I'll not die. I'll survive you."

Spencer stopped and fought off a long spasm of coughing. The first bullet broke the window and the cold November night air was rushing in. He kicked off his blanket and staggered toward Percy.

"I'm going to bite you," he yelled, his voice spluttered and his mouth frothed around the edges, "and you'll die just like me."

Percy stepped back, toward the door, grabbed a chair and was holding it as a shield between Spencer and him.

Attempting to get closer to Percy, Spencer tried to knock the chair out of his hands.

Percy hollered at him. "It's nobody's fault but yours that you've got sick. You had a young and beautiful wife, a good person, whom you didn't deserve but it wasn't enough for you. You fooled around who knows with whom and how many times, unprotected, only God's blessed mercy prevented you giving the sickness to her. She was lucky she didn't get sick because of you. Did she ever tell you that? You almost killed her too. Do you care about that aspect of your irresponsibility?"

Spencer grabbed another chair and attacked Percy. "I don't care. I must kill you first. I hate you. What are you doing in my house?"

"Your wife hired me. I do chores around the house for the room."

"Is sex included in your pay?"

"No. I told you before. No."

"Liar," Spencer bellowed hoarsely and plunged ahead.

Percy kicked the gun to the corridor, jerked the chair away from Spencer, jumped out and shut the door behind him. He put the chair against the knob and listened.

Spencer fell on the floor, without his blanket, and the cold air kept coming in. He shivered, coughed with terrible spasms, but Linda was still asleep and nobody heard him. Left alone in the cold his end approached.

Percy cursed, picked up the gun and ejected the magazine. To shake the bullets loose he hit magazine to the doorframe and bent down to pick them up. Placed the shiny projectiles in his pocket, put on an overcoat and went downstairs.

Heading straight to the front door he took his car and

drove to Tilly Pond. Looked at the dark water and flung the gun away, far out and aiming to the middle. The weighty weapon landed with a big splash and he watched the tiny waves circling to the shore. Disturbed ducks quacked noisily; he threw the bullets and the magazine at the birds, missed and soon the lake settled back to quietude.

He sat down on a rock. Still upset, he wasn't ready going back and face Spencer's wrath. Feeling cold and hungry he thought having a midnight snack would do him a world of good.

Drove to McDonalds in Stamford and ordered hot chocolate and apple pie at the drive in. Eating at the outside picnic table he watched a group of young people in baggy pants and huge parkas staring at him with intimidating glare.

One came closer and said provocatively. "What do you need, man?"

"Nothing."

"Then what are you doing here?"

"Domestic violence."

"She kicked you out?"

"Her husband."

The man in the parka grinned understandingly. "Stop fooling around, dude." Throwing a furtive glance over his shoulder he asked worriedly.

"You are not a cop, are you?"

He stepped closer and under the light Percy recognized him. He was locked up a few cells away from him at Bridgeport Correctional.

"I know you." Percy said.

"No way, dude."

"Bridgeport, in the joint."

With sudden jitteriness he wheeled around his heels, jumped up and slapped his open palms against Percy's. "That's right brother. How did you get out?"

"They dropped the charges."

"No shit. Are you sure you don't need anything."

"I need peace. So I can finish my work."

"What work?"

"My book."

"Cool." He said approvingly and wobbled back to the dark side of the parking lot.

Hours later, Percy went home. The house yawned to him with awful emptiness. Seeing Linda still asleep he didn't feel like checking on Spencer. He threw himself on his bed and quickly fell asleep.

Around ten, far too late for her, Linda woke up. The house surrounded her with an unusual lack of life. She glanced at Percy's room. His head lying above the comforter she heard his rhythmical, slow in and stretched out exhale, relaxed breathing. Sleeping soundly, Percy appeared beyond productively usable.

"Sloth," She mumbled and set out to check on Spencer. Still half asleep she squinted with suspicion at the chair leaning against the doorknob. Fearing wrong she pushed it aside and forced her way in.

Saw Spencer lying on the floor. He didn't move and didn't seem to breathe.

She let out a stifled cry, "Oh, my God," and crouched down, her nightshirt, stretching tight at the bottom slipped above her knees. She touched Spencer's wrist and checked his pulse. He had none. He was dead. His reproaching eyes, wide open and still showing pain eyeballed her with a cold, unearthly stare. He was staring directly between her legs. She shivered at the hideous thought, bent forward and closed his eyes.

His skin already felt cold, looked grayish pale, frightening but harmless.

Feeling sorrow she touched him again and told him what came to her mind. "Spencer, it could have been different. Why did you marry me if you didn't love me? Why did you have to beat me? What did I do wrong? Now it's over. I kept my word. I took care of you, in sickness and in health. Now I'm free. You had everything and you threw it away. Why? Only you would know. What have you done to get this horrible sickness? What have I done to deserve what I had to go through? I hope you are not mad at me. Go in peace and remember only the nice things about us. We must have had some. I was young and gullible and you'd impressed me. How would I have known it better? How would I have known your secret desires? Was it worth it? It's too late for you. I'm sorry."

She ran her fingers on her dead husband's face, caressed his skin and continued her lament. "Life has to go on and it will go on, and at the end the living triumphs over the dead. Sorry I feel that way, but I'm young and I'll have my life. As much as you have abused me and I had to suffer taking care of you, you rewarded me hundredfold. I grew up and now; thanks to you I'm wealthy. Your life continues in me. Except that I'm smarter and more intelligent than you ever were. You grew up in Darien. You had a rich and sheltered life. You thought nothing bad could happen to you. I knew it better; I learned my lessons the hard way. I have seen my mother being arrested, handcuffed and dragged away screaming. Indifferent social workers seized me. I wanted to touch my mother's hand but they held me back. I knew life offers only few chances, more to others less to some. But we all make our decisions and our life is guided by the choices we make. I stayed clean and abstained. I've had my hot sweaty nights alone in my bed, I had my temptations I have seen my friends getting pregnant and getting diseased. I choose to stay healthy. It was my choice, I paid the price in loneliness but at the end, and this is not the end for me, the biggest asset is still mine, my health; my good health."

She stood up, backed away and looked at Spencer one more time. His eyes closed, he didn't look much different than sleeping off one of his deliriums.

She talked again, "Sorry, Spencer but I'm going to marry Percy. He was good to me when I was down. He adored me and held me in the highest esteem when he didn't know if I was going to make it. He loved me and you didn't. He never hit me; he never yelled at me he was there for me when I needed him. He's my man. I love him and now I can be his, forever."

She left her dead husband, dialed 911 and waited. At her twenty years of age she still had her life ahead of her. The house was hers. A million dollar in the bank was hers, she had the car and she had the love of his life sleeping in the next room. And she wasn't ashamed for any of it. She didn't have to.

The Lawrence Funeral Associates properly buried Spencer, next to his mother at the Spring Grove Cemetery, across the street from the police station. Few weeks after the burial, Linda started her new job at the Darien Police. For now she had a desk job but in September they scheduled her entering the Police Academy at Meriden.

Linda and Percy went to the St. Ladislaus Roman Catholic Church on Cliff Street in South Norwalk. Father Burke listened to their story and agreed to marry them, contingent on getting their baptism certificates. He recommended a six weeks marriage preparation course and invited them to become members of his parish.

The wedding took place the week after Mother's day in May on a beautifully sunny, late springtime Saturday afternoon. People filled the church pews to capacity. Parish members, young and old, Irish and Hungarian, loved the young couple, Percy's parents and sister sat in the front row. Dozens from the Darien police, including Barbara and Francis showed up and sat in the back.

The organist began to play and Linda in her snow-white, long wedding gown and clinching to the arms of Sean Doherty walked down the aisle. At the altar, Percy, in his shiny black tuxedo, proudly waited for her. David, his brother the best man, envy lurking within his awkward grin stood next to the groom.

David couldn't think of saying anything nice and kept his mouth shut.

Father Burke, after giving a truly inspiring marriage speech, pronounced them man and wife. The ceremony ended and as they walked back to the front door hundreds greeted and congratulated them. Outside the bright sun of late springtime smiled down with blessings and happiness on the newlyweds and a feeling of cloudless joy overwhelmed all other emotions and erased all the bad memories of their stormy past.

The reception took place at the St. Ladislaus Social Hall, next door on Sound View Avenue. The caterers brought in plenty food and drinks for the near three hundred guests and a Hungarian band provided boisterous music with plenty of fast czardases.

Percy taught Linda how to dance czardas. He put his hands on her strong hips and made her to put her hands on his broad shoulders. He looked straight into her eyes and showed her two steps to the left and two steps to the right. With caring admiration, Linda lost her gaze in his proud stare. She swayed her skirt with the steps, pulled her shoulders back and thrust her breasts out to provoke. He accepted the delightful challenge and gently fondled her waist. The hypnotic rhythm of the music mesmerized the dancers and they moved with passion and fire. Natural talents for dancing, they kept up with the speeding pace, stomped their feet on the floor and swayed back and forth with charming grace and old world elegance. Linda swirled around and Percy held her hand with blissful glee and happy appreciation that she had chosen him for her lifelong mate.

Past midnight his friends asked Percy to play and sing a song dedicated to his newlywed wife. He readily obliged and sat down at the piano when the band left for a break.

Linda looked at him and there was encouraging glee in her sparkling eyes. "Play something cheerful. No more sad songs, Give me a lively tune."

Percy winked at her, run a few accords on the keyboard and took a deep breath.

"That blonde is there, truly pretty,
The brunette is really sexy,"

His tenderly adoring eyes looked at Linda with unearthly

devotion. She smiled back and swayed herself to the rhythm. He continued the song.

"But the read-head, she is the best,
She is the true lovely goddess."

She wrapped her arms around him, kissed his still joyfully singing lips and whispered into his ear. "I'll eat you alive tonight. Where do you learn all these songs? Do you have any more?"

He said, "Hundreds, enough to last for a lifetime."

On their wedding night they consummated their marriage. They made love all night long, again and over again. They imposed neither limits nor restrictions. There was no shame or bashfulness, only youthful and all encompassing healthy, satisfying and God consecrated marital sex.

Chapter Thirty-Five

The probate court nullified Sclafani's purchase of Pamela Leicester's home and awarded ownership to her orphaned son, Joshua. Joshua insisted selecting Percy and Linda as his legal guardians.

Percy rented the Leicester house to a banker from Chile for $5,000 a month. Linda and Percy decided to adopt Joshua and raise him as their own. Joshua moved in with them and happily returned to the Darien Junior High on Middlesex Road. He proved to be an excellent student and soon made the high honor roll. He had the highest respect for Percy and revered Linda. He truly understood their sacrifice and rewarded them with good behavior and love.

Barbara Doherty divorced Sean and moved in together with Francis Dubois. To avoid local gossip they moved down to Land O'Lakes, Florida where they purchased a three-bedroom villa at the exclusive, Caladesi Lake nudist colony. The Pasco County Sheriff's Department hired Francis and Barbara became a hotel receptionist at the resort.

Percy and Linda accepted Barbara and Francis invitation to spend their next year vacation at Caladesi. Scheduled for mid April they were to stay in their guest room for two weeks.

Time quickly passed and soon they were on their way down to Florida. Arrived to Tampa around noontime, rented a car at the airport and drove North on Route 41.

Seeing the colorful and inviting sign, Percy turned to Linda. "Are you sure you're going to be comfortable here?"

"I'll be all right," she replied and there was a mischievous glint in her eyes, "if you let me be myself."

"I would love to see you walking around without a stitch for two weeks."

"What about other guys watching me?"

"I'll be proud of you."

She playfully hit his knees. "You, silly man, you are one sick of a deviate."

He squeezed his wife's thighs and shamelessly encouraged her.

"I see nothing wrong with parading au naturelle on Nude Main Street, USA."

The guard checked with Barbara, gave them their passes and pushed the button to open the wrought iron gate. A hundred feet inside an older man, covered head to toe with abundant body hair, rode his bicycle. Except his shoes he wore nothing and his portly fat but naked bottom hang down on both sides from the small bicycle seat.

Seeing him Linda chuckled. "Look at that hairy baboon sitting on the grinding wheel."

"Wait until they see your butt."

The uncalled remark offended her. "Nothing is funny about my butt. Just watch when they see you, my friend. With your oversized ding-dong you're going to freak out the local ladies."

He laughed, "No way, unless they see you standing right next to me."

Along a long lagoon they reached their destination, the hedonistic retreat of Barbara and Francis. The two lady lovers came out to meet them. Loosely tied around their bodies, both had colorful wrap around sarongs and seemed to have nothing underneath.

They greeted Linda and Percy. "Welcome to paradise. Come on in."

The four hugged, kissed and went inside. The large villa looked plenty comfortable for four. Decorated tastefully, it was airy and had glass and wrought iron Florida style furniture with pastel colored sofas and chairs. Upstairs they found three large bedrooms and Barbara gave them the one, next to theirs, overlooking a large lake with vistas of a sandy beach and the elegant 50 million dollar clubhouse on the other side.

Seeing the positive impact their place made on their guests Francis asked. "Can we give you two a guided tour of the facilities?"

"By all means," they volunteered, "let's go."

Hesitating she looked at her guests. "Not like that."

"Like what?" Linda asked.

"Not in textiles. Lose your clothes."

Linda and Percy burst into happy laughs. Percy said. "I guess if you are in Rome you do like the Romans do."

From under her short skirt Linda pulled off her panties and threw them at Percy. "I'm done."

"My foot you are," Barbara answered, "take them off all, girl."

"You do it first," Linda procrastinated, "I'll do it after you."

"No problem." Barbara and Francis giggled provocatively and untied their sarongs. Percy stared at them in disbelief. They crossed this seemingly impenetrable barrier with such ease and natural grace he couldn't believe his senses. Naked, they both looked lean and years younger than they were in Darien. They had full suntans without white bathing suit prints blemishing their skin. Standing naked they shamelessly withstood his staring directed at their uncovered bodies.

"What are you still waiting for?" They asked.

Linda turned around, unbuttoned her shirt, threw it on the sofa, and took off her bra. Covering her breast she turned back. "Ta-taa, give me a drum roll."

Percy beat a mad rhythm on the table and yelled. "Take it off, take it off."

She turned her back toward them again, shook her ass and lifted her skirt up. "Happy?"

"Take it off."

She unbuttoned the skirt on the side, made a big wide circle with her hips, then let the garment drop and spread her arms.

"Viva nakedness." She yelled and ran to hide behind Barbara's back. From behind her she challenged her husband.

"Percy, shame on you, three naked ladies and you are still fully clothed."

Percy gave up and took off his protective textiles. When naked he looked at the three women but saw no interest in their eyes. Felt embarrassed, cooled off and like a docile mule followed them to outside to the walking path that meandered directly in front of the house. Walking behind the three women he watched in bewilderment their big, sexy and bare behinds swaying a few feet away from his nose.

A gentle breeze came in from the lake and eased the strong sunrays heating up their shoulders and naked buttocks. Percy and Linda soon discovered the delightful feeling of total freedom and trusty friendship and felt completely uninhibited and comfortable of being naked in public, although of course only within the walls of the private resort.

The walking path went winding around two lakes, took them along expensive apartment buildings and luxuriously built private homes. Naked people walked and jogged and everyone greeted everyone with respect and friendly kindness.

They admired how well the buildings fit into the natural surroundings, with the majestic oak trees, the placid lakes and the lush landscaping.

They walked past by the tennis courts, three made of clay and three hard surfaced, observed the spacious children playground, saw the petanque courts, the sand valley ball courts and saw the inviting motel building.

Seeing the tennis courts Percy announced. "I'm going to play tennis tomorrow morning."

"What am I going to do, dear while you are so selfishly indulging in your private pleasures?" Linda asked.

Barbara answered Linda's question. "Don't worry dear. We're going to take care of you. Nobody gets bored around here."

A large circular driveway rose to the expansive entrance of the huge and elegant clubhouse. White stone lions and naked nymphs guarded the front door and passing by them they entered. A lady greeter checked their passes and they just stood there in awe. They admired the statues, the big brass flowerpots, the modern nightclub, the large sports-bar, the refined piano bar and the first class restaurant. Downstairs they looked at the fully equipped health and exercise gymnasium facilities and at an elegant store for fancy and provocatively sexy outfits and lingerie.

After the initial introduction tour they returned with towels and lay them out, as the rules of conduct required, on lounge chairs next to the pool.

They comfortably stretched out on the chairs. *What a lifestyle,* Percy thought and peeked at his wife. She closed her eyes and seemed only concerned to eagerly absorb the rays of the sun onto her skin.

When felt too hot and had too much sun they went to the big pool under the swaying palm trees and flowery magnolias. They stood under the waterfall and let the water massage their shoulders and derrieres. Later mounted floating mattresses and hovered between the skies and the blue water with timeless and heavenly feelings. Percy pushed Linda around and splashed water on her belly. It tickled her and he liked watching the beads running down to her delightfully matured, black and abundantly thick pubic hair.

Later, all four of them sat in the hot Jacuzzi tub and picked up friendly discussions with other guests in the long conversational pool.

Club members accepted Barbara and Francis the way they were. Nobody ever questioned or remarked at their relationship. They lay naked next to each other, acknowledged appreciative glances from male members but never let any single man get closer than the two women deemed it comfortable.

In the evening, after taking together a long and cheerful outdoor shower they dressed up in revealing dance clothes and went to the nightclub.

The music sounded powerful, modern and delivered by a best, state of the art sound system. By ten o'clock dozens of couples hopped, jigged and shuffled their feet on the dance floor. Most women wore only short skirts and no underwear; many went topless and danced with careless delight and indulgence in their selected lifestyle.

By midnight half of the floor crowd danced naked and the music turned into deafening crescendo. Young and attractive women, mostly tall and skinny southern beauties went up and danced on the stage. Nobody touched anybody. All remained for the eyes and nothing was allowed for the hands.

The excellent air conditioning and the lack of most clothes eliminated sweating and the swirling kaleidoscope of human bodies held out and saved their owners from dehydration and heat exhaustion. The dance lasted past midnight and the four friends walked home, tipsily but more or less straight forward, across a flimsy footbridge over an alligator infested pond and back to their villa.

Early morning the eastern sun shone into the bedrooms. Percy woke up first. He kissed and fondled Linda but exhausted and sleepy she only turned to her other side. Percy gave up, perhaps too easily, and took his racket and headed out to test the opposition on the tennis courts.

Minutes later Linda woke up and saw him walking toward the courts, naked and only with his tennis racket under his arm. She pulled away from the window and went to check on their hosts.

In their king size bed Barbara and Francis were sleeping together in the nude. Barbara lay on her side. Her large touchy and raised round hip invitingly beckoned to Linda. Francis slept on her belly. She spread her legs apart and revealed her strong and appetizing innermost feminine treasure in between.

Linda contemplated climbing onto the bed and sandwiching herself tightly in the middle. She imagined their naked bodies pressed against hers. She stood there with the pounding heart of an excited explorer about entering un-chartered territory. She kept quiet and waited. Hyperventilating and aroused she felt butterflies licking and dancing wildly inside her belly.

First Barbara moved. The presence of a warm and naked body of her lover close to hers made her to feel secure. She squinted up with her sleepy eyes and saw Linda, standing there naked and curious. She didn't have to say a thing. Not a hint. She knew what Linda expected her to do.

Francis turned on her back and spread her legs wide apart. Barbara slid down and pushed her head in between. Francis received her delightful kiss and demanding more moved her hips. Barbara waited to see if Linda was still watching and when she saw she was, she pressed on.

She whispered into Francis' ears. "Linda is looking at us."

Feeling Barbara's advances Francis released her own self from all binding conventions, trusted her lover, her significant other with a serious, unbreakable lifetime commitment and let her do what she wanted to do. Barbara lips pressed down on her and her tongue slipped inside. She buried her face and Linda kept admiring them. Excitement emerged from depths within and until now existing unbeknownst to her. They displayed secrets she couldn't imagine, until she has seen them with her own eyes and she was tempted to join.

Barbara fondled Francis buttocks reaching with her fingers inside and easing them out. Francis pulled up Barbara and kissed her mouth. She tasted her lips, still soaking wet with her own love juices, parted her lips, pushed her head into the soft pillow under and made her tongue dance around inside her mouth.

Later they changed positions and continued on uninterrupted. Much later they looked up and saw that Linda was gone.

Linda watched them with bewildered amusement. She admired their commitment to each other, she knew they loved each other and would have been unhappy in any other man-woman relationship. She wasn't about being judgmental, their love was pure and they proved their commitment and they owned no explanation to anyone.

But she didn't want to have any part of it. She fought hard for Percy, she endured terrible suffering, an agonizing wait to be his wife and now when she had it, she couldn't throw it away for moments of lust and experimenting. She thought of Spencer. His weakness destroyed him. He couldn't resist the temptation and paid for it with his life.

She loved her husband, and she had her self-imposed limits. She didn't want to have a double life; she couldn't deceive her one and only love, her husband, Percy. It didn't matter if Percy approved or not, if he wanted to play for fun, brag or write about strange experiences. True love still existed, in spite of all the Internet sex, all the chat rooms, all the swinging sex clubs, all the love for sale and all the people seeking gratification without making commitments. And she had found it. Heavenly providence repaid her for all her childhood sufferings and rewarded her with the love and tender care of Percy. She slowly withdrew and walked outside.

Following the path Linda soon reached the tennis courts and saw Percy playing hard and beating his opponents, the best ones in the club. He saw Linda standing outside and saw his partners admiring her.

"Is this your wife?" They asked.

"Yes, she is."

"Nice."

She yelled to him. "I'll meet you in the clubhouse. After you had enough tennis, have breakfast with me."

Ten minutes later, hungry and exhausted from the three gruelingly competitive sets he played, he was glad to sit down and enjoy being served.

Linda sat down, buck-naked in his lap, wiggled her ass down onto his penis and French kissed him on the mouth.

"What?" He said. "What's going on here? Why do I deserve this? Is there something I should know about?"

"Yes, dear love." She said, "I need to tell you something."

"Oh no," he smiled coyly, "Something about Barbara and Francis."

"No silly, leave them alone. They are happy with each other as is. Remember us. We're against the whole world, just the two of us."

"Yes?"

"But that is about to change."

"Don't say. I can't even bear the thought of it."

"You silly husband, you," and she kissed him even deeper inside his mouth. "Don't be afraid. Don't you have faith in me?"

"Tell me then, what is it?"

"We are pregnant."

The news took his breath away. Gasping for air he answered and there was pride and sense of accomplishment in his voice. "That's wonderful. Boy or girl?"

"What's the difference? He or she is going to be writer anyway."

"Better be a girl."

"Why?"

"She is going to be a sexy redhead like you."

They giggled conspiratorially and Linda spoon-fed her wonderful and understanding husband.

The two weeks passed by fast. All four truly enjoyed it and they became bonded for life. They truly respected and liked each other. The way they were, different and many worlds apart but in agreement in one thing. Live and let live. Don't force your opinions or lifestyle on anyone.

Back in Darien a large brown package waited for Percy, he received the complimentary copies of his first book. He opened the box, pulled out a copy and showed it to Linda. "Here is my book. You can read it now."

She took the book in her hands, flipped through the pages and looked at the cover.

"The Legend of Red Rose Circle," She asked.

"Yes."

"Our story?"

"Yes."

Smiling with bittersweet approval she told him. "I sure hope you can write the next one about someone else. I don't want to go through again anything like what's probably divulged in this book."

He laughed, "Of course not. But our story had to be told the way it happened."

The End